E.R. PUNSHON
DEATH AMONG THE SUNBATHERS

Ernest Robertson Punshon was born in London in 1872.

At the age of fourteen he started life in an office. His employers soon informed him that he would never make a really satisfactory clerk, and he, agreeing, spent the next few years wandering about Canada and the United States, endeavouring without great success to earn a living in any occupation that offered. Returning home by way of working a passage on a cattle boat, he began to write. He contributed to many magazines and periodicals, wrote plays, and published nearly fifty novels, among which his detective stories proved the most popular and enduring.

He died in 1956.

Also by E.R. Punshon

Information Received
Crossword Mystery
Mystery Villa
Death of A Beauty Queen
Death Comes To Cambers
The Bath Mysteries
Mystery of Mr. Jessop
The Dusky Hour
Dictator's Way

E.R. PUNSHON

DEATH AMONG THE SUNBATHERS

With an introduction
by Curtis Evans

DEAN STREET PRESS

Published by Dean Street Press 2015

Copyright © 1934 E.R. Punshon

Introduction Copyright © 2015 Curtis Evans

All Rights Reserved

Published by licence, issued under the UK Orphan Works
Licensing Scheme

First published in 1934 by Ernest Benn

Cover by DSP

ISBN 978 1 911095 32 3

www.deanstreetpress.co.uk

INTRODUCTION

"It's a place for them sun bathers," Ashton explained. "Sit out there on the lawn without any clothes on, they do, and if there ain't any sun, there's rays instead. A fair scandal I call it."

Various British naturist, or nudist, organizations, such as the Sunbathing Society, the Sunshine League and the Sun Ray Club, began forming in Britain during the Twenties. In 1927, one sunbathing enthusiast, a Captain H.H. Vincent, was arrested and fined for indecent exposure after he arrayed himself, in an Edenic eruption of enthusiasm, bare-chested in Hyde Park. A man's exposing the upper part of his body in such a location was "likely to shock persons of ordinary sensibility," concluded the censorious sentencing magistrate. Undaunted as well as unclothed, naturist groups carried on their activities in private; and by the 1930s, according to Philip Carr-Gomm's *A Brief History of Nakedness* (2010), "nudism had reached the height of its popularity in Britain," drawing emphatic vocal support from such reliable controversialists as Havelock Ellis and George Bernard Shaw. In 1933, as the Nazis banned nudism in Germany, George Bernard Shaw in England's *Sun Bathing Review* called on individuals to rid themselves "of every scrap of clothing that can be dispensed with."

With *Death Among The Sunbathers* (1934), E.R. Punshon clearly was taking timely advantage of a fad that had attained newspaper notoriety in the western world. Nor was he the only Thirties mystery author to do so. Ellery Queen's *The Egyptian Cross Mystery*, which partly concerns the activities of an American nudist colony, actually preceded *Death Among The Sunbathers* into print by a couple of years, while Traill Williamson's *The Nudist Murder* (1937) and Gladys Mitchell's *Printer's Error* (1939) followed not long afterward. Although naturism is not involved in Dorothy L. Sayers's *Murder Must Advertise*, which slightly preceded into print *Death among the Sunbathers*, there is a certain similarity as well between these two novels, which I will leave discerning readers to discover for themselves. One may reasonably assume, I believe, that Punshon closely read Sayers's detective novels, the Crime Queen in 1933 having done much to boost Punshon's own career as a writer of detective fiction with her rave review of *Information Received*. (See the introduction to *Information Received*.)

In *Death among the Sunbathers* young Constable Bobby Own and his mentor, Superintendent Mitchell, confront another murder, this time that of Jo Frankland, a prominent woman journalist. When Frankland is pulled dead from a burning wrecked car, it is quickly discovered that her death was due not to crash injuries but rather a bullet fired out of a Browning automatic. Shortly before her death Frankland had visited Leadeane Grange, a property owned by a naturist group, the Society of Sun Believers. (Originally, notes Punshon wryly, the group was known as the Society of Sun Worshippers, "but the last word had been altered on the representation of some of the local clergy, who feared misunderstanding.") Was Frankland simply seeking material at Leadeane Grange for another colorful nudism story, or was she after something else? Superintendent Mitchell and Inspector Ferris are tasked with discovering the truth behind Frankland's brutal slaying. Constable Bobby Owen is less in evidence in this novel than he was in *Information Received*, though we do see a great deal of "Bobs-the-Boy," a pugnacious old lag with a mysterious agenda of his own.

E.R. Punshon received some contemporary criticism from reviewers for incorporating thriller elements into *Death Among The Sunbathers*. The novel was deemed something less than a simon-pure detective story and, unlike *Information Received*, it was never published in the United States. Yet this was not the first time Punshon had merged two strains of mystery in his detective novels.

In Punshon's earlier Inspector Carter and Sergeant Bell series, two of the five novels—*The Unexpected Legacy* (1929) and *The Cottage Murder* (1931)—are distinctly thrillerish. The boundaries between thrillers and true detective fiction became more firmly delineated in the 1930s, after rules distinguishing the two forms of mystery were promulgated by such authorities as Father Ronald Knox, S.S. Van Dine and Britain's Detection Club. Among other things, true detective novels were expected to refrain from reliance on such thriller devices as untraceable poisons, supernatural manifestations, fantastic pseudo-scientific gadgetry, twins, gangs and criminal masterminds. I leave it for readers to see for themselves just what ostensibly extraneous thriller matter finds its way into *Death Among The Sunbathers*. For the rest of the 1930s Punshon generally would be scrupulous in abiding by these distinctions. Most modern readers, I presume, will concern themselves with such aesthetic deviations less than some of Punshon's more absolutist contemporaries did.

With justice having triumphed in *Death Among The Sunbathers* due to the good offices of the law, Superintendent Mitchell informs Constable Owen at the conclusion of the novel that the copper's job is never done. "There'll be a little job waiting for you on the east coast," Mitchell tells Bobby. "There's something on there apparently that's worrying the local people because they can't make out what it is. So they've asked us to send down a youngster able to show at a country house as an ordinary guest and warranted not to give himself away by eating peas with a knife or putting his feet on the dinner table or doing anything else natural and friendly and sociable. Also required to be good-looking, smart, and intelligent. Think you fit the bill?"

"Yes, sir," answers Bobby, evidently having shed some of his modesty in *Death Among The Sunbathers*. The exciting events he experiences at the east coast country house are detailed in the next E.R. Punshon detective novel, *Crossword Mystery*.

Curtis Evans

CHAPTER ONE

The Burning Motor-Car

A SLIGHT defect had developed. Nothing of much importance, but it needed attention, and since just here the road
was dangerously narrow, since also close behind was the
sharp bend they had just come round, and as, moreover,
darkness was now beginning to set in, Constable Jacks, the
careful driver Superintendent Mitchell always chose when
he was available, decided to take precautions. Near to them
was a large, imposing-looking house with a wide drive
sweeping up to it, and prudently Jacks backed their car a
yard or two up this drive, of which the gate fortunately
hung wide open. In that way the rather narrow road itself
would be left free, and if any car did happen to round the
sharp bend in it at the speed at which cars do occasionally
take sharp bends, there would be no risk of any accident
occurring. Satisfied with the precaution thus taken, Jacks
alighted, got out his tools, and set to work.

Mitchell descended, too, to stretch his legs, as he said. He
was a big, generally slow-moving man, with a pale, flat face,
small, sandy moustache, deep-set grey eyes, and loose,
loquacious lips that at sudden, unexpected moments could
set in thin and rigid lines. His companion, Inspector Ferris,
followed, a big, bluff, hearty, smiling man, whose chief merit
as a detective was not so much any special subtlety of mind
or insight into things, but a devastating, almost awe-inspir-
ing patience that permitted him to sit and wait for hours,
and to be, to all appearance, as fresh and alert at the end of
the vigil as at its beginning. He and Mitchell had been on a
visit to Lord Carripore, chairman of Universal Assurances, a
company somewhat badly hit by a recent series of big fires,
including one on a transatlantic steamer, that Lord Carripore had personally declared to the Home Secretary could
not possibly be accounted for by natural causes. As his lord-

ship was suffering from a bad attack of sciatica, probably a result of sun-bathing, to which he was a recent and enthusiastic convert – though that that was the cause he would not have admitted for one moment – Mitchell and Ferris had been detailed to visit him at his country house. But the interview had proved of small interest. Lord Carripore appeared to have little to say, except that it was all most suspicious, and that his company had been hit to the tune of a quarter of a million, so that the annual dividend would probably have to be reduced, and the shareholders wouldn't like that, might even hint at making changes in the directorate. As, moreover, this prospect, or the sciatica, or both together, had affected his lordship's temper to a most unfortunate degree, the two police officers had been glad to take their leave as soon as they decently could.

'Of course, any assistance we can give, you can depend on,' Mitchell assured him as they were going; 'any information we can be supplied with, we will follow up instantly.'

'I thought it was the business of the police to get information, not to wait to have it given them,' snarled Lord Carripore, wincing at a fresh twinge of his sciatica.

'But we can't get it unless someone gives it us, can we?' Mitchell protested mildly. 'Information received is what we always need before we can take action.'

Therewith he and Ferris took their departure, leaving Lord Carripore writhing with mingled sciatica and temper, and determined as soon as he was well enough to ask the Home Secretary to dinner for the sole purpose of telling him exactly what he thought of Scotland Yard.

Unaware, however, of this determination, Mitchell and Ferris had already forgotten all about his lordship and his more than somewhat vague complaints and doubts and suspicions. It was another subject they were debating, and, as he followed Mitchell from the car, Ferris was saying,

'Well, sir, of course, it's for you to say, but Owen's young, very little experience. I would much rather have a more experienced man for the job myself.'

'Owen's young all right,' Mitchell admitted, 'though you and I were both the same age once.'

'Not long since he was transferred from the uniform branch,' Ferris persisted.

'Earned it,' said Mitchell; 'he was quite useful in that case of the murder of Sir Christopher Clarke.'

'Happened to be on the spot,' commented Ferris, still unsatisfied; 'never struck me as having any more brains than the next man – or much initiative.'

'Educated instead,' explained Mitchell, 'and education just naturally chokes initiative. He's 'Varsity and public school, you know, and you can't expect to have an education like that and initiative as well.'

'Don't hold with it,' grumbled Ferris, 'not with all these B.A.s and M.A.s and A.S.S.s crowding into the force – changes its whole tone.'

'It's a changing world,' Mitchell pointed out, 'and mass production of criminals has got to be met by mass production of police from 'Varsities. As for brains, well, I'm not saying I've noticed Owen has any more than the usual ration, and it's just as well. Too many brains is a fatal thing for any man in any line of life, though, the Lord be praised, few suffer from it. But Owen has got a kind of natural-born knack of being on the spot when he's wanted, and a detective on the spot is worth two —'

He paused, for they could both hear a car approaching at what was evidently a very high rate of speed. A moment later it rocketed round the bend in the roadway they themselves had just passed. It must have been going sixty or seventy miles an hour. Had Constable Jacks not adopted his precaution of backing their car a yard or two off the roadway up this carriage drive, a collision could hardly have been averted. For an instant as it flew by it showed clear in the strong light of their headlamps. They had a momentary vision of a woman at the steering-wheel, her face half hidden by one of the flat, fashionable hats of the day, worn tilted so much to one side that to the uninstructed male eye it seemed such hats could only stick on by the aid of a miracle

9

– or of glue – and by the high fox-fur collar of her coat.

It was the merest glimpse they had as the car shot by and Jacks stopped his work to stand up and shake a disapproving head at it.

'Asking for trouble,' he said, 'going round a corner like that at such a speed – want talking to.'

'Girl driving,' remarked Ferris, rather as if that explained all.

'Hope her life's insured,' commented Jacks. 'She was doing all of sixty m.p.h. – those little Bayard Sevens can travel all right.'

'Alone, wasn't she?' asked Mitchell. 'If she breaks her neck, as she probably will, she'll break it alone, that's one thing. I'm glad I wasn't in that car though – what's that?'

They had all heard the same sound, dull, strange, and ominous, distinct in the evening quiet, where the echo of the roaring progress of the little Bayard Seven seemed still to be hanging in the air, and to it they all gave instinctively the same interpretation. Then, as they looked, they saw a sudden crimson glow develop, shining red through the trees that lined the road, and across the hedges of the fields. None of them said a word. Jacks left his tools lying there, scattered by the roadside, and leaped into the driver's seat. Mitchell, quick enough at need, was already in his place, already had in his hands the chemical fire extinguisher. Ferris, a trifle less quick and active, tumbled after him. Jacks shot the car into the road, sent it flying along to where the crimson glow shone before them.

They came thundering at speed to where the road crossed by a bridge, a deep railway cutting. Their headlights showed them, half-way across, the railing that ran along the side of the bridge smashed clean away. Someone at a distance was running and shouting. Jacks brought the car to a standstill with a fierce grinding of tyres and brakes. Mitchell leaped out and was through the broken railing in a flash and down the steep side of the cutting to where across the rails a shapeless heap of wreckage smoked and burned. Somehow he arrived on his feet, still carrying the chemical extinguisher unharmed in his hands. Ferris, less fortunate, arrived on his back, head foremost. Jacks came last, more cautiously. He had taken time to bring the car close to the gap in the railing so that the light from its headlamps might illumine the scene. The fire was blazing furiously, but it had not yet obtained complete control, for all this had happened in two or three minutes and the chemical extinguisher was efficient. The flames spluttered, died down, smouldered a little. Presently, remained only a few tiny tongues of fire the three men beat out without difficulty. The car, or rather what was left of it, was lying on its side. Within, they could see a dark, motionless, huddled form that told them tragedy was there.

'Lend a hand here,' Mitchell grunted to the others, and added, for the wrecked car was lying right across the lines, 'Hope a train doesn't come along.'

The door of the car had jammed, but they managed to force it open. With some difficulty, and at the cost of a badly bruised hand for Ferris, they were able to disentangle a body from the wreckage. They laid the broken form on the grass at the foot of the steep embankment.

'Past help,' Ferris said, 'must have been killed on the spot.'

Mitchell had taken an electric torch from his pocket. With it in his hand he knelt down by the body.

'A woman,' he said. 'Young, too, poor thing.' And then the next moment : 'Good God,' he said below his breath. 'Ferris, Ferris.'

Ferris turned abruptly, startled.

'Sir !' he said.

'She was alive,' Mitchell half whispered, moved beyond his wont. 'I'll swear she was . . . just for a moment. . . . I saw her look at me . . . as if she wanted . . . something she wanted to say . . . then she was gone.'

'Are you sure, sir?' Ferris asked, more than a little incredulously. 'After a fall like that . . . it must have killed her on the spot . . . going over that embankment at sixty miles an hour . . . and if it didn't, then the fire would have, for it was all round her.'

'I saw her look at me,' Mitchell repeated, his voice not quite steady now, for though his profession had habituated him to scenes of terror and of grief, yet something in that momentary dying look had touched him to the quick, had seemed to convey to him some message he was but half conscious of. 'Young, too,' he said again.

'What I can't make out,' observed Jacks, 'is how it happened – a perfectly good straight road, night quite clear, no sign of any obstruction anywhere. Of course the steering might have gone wrong.'

'Bear looking into,' agreed Mitchell.

A voice from above asked what had happened, and then a man came scrambling down the steep embankment side. Mitchell became the brisk executive. The newcomer described himself as the landlord of a small public house, the George and Dragon, on the road just the other side of the bridge. His establishment did not boast a phone, but there was a call box close by. Mitchell sent Jacks to report to headquarters, to ask for more help, to summon the nearest doctor, to warn the railway people that the line was blocked, for the debris of the car, and part of the railing from the bridge it had carried down with it, lay right across the line. The landlord of the George and Dragon, who gave his name as Ashton, was set to work, too, while Mitchell and Ferris made as careful an examination as was possible of the half-burnt wreckage. But it was Ashton who called their attention to the smashed fragments of a bottle in what once had been the dicky of the car.

'Whisky, if you ask me,' he said. 'There's been whisky there all right – what about that?'

'Bear looking into,' agreed Mitchell, 'whisky explains a lot, and maybe it explains this, too – and maybe it don't.'

'There's the poor creature's hat,' Ferris remarked, pointing to it, where it lay, oddly uninjured, flaunting as it were its gay and fashionable self against the background of dark tragedy.

Somehow or another it had rolled to one side and had escaped both the fire and the effects of the fall.

They found a handbag, too. It was badly burned, but within were two different sets of visiting cards, comparatively slightly damaged. One set bore the name of Mrs John Pentland Curtis and an address in Chelsea, the other was inscribed, 'Miss Jo Frankland', with the same address, and at the bottom the legend, *Daily Announcer*.

'One of the *Announcer* staff perhaps,' Mitchell commented. 'Looks as if Curtis were her married name and Jo Frankland her own name she used in journalism still. Curtis – John Pentland Curtis,' he repeated thoughtfully, 'seem to know the name somehow.'

'Amateur middle heavyweight champion two years ago,' said Ferris, who was something of a boxer himself. 'Beat Porter of the City force in the final, fined five pounds last year for being drunk and assaulting one of our men, but apologized handsome after, and gave another tenner to our man, so he didn't do so bad, and another tenner to the Orphanage.'

'Wonder if it's the same man,' mused Mitchell.

They examined again the side of the embankment where the car had somersaulted down the steep incline, tearing earth and bushes with it, and they examined also the surface of the road. But the weather had been dry, the road surface was newly laid and in good condition; they found nothing to help them. Apparently the car had shot right across, across the pathway, through the railing, down the side of the cutting, and what had caused such a mishap on a perfectly good straight stretch of road there seemed nothing to show.

By now help was beginning to arrive. A breakdown gang had appeared to clear the line under the superintendence of Ferris. Photographers and other experts were on the scene. Mitchell was kept busy directing the operations, but when a local doctor came at last – there had been difficulty in finding one – he left his other activities to take the newcomer aside for a moment and whisper earnestly in his ear.

That the unfortunate victim of the accident was past all human aid was plain enough. Nevertheless the doctor carried out a very careful examination, and when he finished and came back to Mitchell there was a look of strange horror in his eyes.

'There are injuries enough from the fall to cause death,' he said; 'the spine is badly injured for one thing. There's the fire as well, the lower limbs are terribly burnt.'

'The actual cause of death,' Mitchell asked, 'can you say that?'

'There is a bullet wound in the body,' the doctor answered. 'She had been shot before the accident happened.'

CHAPTER TWO

Two Motor-Cyclists

IN all such tragic occurrences, much of the work that has to
be done is of a purely routine nature, and Mitchell was soon
satisfied that all that custom, regulation, and experience
prescribed was being correctly carried out. Now that there
was nothing to be seen to here that others could not attend
to just as well, he began to think of departing on errands
that seemed to him more pressing. Then Ferris with a touch
of excitement showing beneath his calm official manner
came up to him.

'A pistol's been found, sir,' he reported. 'A point thirty-
two Browning automatic. It's been pretty badly twisted up
with the heat, but it makes it look to me as if it might have
been suicide. If she shot herself, going at that speed, it would
account for the way the car swerved off a perfectly straight
road and went down over the embankment.'

'So it would,' agreed Mitchell. 'Bear looking into . . . only
I can't help remembering the way the poor thing looked at
me just before she died. Sort of surprised she seemed and
indignant, too, asking for help, protection, asking what I
was going to do about it – that's how it seemed to me. You
think I'm going silly, Ferris, talking a lot of fanciful rot.'

'Oh, no, sir,' answered Ferris, in a tone that plainly meant,
'Oh, yes, sir.'

'I don't wonder,' Mitchell said, answering not the words
but the tone. 'All the same, Ferris, you might have felt the
same if you had seen the look she gave me. Too late for help
or protection we were, but anyhow I can see whoever did it
don't escape.'

'Don't quite see myself,' Ferris observed, in his voice a
carefully restrained note of incredulity, 'if you don't mind
my saying so, sir, how she could possibly have been still alive –
shot through the body same as the doctor says, all smashed

up going over the embankment at sixty per hour, and then in the middle of that blaze till we came up. But if she was, sir, and you're sure of it – why, that goes to show she must have been shot only just the minute or two before the thing happened. And that looks like suicide again.'

'I don't know that that follows,' Mitchell objected; 'it might have been done some time before – she might have been lying unconscious till the shock of fall and fire brought her back to life for a moment just before the end came. For life's a rum thing, Ferris, and I've read stories of men having been executed by beheading and the head showing signs of consciousness afterwards, as if life still clung to it. Anyhow, I'm certain there was life and meaning in that poor creature's eyes for just the moment when she looked at me, and I'll swear she was asking what I meant to do about it.'

'Yes, sir,' agreed Ferris, slightly in the tone of one humouring a child's fancies, while to himself he thought that after all Mitchell must be getting near the age limit and no doubt his years were telling. He went on, 'I sent Jacks to find out at the pub up the road if they had heard anything like a shot. I thought we had better inquire before they got to know about the pistol, or half of them would most likely be ready to swear they heard the report and believe it, too. People will swear anything, you know, sir, once they let their imaginations go.'

Jacks came up and saluted.

'No one at the George and Dragon seems to have heard anything, sir,' he said, 'not even the sound of the smash. Anything they did hear, they just thought was something on the railway; they seem sort of trained not to notice noises on the line. But it seems a lady driving a Bayard Seven stopped there this afternoon to ask the way to Leadeane Grange. I don't know if you would like to speak to Mr Ashton yourself, sir.'

Mitchell nodded acquiescence. Ashton, interested and busy, was not far away. He remembered the incident clearly. He was certain the car had been a Bayard Seven. To the driver of the car, however, he had apparently given less attention. That she had been a woman, and young, was about all he could say.

'She wanted to know if she was right for Leadeane Grange,' Ashton said. 'I told her all she had to do was cross the bridge and keep straight on.'

'Leadeane Grange far? Who lives there?' Mitchell asked. Ashton permitted himself a grin.

'No one don't live there,' he said. 'Not more than three miles or it might be four, but there's no one lives there.'

'How's that?' Mitchell asked. 'How do you mean?'

'It's a place for them sun bathers,' Ashton explained. 'Sit out there on the lawn without any clothes on, they do, and if there ain't any sun, there's rays instead. A fair scandal I call it.'

Mitchell asked a few more questions and gathered that Ashton cherished a faint grudge against the sun-bathing establishment, partly on those high moral grounds which make us all disapprove of the activities of others, and still more because, though since it had come into existence it had greatly increased the traffic passing by, none of that traffic ever stopped at the George and Dragon except to ask the way.

'I get fair fed up,' he admitted, 'telling 'em to cross the bridge and keep straight on – a poor skeleton lot if you ask me, that look as if a good glass of beer would do 'em more good than sitting in the sun dressed same as when they were born. Only I will say I seem to remember she looked better than most, and so did the fellow on the motor-bike that caught her up.'

Ferris interrupted suddenly. He exclaimed :

'Leadeane Grange? Of course, I thought I knew the name – it's where Lord Carripore said he was the other day, where he caught his sciatica most like, though he wouldn't admit it.'

'That's right, I remember now,' agreed Mitchell. He turned back to Ashton. 'Fellow on a motor-bike caught her up?' he asked. 'Do you mean he stopped her?'

'Yes, following her he seemed,' Ashton answered. 'He

slowed down outside my place and I was just wondering whether he would be taking something or whether he was another of 'em wanting to know the way where he could have a sun bath instead of a regular Saturday night like everyone else, when he caught sight seemingly of the Bayard Seven on the top of the rise beyond the line and went off on top speed – fair vanished he did, doing eighty or more.'

'Did he catch her up, do you know?'

'Couldn't help, moving at that speed. And when he did they had a sort of row together seemingly.'

'Did they, though?' exclaimed Mitchell, interested. 'Could you see them? or hear?'

'It wasn't me, it was George,' Ashton explained. 'He was in a field close by where the fellow on the bike overtook her, and he says he could see 'em throwing their arms about, so to speak, and kind of hollering at each other.'

Mitchell expressed a wish to see the George referred to, who, when produced from the constantly augmenting collection of spectators doing their best to get in the way of the police and busily telling each other all about it, proved to be a not very intelligent, middle-aged labourer. All he had to say was that he had seen the motor-cyclist overtake the Bayard Seven, had seen the car stop, and had gathered from their gestures and their rather loud voices that the motor-cyclist and the driver of the Bayard Seven were quarrelling. Finally the lady banged her car door and drove off faster than before, and the motor-cyclist returned by the way he had come. George had not been near enough, however, to catch any of the actual conversation, nor had it occurred to him to try, and of course no one had thought of taking the number of the cycle, though the make – it was a B.A.D. – had been duly noted. The description of the cyclist himself was hardly more satisfactory – full, reddish face, dark hair and eyes, small dark toothbrush moustache, was about all Mitchell succeeded in obtaining from Ashton and George together, and one of them was certain that he was wearing overalls and a cap, and the other was sure that he had been wearing a leather coat and no hat at all. It did not seem much to go on, but Ashton, a little jealous of the success of George and the attention his story had excited, remembered now that another motor-cyclist had preceded the arrival of this one. He, too, had asked the way to Leadeane Grange, but he had not proceeded there, and after sitting outside the George and Dragon for nearly an hour with a glass of lemonade he never touched, as if waiting for someone, had fiinally gone off back again by the way he had come in the direction of town.

'And I wasn't sorry we was closed except for minerals and such like,' Ashton added, 'for it was easy to see he had had all the drink was good for him.'

'He could manage his cycle all right?' Mitchell asked.

'Oh, yes, it wasn't that he was far gone, only you could tell all right by the funny look in his eyes and the way he tripped in his talk every now and again. In our line you soon get to know when a man's had his whack, same as this chap had – and then some.'

'What was he like?' Mitchell asked.

Ashton looked worried.

'I should know him again,' he said, and seemed to think that a fully satisfactory reply.

About all that further questioning extracted was that the stranger had been a big man and either fair or else dark, Ashton wasn't quite sure which. He was nearly as indefinite about everything else, and then suddenly he brightened up.

'There was one thing I noticed,' he said. 'He had a bit of a thick ear, same as if he had done a bit of boxing in his time.'

'A point to remember,' conceded Mitchell; and saw that Ferris, too, had noticed the significance of these last words.

'If that was Curtis and he did it,' Ferris muttered to the superintendent aside, 'and we went at once, we might get him red-handed so to speak.'

'Not likely to be as easy as that,' Mitchell answered, as he and the inspector, followed by two plain clothes men, climbed into the car Jacks was soon driving Londonwards again. 'Anyhow, we've made some progress. Two mysterious motor-cyclists, one of them seen quarrelling with her and one of them possibly her husband – but no proof, Ferris, remember, that that lady in that Bayard Seven was identical with this other one, and not too much chance of identifying either of the cyclists on the evidence of George – or Ashton either. But it'll bear looking into, bear quite a lot of looking into.'

'I don't know if you noticed it, sir, and I dare say it's only a coincidence,' Ferris observed, 'but the description of the man the lady in the Bayard Seven is supposed to have been quarrelling with would fit Mr Hunter, of Howland Yard.'

'Why, so it would,' admitted Mitchell. 'I hadn't thought of that, but then it would fit plenty of others as well – fit hundreds of other men. Bear looking into all the same. We'll have to set Owen on to that. I rather wish Owen had been here to-night – might have proved useful.'

Ferris looked as if he did not share that opinion. He was in fact slightly jealous of Owen, a young man not long in the force who had certainly done well in the case of the murder of Sir Christopher Clarke, but probably owed his success more to luck than anything else. Mitchell, however, had certainly taken a fancy to him, and seemed inclined to think at once of him whenever any special mission needed executing. Mitchell went on as if talking more to himself than to Ferris :

'It's none of it clear. Whoever it was quarrelled with who-ever the lady may have been, seems to have left her and gone straight back to town. And if it was Curtis who hung about outside the George and Dragon, he seems to have gone off before the Bayard Seven lady appeared, and to have gone off back to town, too.'

'Ashton said he had been drinking,' Ferris remarked. 'When a man's been drinking —'

Mitchell nodded an agreement.

'Oh, it'll bear looking into,' he said, 'and the first job in-dicated is an interview with Mr Curtis.'

When, however, they reached the Chelsea address they had discovered in the burning car – it proved to be on the first floor in one of those large, new blocks of flats that are springing up all over London – it was to find themselves unable to secure any answer. They knocked and rang in vain. Then they tried ringing up from an adjacent call-box without getting any reply. The porter in charge had seen both Mr and Mrs Curtis go out as usual that morning, one to his place of business, one to the office of the *Daily Announcer*, where, as Mitchell had guessed, Mrs Curtis was on the staff, but did not think either of them had returned. The daily woman they employed was only there in the mornings and had gone long since. There seemed nothing for it but to wait till Mr Curtis should return; and so, leaving one of the plain-clothes men there on watch to notify them the moment he appeared, Mitchell and Ferris went on to the office of the *Daily Announcer*.

CHAPTER THREE

The 'Daily Announcer'

THE *Daily Announcer*, one of those great national papers that to-day provide the people of this country with all their needs, from their opinions and beliefs down to their sets of standard authors in best imitation half calf, possesses, as all the world knows, offices in Ludgate Hill that for their magnificent modernity have become one of the sights of London, so modern indeed as to make those of their most up-to-date Fleet Street rival appear almost antediluvian. Nowhere in the building is any material used save rustless steel that is for ever as bright as though a regiment of charladies did nothing but polish it all day long, and glass of the new type that is warranted to keep out all those harmful rays that nature so inconsiderately mingles with its sunshine. Even the easy chairs in the waiting-room are of shining steel; and the gossip that says that those in the editor's private sanctum are of homely wood upholstered in the style that father knew, is most likely merely malicious – but only those can tell for certain who have ever penetrated into that awesome chamber, and they are too few in number, and most likely in any case too dazzled by the splendour of the presence, for their evidence to be available. A superb house telephone system enables every member of the staff to comunicate with anyone else in the building without leaving his desk, and it is often possible to ring up the man in the room across the corridor opposite yours, and then get up and go and have your talk with him, and come back again to find you have already been put through.

In fact, the *Announcer* is the last word in efficiency. Wherever a machine could do a man's work, a machine was installed. As for their news service, that functioned with a really marvellous certainty and speed, and this evening for instance they had already the news of the tragedy on the

Leadeane Road, though not as yet the further fact that it was murder and no accident that had occurred. But already reporters were out, gathering every detail.

The news editor, Mr Reynolds, hearing of the arrival of two high Scotland Yard officials, received them himself, for his instinct told him at once it must be more than a mere accident, however tragic. And when he heard that foul play had taken place, he was shocked as a man, distressed as a colleague, and as a news editor thrilled with the thought of the headlines with which he would be able to bring out the next morning's issue. 'Exclusive *Announcer* interview with Police Chiefs' would be the smallest of them.

Miss Frankland, Mrs Curtis in private life, was, he said at once, a valued member of their staff. She had been with them some years, an extraordinarily capable, energetic journalist, whose heart and soul were in her profession; ambitious, too, for it was known she cherished the hope of becoming some day the first woman editor of one of the great national papers. After all, as she was accustomed to say, a woman had already been a Cabinet Minister, and why should not another woman climb to still more dazzling heights and win through even to the editorial chair of one of the great dailies? A dazzling thought, but what man has done, woman will do.

Two or three years before, she had married, a weakness in a woman with a career, but she had been wise enough to let it make no difference to her work. Indeed, it was a standing joke in the office that on the eve of her wedding she had offered to put it off for a day or two, if no one else could be found to fill a certain assignment. Fortunately so extreme a measure had not been necessary, but it showed how keen she was.

'Not long ago,' added Mr Reynolds, to emphasize still further this point, 'we had to ring her up on an emergency story one night she and her husband were giving a dinner-party to some friends, and she came right along and never said a word.'

'Well, now, think of that,' murmured Mitchell when Mr

Reynolds paused for him to express his admiration, but all the same in private Mitchell wondered if husband and friends had been equally complaisant, or whether they, or at least the husband, had been tempted to say perhaps a word or two. Then he asked, 'Is Mr Curtis the gentleman who was well known at one time as an amateur boxer?'

Mr Reynolds had no idea. The sports editor might know, but he did not. It was evident that Mr Reynolds's interest in his staff was as entirely confined to their journalistic abilities as his interest in the universe was confined to its ability to provide headlines for his next issue – a man of one idea, in fact, which accounts for his value, his standing, and his reputation.

It appeared, however, from something else he said that Miss Frankland's standing in the office permitted her a certain initiative, and it was at her own request she had been allowed to go that afternoon to visit the sun bathing establishment at Leadeane Grange in order to write it up.

'Though the *Daily Intelligence* did it a month or two ago, added Mr Reynolds, 'so what made her think of doing it again I've no idea – unless,' he added thoughtfully, 'she was on the track of some scandal – a lot of Society people go there.'

To Mr Reynolds, Society had but one interest – that of providing a scandal now and again. But he admitted that so far as he knew the Leadeane Grange sun bathing establishment was conducted with the utmost discretion.

'Lot of well-known people go there – latest fad, you know. Lord Carripore goes twice a week regularly – I know that because we had to send there to interview him about the big fire that took place on one of the American liners the other day.'

' I remember that,' agreed Mitchell. 'Now I come to think of it, it was there I had to send Owen to look for him with that note from the Commissioner,' he added to Ferris, and then explained to Reynolds, 'Owen's one of our young men. Lord Carripore wants us to make some inquiries, but they haven't come to anything so far. You have no idea if there was anything special that took Miss Frankland there?'

'You might ask Miss Martin if you like,' suggested Mr Reynolds; 'she runs our woman's page and was very friendly with Miss Frankland. Most likely Miss Frankland had something in her mind. She had a wonderful nose,' he added admiringly.

'Nose?' repeated Mitchell, slightly puzzled.

'For news,' explained Reynolds. 'She could smell out a story quicker than almost anyone I've ever known. Of course she went off on a false scent at times, like everyone, but I wouldn't mind betting there was some reason she had for being keen on visiting Leadeane, though it may have been just she thought she could write it up better than the *Daily Intelligence* people did.'

Then in his turn he began to question Mitchell very gently, very discreetly, very thoroughly, and Mitchell answered almost like a good little boy in Sunday school, so free and frank and innocent he was, till when he rose to go, and while Reynolds was already visualizing with excited approval the splendid headlines he would splash across the issue now preparing, Mitchell launched his devastating, sledge-hammer, high-explosive knock-out.

'Of course,' he said, 'all that's quite confidential, Mr Reynolds, entirely between ourselves.'

Less cruel would it have been to dash a cup of cold water from the parched lips of one dying from thirst. Mr Reynolds nearly wept. He tried to wheedle, coax, protest, but Mitchell clung to that word of power 'confidential', and leaving behind them as nearly heartbroken a news-editor as imagination can conceive, they made their way under the guidance of a messenger boy, through a labyrinth of passages, past a series of rabbit hutches miscalled offices and a good deal less modern than the exterior of the building promised, to the room where Miss Martin would have been waiting for them, had not the phone message warning her of their arrival somehow gone astray.

However, she was not far off. Like, by now, everyone else in the building, she had heard of what most of them still believed to be the accident to their colleague. It had evidently been a great shock to her, and she was eager for details, but she, no more than Mr Reynolds, had any idea what had made Miss Frankland suddenly desirous of writing up the Leadeane sun bathing. She admitted that in her view sun bathing had now dropped from the news class into the category of the accepted. She could only suppose that Miss Frankland had seen her way to make something of it. Anyhow, anything she wrote would always have been sure of favourable consideration. Miss Martin evidently knew more, too, than Mr Reynolds had done of Miss Frankland's private life. She knew she had a sister, for instance, named Sybil, who lived with their mother in Ealing. She gave Mitchell the address. The father had died, she thought, many years ago. Mitchell's further question as to whether Miss Frankland had any known enemies, either private or journalistic, evidently startled Miss Martin a good deal.

'Good gracious, no,' she declared. 'Jo was amazingly popular. What makes you ask that?'

'I have a reason,' Mitchell replied. 'About her husband; do you know if they got on well together?'

'They were tremendously in love when they got married,' Miss Martin answered evasively. 'Jo was a perfect idiot about him.'

'And after the marriage?' Mitchell asked.

Quite plainly Miss Martin did not very much want to answer. But she gave way to Mitchell's gentle insistence and admitted that certain differences had arisen. Both were strong-willed, somewhat egotistic people, self-willed and hot-tempered. All the same, there was no doubt, Miss Martin insisted, that they were still amazingly in love with each other. Mitchell referred to the story Reynolds had told of the interrupted dinner-party when Mrs Curtis had been summoned from her husband and guests to attend to some journalistic errand.

'I wondered a little how Mr Curtis took that,' Mitchell remarked : and Miss Martin had to admit that Mr Curtis had failed to take it quite as one would have hoped.

'He never seemed able to realize that a journalist must put her paper first,' observed Miss Martin. 'On principle.'

'Ah, yes, on principle,' observed Mitchell. 'Wonderful thing – principle.'

'Poor Jo was very upset about it,' Miss Martin added. 'Then, too, I don't think Mr Curtis quite understood the way she had to go about – I'm not sure sometimes he wasn't rather jealous because she met so many people he knew nothing about.'

Mitchell asked a few more questions, and then told her gently that the reason for his asking them was that her friend had met her death not by accident but by murder. It was a great shock to Miss Martin, who indeed seemed at first hardly able to believe it. She was so shocked indeed that she even forgot the news value of the information and could think of nothing but the tragedy. And she told them that that very afternoon, just before the unfortunate Jo Frankland had started out to get her story, Mr Curtis had called at the office and had made a most unpleasant scene.

'I think he must have been drinking,' she said. 'I don't know what it was about, I only heard of it afterwards. I expect Wilkins, the porter downstairs in the hall, could tell you.'

The two men thanked her and went away to find Wilkins, who inhabited the great entrance hall downstairs, all in marble and gold, the pride, for its great sweep and splendid lines, of the architect who had designed it, but who had never in all his dreams bargained for the little hutch, half glass half wood, that had now been erected by the side of the great central stairway, to the somewhat doubtful improvement of its upward spring. From this erection Wilkins watched to make sure no unauthorized person penetrated to the mystic realms above whence day by day proceeded the *Announcer's* version of the version they had received of the reported facts of what it was believed might possibly have happened during the last four and twenty hours.

Wilkins, duly impressed by the fact that he was talking to a police superintendent – though he had stopped once without turning a hair an authentic film star from ascending those stairs, and had made even the writer of the current best-seller wait while his card was sent up in the usual way, nor in either case had lightnings from heaven destroyed him – proved communicative. He, too, had heard the news of the accident, as he still believed it to be, and showed himself quite human in his concern. Too bad, too, he thought, after the flare up there that afternoon. It might be worrying about that, he thought, had caused the accident, for generally Miss Frankland was a good, careful driver.

Mitchell asked for details of the scene Wilkins had talked of and with some hesitation Wilkins gave them.

'But, you understand, sir,' he said, 'Mr Curtis had been drinking, or he wouldn't ever have talked the wild way he did.'

'What was that?' asked Mitchell.

'It was some place where he had seen her, he said,' Wilkins explained. 'Howland Yard, it was, I think, and a Mr Keene with her, or following her. So Miss Frankland told him off, bitter like; not much she said, but the way she said it, spying, she said, and then he whipped out a pistol and showed it her.'

'Did he, though?' exclaimed Mitchell, startled this time. 'That was going a bit far.'

'Gave me a bit of a turn,' Wilkins admitted.

'Did you see what make it was?' Mitchell asked.

'One of those automatics – a Browning automatic – point thirty-two calibre most likely, but I'm not sure,' Wilkins answered. 'I heard him say, "You had better be careful – you and Keene, too." She stood up to him well; blazing with anger she was. "I'll never forgive you for that, John," she said, and he gave her a queer, sick sort of look, as if he knew she meant it, but only just that moment knew what he had done. So then he put the pistol back in his pocket and walked straight outside, and I wasn't sorry to see him go either. Miss Frankland stood looking after him. Then Mr Freeman came in and started talking to her. Of course he hadn't any idea of what had been going on, and she answered him just as cool as could be.'

'Who is Mr Freeman?' Mitchell asked.

'Well, he was one of the gentlemen here,' answered Wilkins, 'but he got the push two or three months back – something went wrong, we missed a story and they thought it was his fault. So he got the push and I did hear he had been through a bad time, jobs not being so easy to get along of now. He had been asking Miss Frankland to try to help him to get back, and she had been doing her best, but, lor', you know yourself, it's a sight easier to get pushed off than to get pushed on again.'

'Why was she interesting herself?' Mitchell asked. 'Were they specially friendly?'

'Oh, no,' answered Wilkins, 'only Miss Frankland was like that, always ready to help you if she could – wasn't a better liked lady in Fleet Street.'

On the general popularity of Jo Frankland, Mitchell allowed the good Wilkins to dilate for a moment or two, and then, satisfied there was no trace of any secret enmity to be discovered in the *Announcer* office, he suggested to Ferris that they had better be pushing along to Ealing to see what the relatives had to tell them.

'For up to the present,' he commented to Ferris as they made their way towards their waiting car with Jacks still at the wheel, 'up to the present we don't seem to have hit on much in the way of a motive.'

CHAPTER FOUR

The Ealing Villa

'Rummy,' commented Mitchell again as he settled himself in his seat in the car, 'Rummy that Howland Yard keeps popping up – you remember, Ferris, you thought the description of the second motor-cyclist answered to Hunter's. Can it have been his place in Howland Yard Mrs Curtis was visiting? But then who is Keene? Have to put Owen on to that.'

'Yes, sir,' agreed Ferris, 'but if you ask me, it seems to be getting pretty clear. Jealous husband on the booze, threats and pistol and all. Looks plain enough to me.'

'Think he can have been in the car when we saw it pass us?' Mitchell asked. 'If he did it, he must have been either in the car or have joined her somehow afterwards.'

'I've been trying to work that out,' Ferris answered. 'Curtis might have been in the car; none of us saw him, but he might have been there all the same, though it's not likely. We all thought at the time she was alone, and I would be pretty near ready to swear to it myself. But going at the rate that car was travelling, it ought to have got to where the smash happened quicker than it did.'

'You mean,' Mitchell observed thoughtfully, 'there was a longer interval between our seeing the car pass and our hearing the smash than there would have been normally, if the same speed had been kept up?'

'That's right,' said Ferris. 'In my humble opinion it's on the cards that Curtis was on the road, waiting for her perhaps. If the car slowed down or stopped, which it is next to certain it did, it must have been for some reason. What? But with all this talk about motor bandits and the rest of it, in my humble opinion no woman motorist, driving alone after dark, would be likely to stop unless it was for someone she knew. But if she recognized her husband, for instance, it would be perfectly natural for her to slow up.'

'What do you think happened then?' Mitchell asked.

'Why, he was crazy with drink and jealousy and we know he had a pistol. Perhaps he thought she had come straight from meeting someone. He shot her and then ran the car over the embankment. Possibly he climbed down afterwards and set it on fire in the hope of concealing the crime. He could easily get away afterwards along the line without any risk of being seen or leaving any tracks.'

'Almost good enough to put before Treasury Counsel,' agreed Mitchell. 'Anyhow, I think it's right there was a slight delay of some sort after she passed us, before the thing happened. The question is, why? Was it because Curtis stopped her? Or was it someone else? Or was it for some other reason altogether?'

'Odds on the husband, in my humble opinion,' pronounced Ferris.

Mitchell leaned forward and spoke to Jacks, who stopped the car almost immediately on coming at once in sight of the call box he had been told to look out for. Mitchell alighted and, after using the phone, returned to the car. The man he had left on watch outside the Chelsea flat had been instructed to report the moment any sign of life or movement was visible there, but so far it seemed nothing had been heard from him. Plainly therefore Curtis had not yet returned, and Ferris nodded complacently at this confirmation of his theory.

'Most likely he's making for the continent,' he said. 'Don't you think, sir, it might be as well to have all the continental boats watched?'

Mitchell agreed that the precaution might be useful and went back to the phone to ask that it should be done. Once they were on their way again, he remarked thoughtfully:

'I wonder why she was so keen on writing up this sun bathing place? I thought that seemed to puzzle them quite a lot at the *Announcer* office, and I must say I should have thought myself sun bathing was a bit stale news by now for an up-to-date paper. Bear looking into, that.'

'In my humble opinion,' declared Ferris, 'there was someone she wanted to meet, and sun bathing was a handy cover.'

But Mitchell shook his head.

'Plenty of opportunities for a woman working on her own to meet anyone she wanted to without telling all the world where she was going,' he objected. 'Besides, she didn't sound like that sort to me; too keen on her work, too ambitious, to be fooling about with any other man when most likely she was half sorry about tying herself up to her husband. I agree if we can get young Owen to identify the second motorcyclist who was seen quarrelling with her as Mr Hunter, of Howland Yard – it'll look a bit different. But if she was going to Leadeane Grange to meet him, why did he wait for her on the way and start a quarrel at once? Don't seem to fit in.'

'Main points,' commented Ferris, 'are, so far – (1) Find Curtis. (2) Check up Curtis's movements this afternoon from time seen outside George and Dragon. (3) Check up possible identification of Hunter, Howland Yard, with second motorcyclist. (4) What was cause of apparent stopping of deceased's car after passing us? (5) What was connexion between deceased and Howland Yard?'

'Instruct Owen accordingly,' said Mitchell. 'Further, why did deceased want to write up the sun bathing place, and who is the "Keene" Curtis talked about according to Wilkins? Is it possible that is another name for Hunter?'

Jacks brought the car to a standstill and said to them :

'This'll be the place, sir, I think.'

They had stopped before one of those small 'semi-detached villas' common in Ealing as in most of the other London suburbs. The lighted windows, a bustle of people about, several cars standing in the roadway, told that something unusual had happened. Mitchell guessed correctly that already news of the tragedy was here, nor was he sorry to be spared the task of breaking such tidings to the relatives. From the scene of the catastrophe itself, and from all the newspaper offices, reporters had swarmed on that little Ealing house, anxious, each and all, to be the first to tell of what had happened, for every news editor in town wished to be able to say, and intended to say, whether able or not, 'The first news of the tragedy was brought to the victim's relatives by our representative.' Their task, too, it would be to describe in language of discreet emotion how the intelligence was received, since these are days when private grief must not hide from public curiosity, to secure also photographs for the back page, and above all to get word of the whereabouts of John Curtis, of whose odd disappearance some rumours were already circulating and an interview with whom for the morning's issue was plainly indicated as desirable.

Most of the newspaper men knew Mitchell, and they swooped upon him in a flock, avid for more details. But he by long practice knew how to answer at length, with the greatest frankness and friendliness, while saying precisely nothing, and on his side he learned from them that that Mrs Frankland and Sybil Frankland, Jo's mother and younger sister, the inmates of the house and her only near relatives, already knew the dreadful truth that what had happened had been not accident but murder.

It had been altogether too much for the older lady, who had retired to her room in a state of almost complete collapse. But Sybil, though dreadfully pale and shaken, appeared quite collected. This story indeed of her sister as the victim of a sensational and inexplicable murder was one that she seemed hardly able to realize as actual fact. She had the air of expecting every moment to wake from what would prove to have been only a bad dream. Probably till now murder had seemed to her a thing one read about, a thing in books or newspapers, far off and unreal as dreams and fairy tales; that such a thing could enter into her own life she found difficult to grasp. All the time she kept looking towards the door, as if expecting to see Jo herself come walking in with her long easy stride that went so well with her tall figure, ready to laugh and explain in her jolly way that it was all part of those odd journalistic activities that Sybil for her part had always found bizarre and bewildering enough.

In appearance Sybil was small and slight, with nothing of her unfortunate sister's height and somewhat imposing presence. But if her appearance was less striking, she was none the less very pretty in her quiet and pleasant way. Jo, no one could ever have passed at any time without notice. Sybil could easily have slipped by without earning a second glance, but less easily could anyone have been in her company for ten minutes without being aware of a certain gentle attractiveness she possessed. She was fair, as her sister had been, with sunny hair, less tortured by the hairdresser than the present mode commands; blue, candid eyes; and a lovely complexion on which she had the good sense to inflict no cosmetics save sun and rain and the fresh air of heaven, and also with a very engaging little smile that in more normal times, but not now, came and went in a shy, unexpected way, as if at her own secret thoughts. A certain clear roundness of outline her small, firm chin showed suggested, however, that she had her own viewpoint and one she would not change too easily, though at the moment it was distress and terror and sheer, utter bewilderment her features expressed most clearly.

When Mitchell explained who he was she took him into the little drawing-room. She had no idea, however, where her brother-in-law could be. She could not understand his absence. She had rung up, she said, the Chelsea flat two or three times already, without getting any reply. To further questions she admitted, indeed there was no use trying to conceal what was so well known, that there had been a certain amount of disagreement between husband and wife, but she insisted with evident conviction that at bottom they had been still devoted to each other.

'It was only that John was a little jealous of her work,' Sybil said.

And when Mitchell went on to ask her outright if she thought it possible Curtis could be guilty of the murder, she showed herself so horrified, so amazed, and in a way so amused, at a suggestion that had evidently never entered her mind as even the barest of possibilities, that Mitchell had to pacify her by explaining it was merely a theory their official position forced them to consider.

'We have to think of everything,' he told her, 'especially when it's a case like this and we can't find Mr Curtis, or anyone to tell us where he is. You can't give us any hint, Miss Frankland, of any enemy your sister had, or of anyone who could have a reason for doing her harm?'

Then just for a moment there passed in her clear, blue eyes the shadow of an awful fear, passed and was gone again in a flash, as if resolutely thrust back into the unconscious.

'Have you thought of something?' Mitchell asked quickly.

She shook her head. Her expression grew almost defiant. She said,

'I'll ring up the flat again and see if John is back yet.'

Before they realized it she was out of the room, at the phone in the hall, and Mitchell muttered somewhat sourly to Ferris,

'She did that to get time – there's something she's thought of, something she's afraid of.'

'Have to get it out of her then, somehow or another,' growled Ferris, looking a little less hearty and smiling than usual.

But Mitchell shook his head.

'She won't let it out to herself just yet, much less to anyone else,' he remarked. 'Not for a time. It looks to me there's something in her mind she won't confess even to herself, won't admit could be possible even. Whatever it is, it'll bear looking into.'

Sybil came back into the room. She had obtained no reply. And now a certain change had come over her; she was more guarded in her replies, more watchful in her manner. Her answers were briefer, too, and she was more apt to plead ignorance. She repeated emphatically, however, when Mitchell returned to the point, that her sister had had no enemies. It was absurd to suppose anyone could have wanted to murder her. It was all some dreadful mistake. As for suicide, that was quite unthinkable – on the very threshold of a career that promised to be brilliant? Whatever the explanation, it was not suicide, of that Sybil was sure.

'She would have known it would have killed mother,' Sybil added.

'And you can't suggest who the man could be I described to you who was seen to stop her car and apparently engage in some dispute with her,' persisted Mitchell.

'I can't even think of any little man she knew,' Sybil answered.

'I don't think I said little exactly,' Mitchell remarked.

'I thought you said it was a little man?'

'Description,' said Ferris, reading it from his note-book, 'dark, medium height, good-looking – not much to go on.'

'Well, I can't think of anyone she knew like that. Or anyone I know, either,' Sybil declared with a certain decision and at the same time with a certain air of relief.

There came a knock at the door, and one of the waiting journalists put his head in.

'Oh, Miss Frankland,' he said, 'there's a chap here who says his name is Keene, says you know him and he must see you. I told him I would let you know he was here.'

CHAPTER FIVE

'Bobs-the-Boy' Appears

THAT Sybil welcomed this interruption as a relief from questioning she was beginning to feel a strain, was evident enough. She fairly ran from the room, with but the merest muttered word of excuse thrown to the two detectives; and the journalist, torn for a brief moment between using this opportunity to try to get an informing word or two from Mitchell, and his feeling that the newcomer might be a bringer of fresh news, decided finally to follow her.

Turning to Ferris, Mitchell said thoughtfully,

'Notice the name, Ferris? Keene . . . where does he come in and why was Curtis talking about him?'

Ferris still had uppermost in his mind his theory of the jealous husband.

'Looks to me as if this girl knew something,' he remarked.

'I should put it this way,' Mitchell said. 'There's something in her mind, but what it is even she herself hardly knows yet, and she's doing her level best not to know. Interesting to see if this Keene is a tall man.'

'Tall? Why?' asked Ferris, slightly bewildered.

'If you noticed,' Mitchell explained, 'she wanted the motor-cyclist seen quarrelling with her sister to be a small man. The description said medium height, and you said medium height, and twice over she turned that into "little", because she wanted it to be a little man that story referred to, or rather, because she was afraid of his being described as tall.'

'Yes, sir,' said Ferris doubtfully. 'I don't pretend myself to understand all this new-fangled stuff about people knowing what they don't know they know. It's fellows like Owen crowding into the force the way they are doing now that hand out that sort of dope.'

In spite of his respect for his official chief he could not

altogether repress the reproach that burned in his voice, for Ferris was of the old-fashioned type, and had indeed only scraped through the necessary promotion examinations by the special favour of the Assistant Commissioner of the day, who had known his value. Mitchell felt the reproach in his old comrade's voice, and was not insensible to it, but yet stuck to his own point of view.

'I'm a great believer in education,' he said; 'no really good man was ever yet the worse for it, and then, too, the force has got to keep up with the crooks – you don't find them despising education. And if we find a six-footer in touch with Miss Sybil Frankland, then —'

He paused. The door opened and Sybil came in again, followed by a young man who could claim to be a six-footer with a couple of inches at least to spare. He was of rather ungainly build, with a small body for his height, with long, sprawling limbs terminating in enormous bony hands and feet, but with the face of a pouting cherub, so round and smooth it was, with such small, well-shaped, handsome features, wide, innocent-looking eyes and a pursed-up, red-lipped mouth, above which flickered the dawning of a faint moustache that apparently had not yet decided whether to face the world in growth or not. An unusual-looking youngster altogether, Mitchell felt; one of the self-willed, rather spoiled type, and yet easily led as well. Sybil was clinging to his arm with both hands, and remembering that she wore an engagement ring on her left hand, Mitchell guessed they were an engaged couple.

'Mr Keene?' he asked amiably. 'A friend of the family, I believe?'

'Miss Frankland and I are engaged,' Keene explained. 'I came along as soon as I heard. It doesn't seem possible, I couldn't believe it at first.' He added to Sybil, 'I saw some fellow dodging about the garden as I came in – is he another of these journalist chaps?'

'Oh, they're everywhere,' Sybil said wearily.

'You knew Mr and Mrs Curtis?' Mitchell asked him.

'Yes, of course. Jo called at the shop only this morning
... and now ... I can hardly believe it's true even yet.'

'What shop is that?' Mitchell asked. 'Is it yours?'

'Yes. I'm an art dealer; my place is in Deal Street, Piccadilly,' Keene explained. 'Mrs Curtis came in this morning.'

'Any special reason for calling?' Mitchell asked, and it
did not escape his attention that Keene hesitated for a
moment before answering, and that he chose his words with
a certain care as he replied,

'Well, yes ... I suppose so ... Miss Frankland and I are
hoping to get married pretty soon, and Mrs Curtis wanted
us to put it off for a time.'

'Why was that?' Mitchell asked.

'Oh, well,' Keene answered, 'things are pretty bad in our
line ... dad made pots of money; but ever since the slump,
trying to sell a picture is like trying to get a man to back a
horse he knows won't run. If you do try, people just look at
you and then start to talk about the weather.'

'Things pretty bad everywhere, I suppose,' agreed
Mitchell, thinking sadly of certain pay cuts he knew of,
while Ferris heaved a sigh so deep it seemed like a young
gale.

'That's what Jo didn't understand,' Keene explained
eagerly. 'She was doing jolly well herself and she thought
everyone else ought to be – Curtis wasn't all the same. And
then she didn't like the idea of our leaving England.'

'You were thinking of that?'

'Well, I have some relatives out in Kenya – you can pick
up a good farm there almost for the asking just now, and if
you've a bit of money coming in to keep going you can live
on it for nothing nearly and just wait till things get bettter.'

'It wasn't so much that Jo minded our going,' Sybil interposed. 'She wouldn't believe Maurice could sell the business
for enough to give us a start there.'

'Oh, you never know your luck,' Keene observed.

That there had been some friction between Keene and the
dead woman seemed plain, and yet Mitchell felt it was impossible to attach much importance to the fact. No reason-

able motive for murder lay there; one does not murder a prospective sister-in-law for advising a more prudent course than one feels altogether inclined to follow. All the same, the point was one to remember, and Mitchell went on,

'You said Mr Curtis wasn't doing very well in business?'

'Hit like everyone else,' Keene asserted. 'Not that that mattered with Jo earning what she did – well up to four figures, I suppose. He has a bottle factory in Shoreditch somewhere, he bought when he left the Navy two or three years ago.'

'There was a small profit last year,' Sybil put in. 'Not much, but it was a profit, Jo told me.'

Mitchell asked for the address, and Ferris duly noted it down, thinking to himself that the financial position of that factory would have to be carefully investigated. He could remember more cases than one in which a harassed business man's mind had given way and he had sought refuge in murder and suicide. Was that what had happened here? Ferris asked himself.

Something of the same idea had entered Mitchell's mind, and he asked,

'You have no idea where Mr Curtis can be? It seems strange we can get no word of him.'

'I'll ring up their flat again,' Sybil said, and once more she got no reply. 'It's very strange,' she said, coming back into the room with the news of her failure.

'Do you remember ever hearing Mrs Curtis say anything about the Leadeane sun bathing place?' Mitchell asked her. 'Have you any idea why she should think of writing about it?'

'Oh, she was always writing about anything,' Keene interposed. 'Her job,' he said vaguely.

'I told her,' Sybil added, as Mitchell still looked at her as if waiting her own reply, 'that Mr Keene went there sometimes and she was rather interested. I don't know if that's what made her think of writing about it.'

'You go in for sun-bathing then, Mr Keene?' Mitchell observed, and Keene nodded a somewhat sulky response.

But it was not a subject he seemed to want to say much about. He had been there. It was a very well-conducted place. There was nothing out of the ordinary about it. In the first place he went there because Mr Esmond Bryan, who ran it, had become a client of his, and had interested him in it. Personally he was sure it was good for him; Horry Hunter thought the same. He and Horry both felt all the better for their visits to Leadeane.

'Horry Hunter's a chap I know,' he explained to Mitchell.

Mitchell saw that Ferris, always busy with his note-book, had looked up quickly, and guessed that he, too, had noticed this fresh coincidence of names. Mitchell said,

'Is it the Mr Hunter who has a wholesale fur business in Howland Yard?'

Keene looked rather startled, even uneasy, as he answered in the affirmative.

'Mrs Curtis know him, or Mr Curtis?' Mitchell inquired.

'No, not that I know of. Why?'

'We have information Mrs Curtis was seen in Howland Yard this morning,' answered Mitchell.

But both the two young people looked blank at this, and thought there must be some mistake. It was possible Mr Hunter's name might have been mentioned before her, but that was all. They were fairly certain she had never met him; there was no conceivable reason why she should wish to see him, or why she should go to his place of business.

'The only time I ever mentioned Mr Hunter that I remember,' Sybil said, 'was once when something was being said about our going to Kenya. Jo always said we should never be able to sell the business for enough to give us a start there, and I told her we knew Mr Hunter was thinking of doing exactly the same thing – getting rid of his business here, I mean, and starting fresh somewhere else.'

'Had the same idea as you, Mr Keene?' Mitchell remarked, while Ferris's pencil wrote steadily on.

'Oh, I don't know,' mumbled Keene. 'We talked about it sometimes when we met at Leadeane.'

They were interrupted by a sound of someone calling, and Sybil said quickly,

'That's mother, I must see what she wants.'

She left the room quickly and Mitchell asked Keene again – he had put the same question to him before –

'You are sure you can't think of anything to throw light on this affair? If we could get a hint of any motive. . . .'

'I wish I could,' declared Keene emphatically, 'it's an awful business . . . I can hardly realize it yet . . . it'll pretty nearly kill old Mrs Frankland . . . Sybil, too, awful for her . . . I can't imagine why anyone . . . most people liked Jo, one of the jolly sort, got on with people . . . of course she hated me, but that was only because she thought I wasn't good enough for Sybil and didn't believe in the Kenya idea . . . thought it wasn't possible. It was though, and so she would have found out before long.'

'Do you mean you were openly on bad terms?' Mitchell asked. 'Had there been any serious quarrel between you?'

'Oh, no, we were always civil enough when we met . . . of course, we weren't pals exactly, because I knew she wanted Sybil to break it off, but I didn't care because I knew Sybil wouldn't . . . besides I knew it was only because of the money and she thought I wouldn't have enough to make a start in Kenya and so it was cracked to go there. As a matter of fact I have a purchaser at a good price in view, and if it comes off we shall be all right.'

'That's good,' said Mitchell heartily, just as Sybil came back into the room, looking flushed and excited.

'Mother thought she heard someone in the garden,' she said. 'I told her it would be only one of those awful newspaper people, but I went to look and it was that dreadful man, Maurice,' she added to Keene, using his first name, 'you know, Bobs-the-Boy, I saw him just as plainly as ever. What can he be here for?'

'I'll go and look,' Keene exclaimed.

Mitchell and Ferris went with him, but there was no one in the garden. No one, in fact, was visible at all, for even the journalists had retired by now to hand in their reports, except Mitchell's own car with Jacks dozing at the wheel and the plain-clothes man strolling up and down. Jacks's testimony was not very valuable perhaps, for he admitted having been half asleep, but the plain-clothes man protested he had been keeping a sharp look-out; he certainly seemed alert enough, and he was positive no human being could have gone by without being seen. And it was quite certain there was no one now in the garden.

'If anyone was there,' said Mitchell emphatically, 'he was only playing the fool, and if you see Bobs-the-Boy you can tell him so.'

'That's what I think, too,' declared Ferris. 'Playing the fool.'

The plain-clothes man saluted.

'If Bobs-the-Boy is seen, message shall be delivered, sir,' he promised, 'but I am ready to swear no human being could have gone into the garden or come out again without my seeing him.'

Sybil, however, insisted that she had seen the man clearly in the light of the street lamp at the corner; and as they were all four returning to the house, leaving Jacks to continue his dozing at the wheel and the plain-clothes man his watch, Keene said to Mitchell,

'Do you know anyone who calls himself that? I thought your man out there . . . and you, too . . .'

'Well,' Mitchell explained, 'we didn't see anyone, did we? so it's hard to be sure, but there's a ticket-of-leave man, name of Ford, Robert Ford. He was sent away for ten years for burglary last time he was up, but some months ago he was let out on licence. He brags a lot, and he has a trick of saying if there's any job to be done, "Bob's the Boy for that". So he often gets called by that name. It sounds as if it might be the same man.'

They were back in the house by now, and Sybil looked very much alarmed.

'Oh, a burglar,' she said. 'Oh, Maurice, you won't have him any more, will you? Mr Hunter ought to be warned, too.'

'If he's earning an honest living. . . .' Mitchell protested mildly. 'Does Mr Hunter employ him?' he added to Keene.

It appeared that this Bobs-the-Boy was sometimes employed by Mr Hunter at the fur warehouse as an odd job man. He had also recommended him to Keene, who occasionally employed him as a porter.

'I saw him there once,' Sybil explained; 'he was the most awful-looking man you ever saw, just like a . . . a murderer,' she said with a shudder. 'It was the way he walked, I think – and he was in the garden,' she added with conviction, 'for I saw him, and I don't care what that man of yours outside says. I know what I saw.'

'So far as the lady's description goes,' observed Ferris, 'I'm quite of her opinion – regular bad lot so far as looks go.'

'Make a note of it and I'll sign it as the unanimous opinion of all present,' said Mitchell cheerfully, 'but anyhow he's not in the garden now, and he's certainly not in the house, and there was no sign of him in the street, and nowhere he could hide – except our own car, and even if Jacks was half asleep no one could get inside without his knowing – that's certain. So where was he?'

Sybil still looked dissatisfied, though she had no answer to make, since it was clear that neither in garden, street, nor house, was there any trace of the man she thought she had seen. And when Mitchell and Ferris took their departure, as they soon did – though not before once again the Chelsea flat had been rung up without response – she was a good deal relieved by Mitchell's promise that the policeman on the beat should be instructed to keep a careful watch and arrest Bobs-the-Boy at sight if he were seen.

'We can always pull him in if we want to,' Mitchell explained confidentially as they left, 'because he is on licence, and that can always be cancelled if thought desirable.'

CHAPTER SIX

A Question of Hair-Dressing

HOURS are long, the work strenuous at Scotland Yard, when a case so complicated and mysterious as the tragedy on the Leadeane Road has to be dealt with. On their departure from Ealing, Inspector Ferris was indeed free to seek his bed; but Superintendent Mitchell had first to return to his office at the Yard, there to make certain that all the machinery at the disposal of the authorities was ready to be set in motion first thing in the morning in an endeavour to discover what had become of Mr John Curtis.

'And in my humble opinion,' declared Ferris, 'it's odds on, he won't be found alive. Jealousy, drink, murder, suicide – that's what it looks like to me, and common enough, too.'

'It looks a bit like that,' Mitchell had agreed, 'but there's a lot still that'll bear looking into. We haven't got this young Keene placed yet, and there's Mr Hunter, too – is it for nothing his name keeps popping up, or does he come into it somewhere? You notice, too, that the sun-bathing place at Leadeane Mrs Curtis visited before her murder, Hunter and Keene are also apparently in the habit of visiting. Besides, though we knew before that Hunter wanted to get an ex-convict and burglar, with not much ex about it, for his odd job man, we've still no idea why. Why should a business man, a wholesale fur merchant, want a convict out on licence in his employ? Something fishy about Mr Hunter, but is there any connexion with Mrs Curtis's murder? Then there's the jealous husband —'

'On the booze,' interpolated Ferris.

'On the booze,' agreed Mitchell, 'and also an unknown motor-cyclist seen quarrelling with Mrs Curtis – none of it seems to fall properly into place yet, not even the sun bathing.'

They parted then, Ferris returning straight home, and

Mitchell reaching the same destination by way of his office. And when at last, near morning, he did reach home, full of luxurious thoughts of bath and bed for at least an hour or two, he found his wife waiting for him in the hall, looking very sleepy and clad in her dressing-gown.

'I heard the phone going,' she explained, 'so I got up.'

She had written the message down on the pad. It read,

'Curtis seen entering Frankland's, Ealing. Watching house. Owen.'

Mitchell read it with mixed feelings, very mixed feelings indeed. Mrs Mitchell said,

'Isn't Owen that good-looking, nice-spoken young man who was here a week or two ago?'

'Good-looking and nice-spoken?' repeated Mitchell bitterly. 'Is that the way to describe a man who turns in a message like this to a senior officer who hasn't been near his bed for twenty-four hours or so? Well, anyhow, it's one on Ferris, too. I can smash up his beauty sleep.'

He took down the receiver and proceeded to do so, and, though not very hopefully, Mrs Mitchell suggested that he should ring up someone else to accompany Ferris, so that he himself would not need to go. But the Superintendent shook his head. The case had taken hold of him, there was still vivid in his memory that last look the murdered woman had given him; he would not even wait for a cup of tea, though some was ready for him in a vacuum flask.

'Had some and some biscuits at the office,' he explained. 'I must hurry off; can't risk letting Ferris get there first.'

Ferris was there first all the same, but, as instructed, he waited till Mitchell arrived. Together they went up to the door and knocked. Sybil answered their summons and hardly looked startled when she saw who it was.

'Oh, it's you again,' she said.

'Mr Curtis is here, isn't he?' Mitchell asked.

'Tell them to come in,' a voice called.

Sybil stood aside and the two men walked down the passage into the drawing-room. In it was standing a tall, strongly-built man, with fair hair and eyes and regular, well-cut features. At the moment, however, there was a wild distressed look about him. He was unshaven, with bloodshot eyes, his clothing tumbled and disarranged, one trouser leg showing a gaping tear over the knee. He said to them,

'You are police? I've only just heard about – about —' He paused and did not complete the sentence. He said again, 'I've only just heard . . . Sybil rang me up.'

Sybil had followed them into the room.

'I told him to come here,' she said. 'I felt I couldn't tell him on the phone. . . . I said he must come here.'

'Mr Curtis rang you up first, then, I suppose?' Mitchell asked.

'Oh, no,' she replied, 'I had been ringing up the flat all night, and as soon as I got an answer I said he must come here, so I could tell him what had happened. . . . I couldn't on the phone.'

'Sybil told me the flat was being watched,' Curtis explained, 'and I saw fellows in the street – your chaps, I suppose, or newspaper men. So I got out by the fire escape at the back. It leads down into the yard, but near the bottom you can just grab a tree in the garden at the back and swing down there and out into the street behind. But I knew before I got here, for I bought a paper on the way.'

In fact, a copy of that morning's issue of the *Announcer* was lying on the floor. Mitchell noticed that on the front page was conspicuous a photograph of Mrs Curtis.

'Where have you been all night, Mr Curtis?' Mitchell asked.

'In the flat at Chelsea,' he answered moodily.

'We got no answer when we knocked,' Mitchell remarked.

'I heard nothing,' Curtis answered; and then after a pause, as the police officers looked doubtfully at him, 'I was dead drunk. That's why I heard nothing.'

He sat down abruptly, but continued watching them from his heavy, bloodshot eyes, from time to time shivering a little as if he felt cold. He gave the impression that only by a tremendous effort of self-control did he save himself from breaking down completely. He saw them looking at him, and he said,

'You know, it's a bit of a shock to read in the paper your wife's been found murdered.' Then he said, 'I suppose I do look it.'

'Look what?' Mitchell asked.

'A murderer,' he answered, and Sybil gave a little soft wail of uttermost distress.

'I think perhaps you had better not say anything more just now, Mr Curtis,' Mitchell said slowly. 'I think we shall have to ask you to accompany us, and afterwards you can make a statement if you wish to.'

'All right,' Curtis said, 'or now if you like.' He picked up the *Announcer* and laid it on the table. 'Plain enough what they think,' he said. 'I wonder if I can have them for libel? ... Can you have a paper for libel after you've been hanged for something you didn't do? Sorry. I'm talking wildly.'

He got to his feet again, and as they watched they could see him fighting for his self-control. The struggle was almost as visible, it was a thousand times as fierce, as any of those that in the old days he had been wont to put up in the boxing ring. He said in a new and more restrained and careful voice, speaking to Sybil,

'Sybil, could you make me a cup of tea – strong?'

She left the room at once, and Curtis turned again to the police officers.

'It's all right now,' he said. 'I've been a bit bowled over.'

'You were at the flat all the time we were knocking and ringing?' Mitchell asked, a little doubtfully.

'Enough to wake the dead,' Ferris put in.

'But not the dead drunk,' Curtis retorted. 'I was drinking yesterday afternoon. After I got back home, I had more whisky, champagne as well. If the place had been blown up, I don't suppose I should have known anything about it. I didn't know anything till about five this morning I heard the phone going, and when I answered Miss Frankland told me something had happened and I must come along at once.'

Sybil came back into the room with the freshly made tea. Curtis gulped it down eagerly, scalding hot as it was.

'That might account for your not hearing us,' Mitchell admitted. 'I suppose it's not a thing that often happens, is it? Was there any special reason last night . . . ?'

'Yes,' Curtis answered. 'I quarrelled with – with my wife yesterday. I wanted to forget what a fool I had been. I expect you know all about it. It was at the *Announcer* office.'

'Information we've received,' Mitchell said, 'is to the effect that certain threats were used and that you produced a pistol, a small automatic. Of course, you needn't say anything about that if you prefer not to, but that's our information.'

'I don't remember using any threats,' Curtis answered. 'It's true about the pistol.'

'Got it now?' Mitchell asked negligently.

'No. I threw it in the river.'

'Did you now?' said Mitchell, as he and Ferris exchanged glances. 'Rather a pity . . . what made you do that, I wonder? Do you remember what time it was?'

'I threw it away to get rid of the beastly thing,' Curtis answered. 'If you want to know, I felt I had made a fool of myself. I knew . . . I knew it had upset my wife. So I threw it into the river. I don't know the exact time, some time during the afternoon.'

'Anyone see you?'

'Not that I know of.'

'Can you say what calibre it was?'

'It was a point thirty-two Browning automatic.'

'The bullet that killed Mrs Curtis was from a point thirty-two Browning automatic,' observed Mitchell.

'You think I killed my wife,' Curtis said. 'Well, I didn't . . . my God, man, I loved her,' he shouted, and for the moment it almost seemed that he would break down altogether. But he recovered himself. 'That's my affair, not yours,' he mumbled.

49

'Sometimes love's a thing that comes into cases of this kind as well as hate,' Mitchell answered, a little sadly. 'There was a piece of poetry someone made about that once, "Each man kills the thing he loves." There's times when that's true. If you've no objection, I would like a statement of exactly what did happen at the *Announcer* office, and of your own movements yesterday afternoon. If you would rather wait till you've consulted a solicitor, that's for you to say, of course. But it might help us if you would make it now. There's quite a lot in this case will bear looking into – and time counts.'

'I didn't murder my wife,' Curtis repeated, 'but I'll tell you one thing. I'll find out who did and if you don't hang him, I'll attend to him myself.'

He spoke with an extraordinary intensity, so that for the moment they were all silent, silent before that sudden flaming of such fierce resolve. Abruptly Sybil said,

'That's mother calling – I must go.'

She left the room, and when she had gone Curtis went on more quietly,

'I'll tell you what happened. Jo and I had had a row. She was always rushing off somewhere, I never knew where or why. I used to sit and wonder; and then I would have a drink to stop thinking, and it only made me think all the more. This girl here, Miss Frankland, is engaged to a chap named Keene. Decent sort of chap, got an art dealer's business in Deal Street, off Piccadilly; his father made a pot of money. Jo was trying to break off the engagement. She wouldn't tell me why. Keene's an attractive sort of fellow, at least girls seem to think so. I suppose I was jealous. I got wondering why Jo was so anxious to stop Sybil marrying him. Then I saw her in the City and Keene was following her. You could see he was following her. She turned into a side street, a yard with no exit. He followed her. It looked as if they were meeting on the sly. I went and had a drink, and later I went to the *Announcer* office and tackled her. I made a fool of myself. Afterwards I felt pretty sick and I thought I would try to get friends again. I went home and she wasn't there, and I went to the garage where she kept her Bayard Seven. One of the men said she had just gone off in it and had asked him about the best way to get to Leadeane. I knew there was a sun-bathing place there she was rather keen on writing up – Lord knows why, sun-bathing's stale enough news, but she had got it into her head she would like to do it. I had a motor-bike and I got it out. I meant to overtake her on the way if I could. At a pub I knew she had to pass, I waited for a time. She didn't come, so I thought perhaps she was avoiding me or else had gone another way. I gave it up and went back to the flat – and started drinking. After that I don't remember much more till I woke up to hear the phone going and Sybil calling.'

'Did you notice any other motor-cyclist on the road?'

'I suppose so, I don't remember, lots I expect. Why?'

'None you knew or that you noticed in any way?'

'No.'

'Is there anyone Mrs Curtis knew you can think of who used a motor-cycle – B.A.D. make?'

'None that I can think of specially,' Curtis answered.

'You left your own motor-cycle at the garage when you got back, I suppose. Do you remember if anyone saw you?'

'I don't think so. There wasn't anyone about. It is a lock-up place I hire. Not that I noticed much; someone may have seen me for all I know. I was feeling pretty sick, too sick to worry about who saw me. I knew I had about done for myself with Jo.'

'Was it going or returning you threw your pistol in the river?'

'Going.'

'Could you identify the place where you threw it in?'

'No. Along the bank somewhere. I couldn't say within a mile or so.'

'Did anyone notice your doing that?'

'I don't know, I don't suppose so. Why should they?'

'You see,' explained Mitchell, 'I'm trying to get confirmation of what you tell us. I'm afraid I shall have to ask you —'

He paused. His glance had fallen on the copy of the

Announcer lying on the table where Curtis had thrown it, the photograph of Jo the most conspicuous feature of the front page. Reproduced from one extracted from Sybil the night before by an *Announcer* man, it had been taken only a few days before, and showed her wearing one of the new fashionable saucer-like hats, worn tilted miraculously over her right ear till it was a wonder how it stuck on at all. Apparently it was the one she had been wearing when she met her tragic end. Like a man entranced, Mitchell stared at this photograph while the other two stared at him and wondered what it was he saw that made him look so strange. Sybil came back into the room, and Mitchell said to her, yet without moving his eyes from the reproduced photograph in the paper,

'Miss Frankland, have you a photograph of your sister without a hat?'

'Only rather old ones,' Sybil answered. 'That's the only one she has had taken for some time. Why?'

'I wanted to know, I wanted to know,' Mitchell answered twice over, and still he kept his eyes fixed with the same strange intensity on the picture in the paper. He said presently : 'Miss Frankland, has your sister changed her way of doing her hair lately?'

Sybil shook her head, looking a little as if she thought Mitchell had gone suddenly mad. Ferris seemed almost as bewildered. He was looking alternately at the photograph and at Mitchell, as if unable to understand either. Curtis said with some impatience,

'What on earth does it matter about the way she did her hair?'

'Why, it matters this much, Mr Curtis, sir,' Mitchell answered, turning away as if the paper had no longer any interest for him, 'I was thinking I should have to ask you to come along with us, I was thinking I should have to charge you in face of what you've told us. But if it's true Mrs Curtis has always done her hair that way – why, then, I think you're cleared, unless of course fresh evidence turns up. But at present I don't think I need trouble you any more. Come along, Ferris.'

And the Inspector looked an utterly and hopelessly bewildered man till they were outside the house, when just as they were getting into the car he cried suddenly,

'My God, I see it now – why, if you hadn't noticed that, sir, Curtis might have hanged.' He added presently, 'Plain enough once you do notice it – even a description of that photo would be enough for a smart man to see at once what it meant.'

CHAPTER SEVEN

Alarm Given

THE art dealer's establishment in Deal Street, a turning off
Piccadilly, now owned by Maurice Keene, had been founded
by his father a good many years previously. After existing
in somewhat precarious fashion during the pre-war and war
periods, it had suddenly blossomed into huge success during
that boom when people believed that peace and prosperity
were synonyms. For a time all that was necessary to sell a
picture was to have a sufficient stock in hand, and during
that period the profits had been very large. Unfortunately,
the elder Mr Keene, a little over-excited, imagining these
were conditions that would last, much under the influence
of what psycho-analysts would probably call a 'victory com-
plex', had invested practically all those profits, almost all his
working capital, indeed, in more pictures, of which nearly
all, now that slump had replaced boom, remained in the
cellars, insured at a figure far above present-day values. The
famous Rembrandt, for example, for which it will be remembered the elder Keene, shortly before his death, gave a
large sum at Christie's, and concerning the authenticity of
which a sharp discussion raged for a time in the columns of
the art journals, still remained on the hands of his son, in
spite of the fact that a South American millionaire had once
paid a deposit on it. Even so, that square yard of painted
canvas represented a capital of seven thousand lying idle.

'I'd like to burn the lot,' Keene had once said viciously to
that rare bird, a customer, who, as it chanced, was Mr
Esmond Bryan, the head of the Leadeane Sun Bathing
establishment.

One of the sun-bathers, an artist by profession, who had
read paragraphs in the papers about Parisian artists ex-
changing their work by barter for such mundane things as
groceries, cutlets, and clothes, had offered Mr Bryan two or

three landscapes as payment for his subscription to the Society of Sun Believers of Leadeane Grange, and for suitable bodily refreshment needed during his visits there – for the Leadeane Grange restaurant was famous among those who put food high in the list of the many, many things needing reform. Mr Bryan, by no means devoid of business instincts, even though it was said he carried on his establishment at a loss, had called at Deal Street, to ascertain the value of the proffered works. Keene's bitter and perhaps exaggerated comment had been that he had two large cellars crammed with better work by better-known men, and that work of the quality offered could only be got rid of by giving it away with a pound of tea or else by waiting till the fifth of November, when no doubt material for bonfires would be in demand.

'Burning, that's all that quality of work is good for in these times,' he repeated, but all the same Mr Bryan, undismayed, made a small purchase, announced his intention of accepting the two pictures offered him as payment for a year's subscription to the Sun Believers, and, in addition, for a shilling's worth of carrot tea and minced potato peel, or of such other vitamin-crammed, blood-purifying, vitality-giving foods as might be on sale in the Grange restaurant, on each visit that the artist made during the year.

Before leaving, Mr Bryan suggested that Keene would do well to pay a visit to the Grange, declaring that he would very likely find fresh clients among the sun-bathers, all of whom, Mr Bryan asserted with fervour, were devotees of beauty, fanatics of all true art and loveliness, and some of them even provided with that vulgarity of superfluous cash so convenient in his vulgar world. But this invitation, though it had been accepted, had so far had no result in the way of sales, though it had increased Keene's appreciation of such things as roast beef and pork chops.

Indeed, customers seemed to be growing every day rarer birds at the Deal Street establishment. On this morning of the day following the tragedy of the Leadeane Road, not one had crossed its threshold. The only visitors had been hopeful artists – tautology, all artists are either hopeful or dead – eager to add a few more to the innumerable canvases stacked in every corner of cellar and shop, various travellers and pedlars, one or two undisguised beggars, and a fashionable young lady selling tickets for a forthcoming charity ball and hinting not obscurely that the custom of herself and of her numerous wealthy and important friends would in the future bear an exact ratio to the number of tickets now purchased.

But as it happened the manager Keene now employed was a fashionable young lady herself, Helen Duncan by name, fully capable of dealing with other fashionable young ladies and to-day routing the invader with great loss. The salary Miss Duncan received hardly paid for her gloves and cigarettes, but the work provided her with an excuse for being away from a home she appreciated all the more for seeing so little of it. She was quite a good business woman – or would have been had there been any business to transact – really knew something about art and of the commercial as apart from the artistic value of pictures, took a genuine interest in the work; and if she considered herself entitled to take a day or a morning or afternoon off, whenever she felt like it or some attraction offered, that was really but a trifling drawback, especially in these times when there was so little to do. Besides, she was always considerate about this, and when a cocktail party, a visit to a matinée, an afternoon at bridge, claimed her, she was always careful to let Keene know, so that he might have time to cancel any engagement he had made likely to take him out at the same time. She had the additional merit of getting on rather well with the different errand boys, who were now in swift succession the only other employees at Deal Street, and indeed would often be able to get them to stay quite a long time, as much as five or six months sometimes. Also she smoked cigarettes continuously, and she regarded her employer with a lofty and patronizing contempt he resented deeply but dared not show for fear she departed. In her eyes he was a lower middle-class trading person, to whom it was as natural for her to give orders as to the footman at home. But indeed they had a kind of natural instinct for rubbing each other up the wrong way, though they found each other so useful there was at present no prospect either of his rebelling against her domineering ways or of her terminating her connexion with the business. Indeed, more than once she had hinted she would be willing to buy him out, though at a figure which it would have been unduly flattering to describe as a bargain basement price.

'When I feel like making you a present of the business, I'll let you know,' he had answered loweringly, and she had smiled rather maddeningly as she lighted a fresh cigarette and thought to herself that very likely some day soon the liquidator would be willing to consider an offer even smaller. 'And I'll thank you,' he added, making a grab at the waste-paper basket into which she had tossed her match, 'to be a bit more careful, or you'll have the whole place on fire, and I don't happen to want to be burnt out just yet, if it's all the same to you.'

'Rot,' she retorted, 'don't talk silly, that match was out all right.'

'It's out now,' he told her; 'it was alight when you threw it in there.'

'Liar,' she retorted simply.

'If the insurance company knew about you,' he snapped angrily, 'they would double the premium – Lord knows, it's high enough as it is.'

'I don't see why you don't cut it,' she remarked. 'You carry too much by half.'

'Too little, you mean,' he answered, 'so long as that Rembrandt's down there.'

'Well, I've never seen it,' she observed. 'I don't see why you go on keeping it nailed up like that.'

'Because it's sold if it isn't paid for,' he replied. 'I told you that before – the money may be paid and delivery claimed at any moment. That was a condition of the sale, and I'm not going to lose the chance either.'

She shrugged her shoulders indifferently. That Rembrandt had become almost legendary. Personally she doubted sometimes its very existence, certainly its authenticity. As long as she had been there it had reposed in its case, elaborately fastened up, ready for delivery to some South American, who had arranged to purchase it, and paid a deposit on it, but had never either claimed the picture or paid the rest of the purchase money. Still, if the transaction were cancelled apparently two-thirds of the deposit would have to be returned, which would not be convenient, and certainly no other purchaser was in sight for the moment, so the painting, genuine or not, remained in its carefully packed case, waiting to be claimed.

Keene went off then to see some prospective, Miss Duncan suspected mythical, customer in the city, and as he went the latest errand boy, who had been listening with much interest to this fresh passage of arms, and who was passionately on the side of Miss Duncan, put out his tongue at him. Keene saw the gesture in a mirror, but suppressed his natural instinct to turn and box the cheeky youngster's ears. For one thing errand boys are hard to get and harder to keep, and for another it might be useful some day to have a witness to this little conversation.

He took a bus to the City, and getting down near the Bank walked on towards the Tower, turning presently into Howland Yard, where stood some dozen or so of old-fashioned, rather tumble-down houses, most of them badly in need of paint and repair. There was no way out, the only entry being that by which Keene had come in, and all the houses, except one or two which were empty, were in the occupation of various business firms. Number Seven, about half-way down on the left from the entrance, was occupied by 'Business Furs, Ltd', as a large and shining brass plate proclaimed. On the ground floor were the offices, and a large waiting-room where an occasional favoured client might sometimes be permitted to buy a coat at 'warehouse price' instead of at 'West End price' – though it had happened that after the completion of the purchase the new owner of the fur coat was a little inclined to wonder which of these was the higher, or on which side lay the difference. But such sales were comparatively rare, for the business was essentially wholesale. The basement was let off to a neighbouring wireless set manufacturer for storage purposes, and on the upper floors were kept the furs that formed, declared young Mr Horace Hunter, managing director, founder, and apparently almost sole shareholder in the concern, the finest collection in London.

He could – and did – for example boast of eight or ten coats, mink or Russian sable, of such fine quality that by themselves they were insured for six thousand pounds.

'Under-insured at that,' Hunter would say sometimes, though admitting that during the continuance of the present slump it might be hard to find purchasers. 'But once things turn the corner,' he was accustomed to add, 'as they must sooner or later, because slumps don't last for ever, then they'll fetch double.'

There were two big packing cases of blue fox furs as well, also insured for a large sum, and also being held for a better market, and a good deal more of valuable stock. Hunter, in fact, had started in rather a big way at the time when the post-war boom was at its height, and when, since all the world was making money, all the world's wife wanted – and got – the most expensive furs possible. But almost as soon as the business got well under way, the slump arrived. For a time, Hunter admitted, bankruptcy had threatened, for expensive furs had become almost as difficult to sell as pictures. But now, taking advantage of an opportunity that, said Keene ruefully, came no picture dealer's way, he claimed to have turned even the slump to advantage by a large purchase of lower grade furs at a figure so low his re-sale of them at bargain prices had yet shown a very satisfactory profit. Indeed, he used to tell his friends he was seriously thinking of starting clubs in working-class districts on the principle of 'Pay a shilling a week and choose your own fur coat'.

'Though, mind you,' he would add earnestly, 'the really good furs, the mink, the ermine, the true Persian lamb, the blue fox, and so on, like those I have upstairs waiting for better times, will always command their price. The charlady may have her ponyskin to keep her warm, the shop girl may go to work in her musquash, but the rich woman will still want her thousand-guinea mink – I've more than one of that kind upstairs.'

No more than Keene did Hunter employ a large staff, for in spite of his sales of cheaper grade skins he had been obliged to cut down expenses. There were two or three women whose job it was to look after the stored furs, a manager, a typist, and the inevitable, transitory office boy. In appearance Hunter was a youngish man of middle size, round, plump, with dark hair and eyes, a small toothbrush moustache and generally indeterminate features above a chin that slipped oddly away to a point. To-day he was alone on the ground floor, for his manager was upstairs, seeing to some rearrangement of the stock, the typist was out, and the office boy had gone on some errand or another to a furrier five minutes' walk away and so was not likely to be back for another hour or two. He was busy with accounts which in more prosperous times it would have been the duty of the cashier to keep, and these accounts he was scowling over as if he did not find them too satisfactory. His scowl did not lessen when he looked up as Keene appeared, entering by the open door as one who was familiar there.

'What are you so early for?' he demanded. 'What's the idea? The less you come around in daylight the better.'

'I wanted to see you,' Keene answered. He sat down uninvited and took out a cigarette, but put it back unlighted in its case. 'Seen about the murder?' he asked.

'What about it?' Hunter asked. 'Your girl's sister, isn't it?'

'Sybil's sister,' Keene repeated. 'She hated me,' he said, 'she wanted to break it off. I expect she would in time if she had lived, but now she's dead.'

'You're nervy,' Hunter said. 'Better have a whisky.'

He rose to move towards a cupboard in the wall, but Keene said almost violently,

'No, sit down,' and then more quietly as Hunter stared at him, 'You were at Leadeane yesterday?'

'So were you,' Hunter said. 'What about it?'

'Jo was coming from the Grange when it happened,' Keene said.

'So the paper says,' Hunter agreed. 'I left before she did, though. I was talking to a chap in the City at the time she was seen leaving there.'

'An alibi, eh?' Keene sneered.

'If you like,' Hunter answered. 'What's the matter with you? When did you leave?'

'About as soon as she got there,' Keene answered. 'I saw her and I didn't much want her to see me. I told Bryan I would put off my sun bath till another time, and I cleared back to town.'

'Another alibi, eh?' Hunter repeated with another sneer.

'Do you know she's been prowling about this place several times lately?'

'What do you mean?'

'What I say – she's been here more than once. I saw her myself, and Curtis saw her, too.'

Hunter looked disturbed, afraid.

'What did she want? Are you sure?' he asked.

'Wasn't there someone here last week trying to buy a Persian lamb coat, had a letter of introduction, couldn't quite make up her mind, asked if she might come again?'

'Yes. I believe so. Why? I didn't see her myself. I was out. What about it?'

'That was her, that was Jo,' Keene said.

'My God,' Hunter muttered below his breath. 'Are you sure?' he asked again.

'I saw her yesterday morning after I left here. She didn't see me. I was on a bus. I wondered what she wanted. I didn't like it. I knew she hated me, I knew she wanted to get Sybil away. I got off the bus and followed. She didn't see me, but Curtis did; his works are close by, you know, and all round here he has customers he calls on. Perhaps he had seen me before. I think when he saw me, and saw I was following Jo, he got it into his cracked silly head there was something up, that we were meeting on the sly, and he got into one of his jealous fits. I made certain that Jo was really coming here, and afterwards I rang your people up and they said she had been here before and had been talking a lot at large – they didn't know what she wanted, but they didn't think it was a fur coat. Now she's been murdered,' he concluded abruptly.

Hunter made no answer, and they were still silent, still staring at each other, when there came into the room a new personage, one who also had walked straight in through the open door as though he were familiar there. He was a tall, strongly-built young fellow, roughly dressed, a woollen muffler knotted round his neck, his height detracted from by an odd, shuffling, furtive way of walking he had. His features were well enough shaped so that he might have passed as a good-looking youth, had a day or two's growth of beard, and a separation from soap and water that seemed even longer, permitted them to be more clearly seen. A cap he wore pulled well forward served further to hide eyes he habitually kept concealed behind half lowered lids, but that one divined all the same to be alert and watchful. His hair seemed fairly to shine with the oil he had used to plaster it down, and when anything amused him he showed a twisted kind of grin that displayed a black gap in his upper jaw where it seemed a tooth was missing. When he spoke it was with the purest accent of Limehouse. Hunter's greeting to him was not cordial.

'What do you want?' he shouted at him. 'Good Lord, is every cursed fool . . .'

'Keep your hair on, guv'nor,' was the cool response. 'Why shouldn't I be dropping round to see if you've any more odd jobs you can give me same as before – Bobs-the-Boy for the odd jobs and the dirty work,' he said with a harsh chuckle as if at some obscure joke. Looking at Hunter he said, 'Do you know the "busies" are snooping round here?'

'The "busies"?' Hunter repeated.

'The "busies", the "dicks", the "'tecs",' Bobs-the-Boy repeated impatiently. 'The Yard blokes – I've just seen Mitchell, what's one of the big bugs there, and another bird, Ferris his name is, at the top of the yard here, just like two fat cats watching a mouse-hole.'

CHAPTER EIGHT

Curtis Visits Howland Yard

It was with an obvious dismay, even terror, that this announcement was received. Hunter's round, insignificant face had become ghastly pale. Keene showed scarcely less emotion, his lips twitching nervously, his large bony hands pressed together so tightly that the knuckles showed white with the strain. Both of them were staring intently at Bobs-the-Boy, who looked back at them with a sardonic grin, as if he enjoyed their discomfiture. He said suddenly,

'There was a bit of skirt put through it yesterday.'

'What do you mean?' Hunter asked angrily. 'What about it? What's that to do with us?'

'Coming from the Grange at Leadeane, wasn't she?' Bobs-the-Boy went on. He looked again at the other two, his eyes, beneath their half-closed lids, alert and questioning and watchful. 'There's things I've done in my time,' he said. 'But I've never put no one's light out and I never will unless it's forced on me. It's a thing I've never held with.'

Keene got slowly to his feet.

'You mean . . . you mean . . . you dare . . .' he said stammeringly.

'Shut up, Keene,' Hunter interposed. 'Bobs, shut up, too, don't talk like a blighted fool . . . anyone to hear you would think you meant we had something to do with it.'

Bobs-the-Boy jerked his head towards the door.

'What's Mitchell doing out there?' he asked. 'Taking the air? At the Grange, wasn't she? So was you.'

'So were a hundred other people,' Hunter retorted. 'I left long before she did . . . if I had to, I could prove easily enough I was back here while she was still there . . . I don't know a thing about her except it seems she came here once to try to buy a coat.'

'Was that all she came for?' Bobs-the-Boy asked, and

when Hunter for only answer swore at him viciously, he grinned and added, 'Of course, if you've an alibi, why that's all right ... if I had had an alibi they wouldn't ever have sent me up for that ten-year stretch I got.' He turned to Keene, still on his feet, still staring at him with a sort of menacing surprise. 'Your girl's sister, weren't she?'

'What's that to do with you?' Keene said slowly. 'You mind what you're saying, my man.'

'All I'm saying is by way of being friendly like,' Bobs-the-Boy retorted with his perpetual and maddening grin. 'I'm trying to be a pal same as I want you to be to me. ... Nothing to do with me if she was your girl's sister, but Mitchell may think it's something to do with him. You was at the Grange, too, wasn't you? Got an alibi as well?'

'You take care, you take care,' Keene stuttered in a rage. 'You look out, I'll throw you out of the window if you don't mind.'

He looked formidable enough with his great height and long whirling arms, but Bobs-the-Boy only grinned again.

'Keep your hair on, guv'nor,' he said. 'All Mitchell wants is for you to do something like that ... give him a chance to push in and in-ves-ti-gate ... that's what he's after ... in-ves-ti-gation ... and me trying to act the real pal and give you the office and look at what I get for it. All I want to know is where we are. That bit of skirt now, I don't want to be mixed up in no affair like that.'

'Then shut up,' Hunter told him briefly. 'We've got enough to worry us without any flaming insolence from you.' He paused and added rather slowly, as if a new idea had come to him, 'You were at the Grange yourself yesterday, you were to go there, weren't you? Hadn't Mr Bryan told you to?'

'Suppose I was,' Bobs-the-Boy answered sulkily, 'what about it? Anyways, I've got an alibi, too, same as you.'

'Did you see Miss Frankland there?'

'Suppose I did?'

Hunter did not answer. He could not possibly have looked any more ghastly than he had done before, but his nervousness had plainly increased. Keene sat down again. It was he who spoke the first. He said,

'I don't know what all this means.'

'Guv'nor,' Bobs-the-Boy told him, speaking with some intensity, 'it means just what Mitchell's being out there means, and what that means – well, God knows. But I take it there's a warning there to you and me, too, because when Mitchell comes snooping round, most like there's trouble brewing for some.'

'This murder business . . . this girl,' Hunter muttered. He looked at Keene. 'Do you think they're shadowing you because of that?' he asked. 'Do you think you've been followed here?'

'Oh, that's impossible,' Keene declared, but with obvious unease; 'they couldn't . . . impossible.'

'What I want to know,' Bobs-the-Boy insisted once again, 'is what's Mitchell and the other bird after. It was Mitchell his own self, him and Ferris what was with him, as was first to find the body, so he's taking a special, particular interest in finding out who done it. Seems like a fellow called Owen is on the case, too. Mitchell and Ferris are big bugs, but Owen's just an ordinary "busy" as don't count one way or the other – pretty green, too. Now there's Mitchell and Ferris out there together, but I didn't see Owen.'

'You seem to know a lot about it,' Hunter said suspiciously.

'So I do, that's a fact,' Bobs-the-Boy agreed complacently. 'There ain't so much goes on at Scotland Yard but I get to know about it.'

'Don't try to stuff us with that sort of rot,' interposed Keene angrily. 'You wouldn't dare show your nose within a mile of Scotland Yard if you could help it.'

'Of course I wouldn't,' agreed Bobs-the-Boy cheerfully, 'me being out on licence and wanted for failing to report, as required by terms of said licence. Did you think I went to the Yard and asked them to tell me all the news? What I said was I had a way of knowing what goes on there, and that's no lie, neither, for so I have.'

'Anything you say probably is a lie,' Hunter snarled.

'If it's true Mitchell's there,' Keene said suddenly, 'he had better not see me – he would only ask a lot of rotten questions.'

'No,' agreed Hunter, 'no.'

'Nor me, neither,' interposed Bobs-the-Boy; 'if he started on me, he might spot who I was, and then I'd be copped again for not reporting.'

'Does he know you? Would he recognize you?' Hunter asked.

'You can't never tell once you've been through it,' the other admitted with a touch of indignation in his voice. 'Once you're lagged, they bring all the "busies" in one by one to have a chat, so they'll know you again, and they photo you, and they finger-print you, and measure you, and one blasted thing after another, till they know you better than they know their fathers and their mothers. Don't give a bloke a chance no more.'

He spoke as one with an acute sense of grievance, but the others were not listening, for they had heard approaching footsteps, and now there came a loud knocking at the door, the open door through which Keene and Bobs-the-Boy had passed without ceremony.

'There they are,' Keene exclaimed.

'If it's them,' Bobs-the-Boy agreed, but with rather a surprised look, as if in spite of all he had not expected their actual arrival.

'They had better not see either of you,' Hunter said quickly. 'Slip into the showroom there, through that door behind, and out into the passage at the back. There's a door there, it's locked, here's the key. It opens on stairs that go down to the basement. There's another door at the bottom. It's locked, too, but here's the key for it. You'll be all right there, because I can tell Mitchell the basement's let to a tenant and I haven't the key for it – I'll tell him if he wants to search it he must go to the wireless people themselves for the key, and that'll give you a chance to get away.'

He hustled them both out into the showroom, and when

they had vanished he went to the door, where renewed knocking had now attracted the attention of the staff working above.

'It's all right,' Hunter shouted to them, and then added to the man – there was only one – he saw standing on the threshold, 'come in, can't you? The door's open, this isn't a private house. Anything I can do for you?'

He turned back into his office and the newcomer followed him.

'My name's Curtis,' he said.

'What?' Hunter almost shouted, staring at him. 'Curtis? ... not....' He paused and glanced towards the copy of the *Announcer* lying near. 'You don't mean ...?'

'Yes, I do,' Curtis answered. 'I am John Curtis. It was my wife who was murdered last night.'

He spoke a little wildly, perhaps, and yet all the same with a certain air of having himself well in hand. Hunter sat down at his desk. He was very surprised, and though in a way relieved, yet also he was uneasy at this new development.

'I read about it this morning,' he said. 'Terrible affair ... all my sympathy, if I may say so ... dreadful such things can happen ... I was interested because I know the sun bathing place the paper says your wife had been visiting. I was there yesterday ... great believer in sun bathing ... wonderful effect ... seems to bring it home somehow ... I mean knowing the place and having been there only yesterday, just when Mrs Curtis was there too ... have a cigarette? ... a drink? ...'

Curtis shook his head.

'No, thanks,' he said. He was looking at Hunter from tired, feverish eyes. He said, 'You knew Mrs Curtis? she had been here?'

'Well, I've been rather wondering about that,' Hunter answered with a great appearance of frankness. 'One of my people showed me the photo in the paper. I hadn't noticed it much before, but when he said so I began to think it was rather like a lady who was here a day or two back. People come like that occasionally. We don't set out to do a retail business, our trade customers would kick up a row if we did, most likely. But when it's a friend or a friend of a friend . . . private recommendation you understand . . . well, we don't actually refuse a sale. It's a favour in a way, because of course we don't charge West End prices, we sell at our ordinary warehouse price, just what we would charge if one of the big West End shops phoned in a hurry for some special fur they happened to be out of.'

'Was Mrs Curtis a friend?'

'Oh, no, we didn't even know her name or anything about her . . . we don't make any inquiries, you understand . . . If some lady comes here and says she's been sent by a friend we don't worry about asking who the friend is. If she wants to buy, we let her, things aren't so flourishing we can afford to turn down even a small retail sale.'

'Did my wife buy a coat?'

'Can't have, there's no record of any retail sale for some weeks. As often as not, people only come to look round and get an idea about current prices.'

'She had two fur coats, an old one and one she bought last season,' Curtis said. 'I can't understand why she should want another.'

'Well, of course, we don't know anything about that,' Hunter answered, 'but my experience is, no matter how many fur coats a woman has, she's always open to another.'

'Do you know a man named Keene, Maurice Keene, an art dealer with a shop in Deal Street, Piccadilly?'

'I've met him at Leadeane; he's a sun bather, too. Why?'

'He has been here sometimes?'

'He has called in once or twice. I think he hoped he might be able to sell me a picture. I countered by trying to sell him a fur coat for his fiancée. Neither of us succeeded. Why?'

'Did he ever meet my wife here?'

'Good lord, no,' Hunter cried. 'Mr Curtis, what an extraordinary question. I think I must ask what's behind it; what made such an idea occur to you?'

Curtis answered,

'I saw her here once. I saw Keene following her.'

'I think that must be a mistake,' Hunter said. 'Anyhow, I know nothing at all about it.'

'People are hinting I murdered my wife myself,' Curtis said slowly. 'I believe the police half think so. I thought they were going to arrest me last night, I think they would have done only for something about the hat she was wearing, or else her hair; I couldn't make out which, and they wouldn't say.'

Hunter was looking at him in sheer bewilderment.

'You're upset,' he said, 'I don't wonder; awful experience. Don't you think you had better have a drink? Pull you together.'

'I'll never touch alcohol again till I know who did it,' Curtis answered.

CHAPTER NINE

'Bobs-the-Boy' Gives Good Advice

Down below, in the gloomy basement passage, closed at one end by a door admitting into the cellars where the goods of the wireless manufacturer were stored, Keene and Bobs-the-Boy waited together, the ex-convict apparently considering it a good opportunity to deliver a monologue on his experiences of prison life.

At first Keene hardly listened to the voice droning on at his side. Distracted and nervous, he let his companion's talk flow by unheeded. But after a time he found himself forced into listening to the level monotonous tones till at last he said impatiently,

'Oh, keep quiet, can't you?'

'Ah, you're nervy, nervy you are,' said Bobs-the-Boy sympathetically; 'just the way you are after you've been put away a year or two – nervy they all get, and the screws as well. What gets you is every day being just like every other, somehow no bloke can stand that. The old bloke in the wig what put me away said as ten years was the very least he could hand out. Along of me earning full marks because of good behaviour they cut it down to seven and a half, but you can believe me, Mr Keene, sir, you can take it from me – seven years and a half ain't no joke, with you most every day wishing you was dead and done with it.'

'What do you keep talking about it for then?' Keene snapped.

'Along of being scared of going back to finish my time with perhaps a bit more added on,' retorted Bobs-the-Boy; 'along of being mixed up with things the way I am now. What always made me feel so sick is knowing if I had only done what my girl told me, I should have been all right.'

Keene had turned, and in the dim obscurity of the passage he was staring fixedly at his companion.

'Why do you say that? what are you saying that for?' he asked in a whisper that seemed half imploring, half threatening.

'I'm saying it because it's Gospel truth,' the other answered. 'My girl said to me when first I got going with the gang and didn't feel as if I dared go on with them and didn't feel as if I dared draw back neither, she said, "Go to the fellows at the Yard. Make a clean breast of it to the 'busies'." She said, "They won't have it in for you then, you'll be safe, whatever happens." But I wouldn't, more fool me. Thought I could do better going my own way, told my girl to shut her mouth. Lumme, if only I had done what she said, I shouldn't be hiding down here like a rat in a drain. I could go swaggering down the middle of the road just like any one else and not a "busy" in the world would think of looking at me twice – lor', it must be like bleeding Paradise itself to know you're always safe and never no one stopping you to say, "The Inspector wants a word with you, my lad." But I wouldn't listen and when you won't – why, that's what you get, a ten-year stretch.'

Keene without speaking walked away as far as the narrow limits of the passage permitted. Bobs-the-Boy, apparently forgetting him, apparently lost in bitter memories of the past, leaned against the wall, his hands in his pockets, his shoulders hunched up till it seemed they nearly met his ears, his half-closed eyes fixed upon the ground. Keene came back to him. In a low, strained voice, his long arms swinging, his great bony hands opening and shutting convulsively, he said,

'I know what you are saying all this for ... to find out if I'm weakening ... if I'm scared ... well, I'm not. You hear? I'm not. I'm going through with it.'

'Even if it comes to a ten-year stretch, same as I told you I had done?' asked Bobs-the-Boy coolly. 'Well, suit yourself. You must go your own way same as I went mine.'

Keene was breathing heavily. He put his face close to the other's and said in the same strained, unnatural voice.

'I've made up my mind. There's no going back even if I wanted to. It's that or ruin, and I'm going through with it.

That's what you can say I said, if you like.'

'And that's that,' observed Bobs-the-Boy, 'only don't say you never had a chance, and, if you ask me, this place down here is just about right for starting a jolly little fire in.'

'Hold your tongue,' Keene almost roared at him. 'What do you know about it? Nothing to do with you.'

'Now, Mr Keene, sir,' Bobs-the-Boy protested mildly, 'you did ought to give a bloke credit for having eyes in his head and some idea how to use them. I've done what I've been told to do, and had my pay, and never said a word, and never asked no questions, neither. But I've got my eyes, haven't I? brains, too, and if you kid yourself I don't know as well as the next man that you and the other blokes mean to have some nice little fires – one in Deal Street and another here – and if you think I don't know why you and him have been meeting regular at that place where the loonies sit in the sun in their natural – well, what did you think I had got in my brain-box? Putty?'

'If you . . . you . . . you . . .' stammered Keene.

He was more excited than ever; his long arms flew round like a windmill. Whatever it was he wanted to say, he could not get the words out. Bobs-the-Boy surveyed him with a kind of good-humoured contempt.

'Lumme, Mr Keene, sir,' he said, 'if you can't keep your end up better nor that . . . well, where do you think you're going to find yourself when the real thing comes along? You had better take my tip and trot along to the Yard and tell 'em all about it while there's time. That's what I would do if I was in your shoes, feeling the way you do.'

'Do you mean that's what you are thinking of doing yourself, giving us away?' Keene asked darkly.

'Have some sense,' Bobs-the-Boy implored. 'You know as well as I do, fixed the way I am, me on licence and not having reported, with what else they have against me into the bargain – why, I daren't. I'm not like you, I'm not free. But I'm not denying I wouldn't be sorry if you did, so as to be safe out of it. I tell you straight, I'm scared of how all this'll finish.'

'You can drop that sort of talk,' Keene said sharply. 'I know what it means, you've been set on to talk that way. You can tell those who sent you I'm going through with it. I double-cross no man. Understand?'

'Yes, sir,' answered Bobs-the-Boy calmly, 'and though what I said was all well meant, and for your own good, and there's time yet to think it over, and though I'm making no admissions, still if there was anyone who had sent me and told me what to say, why, then, I'll tell 'em just what you say. So we'll drop it, and if you'll let me say this, I do think it was a downy trick to choose that sun bathing monkey house to meet ... nothing suspicious about going there ... harmless cranks is always the last anybody worries about, their crankiness keeping 'em busy, and their harmlessness being took for granted, which is most con-venient at times. All the same, sir, I tell you straight, I'm worried about this here business in the paper. I don't hold with putting any one's light out, I never did, and I don't want to be mixed up with such like. Your girl's sister, weren't she?'

Keene did not answer. He was standing with his arms folded now, as if he wanted to control them. He stared gloomily at his interlocutor and remained silent, but Bobs-the-Boy was sure that he had heard him.

'Don't think,' he asked slowly, a pause between nearly every word, 'don't think ... she was rooting round the monkey house ... along of having suspicioned anything ... anything about barbed wire?'

Keene knew these last two words meant 'fire', for the old rhyming slang still exists, indeed seems continually to be born afresh among those who can hardly have had any knowledge of its history. Probably there is a natural tendency in the oblique and crooked criminal mind to avoid calling a thing by its true name, and a word that rhymes with that name is the substitute that springs most naturally to the tongue when one is required. Keene said,

'How could she know anything about it? That's absurd ... there was no way she had of getting to know ... all she went to the Grange for was to write it up ... she hated me, but God knows I never thought of hurting her.'

'There's a story going about you was heard to tell her to leave you and your girl alone or it would be the worse for her,' the other said.

'If you've been asking questions . . .' began Keene, very angrily, 'you had best be careful . . . What business is it of yours what I said to her?'

'What I want to know,' retorted Bobs-the-Boy, 'is what business it is of mine, and if it's none – so much the better. As for asking questions, there wasn't any need. It's all about the neighbourhood that Mrs Adams what's the charlady there heard you and her quarrelling and you saying that.'

'We weren't quarrelling, and Mrs Adams is a gossiping old fool,' Keene exclaimed. 'All I meant was to tell her to leave us alone. And look here, my man, you be careful what you say.'

'Oh, I will,' the other assured him. 'You don't think she came snooping round here because she was on to – to something? What about Mr Hunter? . . . I suppose there isn't no chance . . . ?'

Keene's patience or else his self-control seemed to break, and he burst into a torrent of abuse, to all of which his companion listened unmoved. When Keene at last was silent, more for lack of breath than for any other reason, he said quietly,

'It's what I said before; all I want to be sure of is that it is no business of mine, for murder's a thing I never did hold with or want to have anything to do with.'

A new idea seemed to strike Keene. He was silent for a time, once more staring hard at the other, though now with a different expression. Then he said,

'I had nothing to do with it, it's only silly to think so. I don't suppose Hunter had either; why should he? But you – you seem to know a lot, you seem very interested, you've talked of nothing else; what are you asking all these questions for, dropping all these hints?'

Bobs-the-Boy for once seemed quite taken aback, disconcerted even. He could not quite control his features, the

75

cackle of laughter he emitted sounded anything but genuine; his voice was less well under control than usual as he answered,

'Oh, it wasn't me as did it, if that's what you're trying to put over. I don't say I've a alibi same as you and the bloke upstairs, but it's not a thing I had anything to do with, why should I? If she suspicioned anything, it wasn't me ... it wasn't me she was trying to take my girl from ... she hadn't come snooping round me, asking funny questions same as she did here. What's worrying me, what's making me interested like, is what for Mitchell and that other bird, Ferris, are hanging round here.'

Keene did not answer, but he was still looking hard and doubtfully at his companion, and then from above Hunter called cautiously.

'You can come up now, both of you ... it wasn't Mitchell ... not the police at all ... it was only Curtis. I don't know what he came for; he asked a lot of silly questions, I had to clear him out at last. A bit off his head if you ask me. I'm jolly glad it wasn't Mitchell anyhow.'

'If it was Curtis,' Keene said as he came slowly up the basement steps into the office again, Bobs-the-Boy following close behind, 'why, then, perhaps that explains what Mitchell was doing here ... They may be watching him and they followed him.'

'That's right,' agreed Bobs-the-Boy from behind, 'explains it, that does.'

'Over this business of his wife's murder?' Hunter asked. 'I thought the account in the paper sounded a bit fishy ... only what did he want? ... Seems he knew she was here that time ... He saw you, too, Keene. ... I think he imagined you and she had been flirting on the quiet. I suppose you hadn't, had you?'

'Of course not,' Keene retorted. 'She hated me like poison.'

'Well, I should keep quiet about that if I were you,' Hunter observed.

'What for?' demanded Keene aggressively, and then with

a gesture towards Bobs-the-Boy, slouching in the background, 'He's been hinting you or I had something to do with it.'

'I only asked straight out, not wanting to be mixed up with such like,' Bobs-the-Boy protested. 'I thought perhaps she had suspicioned something . . . anyways, if I was you, with the "busies" snooping round the way they are, I wouldn't go for to deliver the barbed wire just yet awhile.'

Hunter, who also knew well enough what 'barbed wire' stood for, told him angrily to shut up.

'And don't come messing round here on your own again,' he added; 'wait till you're sent for, or you'll be sorry for it.'

'You mean you'll put my light out, same as — ?' Bobs-the-Boy asked grinning. 'Only that mightn't be so easy, I'm not a bit of skirt,' and when at that, with an angry growl, Keene came threateningly, his long arms swinging, towards him, he grinned again and dodged out of the room and away down the yard with his characteristic swift, furtive, sidelong gait that took him over the ground with such speed.

Staring after him furiously, Keene said,

'I'd . . . I'd . . . I'd like to knock his head off.'

'Well,' agreed Hunter, 'if his light were put out, as he calls it, I don't know that I should worry an awful lot.'

'Do you think he can be trusted?' Keene asked.

'Anyhow, he won't dare say a word,' Hunter declared, though looking a little uneasy all the same; 'not with all they have against him. But I wish he had never been brought into it.'

'He's been hinting to me I had better go to the police, give the whole thing up, chuck it while there's time,' Keene said. 'I suppose it means he's been set on to try me out . . . see if I'm weakening.'

Hunter was looking at him rather oddly.

'He was talking to me like that the other day,' he said; 'as good as advised me to go to the police and tell them all about it . . . I thought perhaps it was you . . .?'

Keene denied it with oaths.

'He's just been trying us both,' he said, 'to make sure we'll stick it.' He paused and then said slowly, 'Anyhow, it's too late for that ... too late for anything ... except to go on.'

'Too late for anything,' Hunter agreed, 'except to go through with it now we've begun.' After another long pause he said, looking sideways and doubtfully at Keene, 'Do you think Curtis ...?'

He left the sentence uncompleted but Keene understood well enough.

'He had been drinking pretty hard,' he said. 'He was half off his head with drink and jealousy ... He threatened her ... He had a pistol like the one found on the spot and he can't explain what's become of his own ... He is known to have been near the spot ... Sybil says they were going to arrest him and then seemed to change their minds ... She couldn't understand why ... Something about Jo's hat or the way she did her hair, unless Sybil got hold of the wrong end of the story ... Anyhow, they changed their minds at the last moment.'

'If he feels they still suspect him,' Hunter said, 'perhaps that's why he came here ... to prove he didn't do it by showing them he was trying to find out on his own.'

Keene had gone to the door and was staring down the yard along which Bobs-the-Boy had just passed and vanished. He came back into the room and said darkly,

'That Bobs fellow was dropping all sorts of hints ... I suppose he —' He paused and swallowed in his throat. 'He couldn't have had anything to do with it himself, could he?' he asked in a low voice.

'Well, why should he?' Hunter asked, and then they were both silent, looking doubtfully and darkly at each other.

CHAPTER TEN

Consultation

AFTER his early morning visit to Ealing, imposed upon him by the unwelcome report Detective-Constable Owen had furnished of Curtis's appearance there, Superintendent Mitchell returned to seek his bed once more. For he was sufficiently advanced in years to have found that he could no longer, as in former times, neglect sleep for two or three nights consecutively without much inconvenience, as still could Inspector Ferris or the still younger Owen. Ferris indeed spent all that day out in the country on a promising clue that, like most promising clues, led nowhere, and all the time, except for a slight occasional tendency to yawn, had shown no sign of having missed a night's rest.

Not that Mitchell allowed himself many hours of repose. By early afternoon he was back again in his room at Scotland Yard where, with the knowledge and consent of the Assistant Commissioner, he set to work to clear up as many of the other cases he had in hand as possible, or at least to get them into condition to hand over to a colleague, so that he might devote himself entirely to the Leadeane Road tragedy.

He was not a man very easily affected – how could he be with so many years of police work behind him and all its contacts with shame and misery and despair? But this case had made on him a deep impression; it had become indeed to him not so much a 'case' as something with which his association was far more intimate and personal. The memory of the look the dying woman had given him was still vivid in his mind, so that sometimes it seemed to him that he had been called as much in his personal as in his official capacity to bring her murderer to justice.

He was still busy with his task when Ferris came in to report on the day's activities and to bring with him a long report from Owen that had just arrived by special messenger, though of course Owen was only one of a score or so of men working on different aspects of the affair.

'Oh, yes, Owen,' Mitchell said as he took it to see what it was justified the use of a special messenger. 'By the way I'm wanting a full report from him about this "Mousey" affair – seems now there are likely to be questions about it in the House. "Disgraceful attempt of the police to prevent ex-convict earning honest living." That'll be the line.'

'Mousey and an honest living,' said Ferris. 'Might as well talk about chalk and cream cheese.'

'Mousey' was the name by which was known a certain receiver of stolen goods recently released on licence and then re-arrested, and his licence cancelled, because of an assertion that stolen property had been found in his possession. But the protests of Mousey – whose real name was Jim Geogeghan, or so he said – that this stolen property had been 'planted' in his house by the police themselves, in order to give them an excuse for re-arresting him on account of an old grudge held against him, had been so loud and shrill that they had reached the ears of a certain member of Parliament to whom the opportunity of appearing as the champion of the oppressed against a brutal officialdom had been irresistible.

And the consequent questions in the House would have to be dealt with very tactfully, since there happened to be more truth in a part, though only a part, of Mousey's protest than it was desirable should be known just yet.

'I've made it all right with the Prison Commissioners,' Mitchell continued, 'but it's going to be difficult to satisfy this M.P. chap, and if he goes on asking questions, it may be jolly awkward, especially as Mousey himself won't say a word. Just shuts his mouth and sits tight, so there's no telling whether we're on the right track with him or not. But all the same, that it was through him Bobs-the-Boy was told to go and work for Mr Hunter in Howland Yard is pretty certain.'

Mitchell went on reading the report Owen had sent in

and paying it the compliment of an occasional puzzled grunt. Now and again he fired off a sharp question at Ferris, who for his part was deep in a book he had just picked up from Mitchell's desk. It was entitled *Made Perfect in Sunshine*, by Esmond Bryan, and was published at three and six net by Esmond Bryan at Leadeane Grange for the Society of Sun Believers (Esmond Bryan, president and founder).

'Find it interesting?' Mitchell asked him abruptly.

'Well, sir, I suppose it's right enough for those who like it,' Ferris answered. 'I'm wondering if you think there's any connexion.'

'So am I,' Mitchell answered, putting Owen's report in its appropriate place in the pile of documents growing ever higher and higher on his desk. 'What's certain is that it was the Leadeane Sun Bathing show that Jo Curtis left the *Announcer* office to write up. Also, we know her husband was wanting to speak to her on her way there, though it seems he failed to find her. We know some unidentified motor-cyclist did catch her up, and that there was apparently a quarrel between them. It is equally certain that she reached the Grange in safety, because Owen saw her there himself. But unluckily Owen left the place almost at once, and what happened after her arrival there, till we found her lying shot through the body in a burning and overturned motor-car at the bottom of a railway cutting, we don't know. But we do know from the way she did her hair that it wasn't her who was driving her Bayard Seven when we saw it go by. That's certain, too. Only what's it mean?'

'I suppose,' suggested Ferris, slowly, 'she couldn't have changed her way of doing her hair, could she?'

'That,' said Mitchell reproachfully, 'comes of your not being a married man, Ferris, a great handicap if you ask me. Women don't change their style of doing their hair the way you change your tie, they change it the way you change your religion – weeks of preparation, consultation, debate, hesitation, terror lest your chances in one world or the other will suffer for it. No, I think we may be sure Mrs Curtis hadn't changed her way of doing her hair that afternoon; done the way it was it had to stay till she had time to spend a week or two with her hairdresser. Besides, I've got a report from the doctor, and he says that though the hair was badly scorched there's no doubt which side the parting was.'

'Well, then,' Ferris asked, 'if it wasn't her we saw driving, who was it?'

'That's what we've got to find out,' agreed Mitchell. 'And was she murdered already then, and her dead body hidden in the car, or was she picked up further on and murdered afterwards? And if she was murdered before, was it at the Grange itself or after she had left the Grange? Gibbons was at the Grange first thing this morning, you know. His report is that Mr Esmond Bryan says Mrs Curtis got there early, though he's not sure of the exact time, and was there all afternoon. He says he is used to visits from journalists, and welcomes them, and lets them go all over the place alone, after he has done his best to answer their questions. Apparently, after Mrs Curtis had finished looking round the place she came back to his office, where he and his partners were having some sort of committee meeting that he says she rather interrupted, and after another long talk when he tried to convert her to the sun bathing cure-all fad, he walked across the lawn with her to the entrance to the old stable yard, where visitors park their cars now. That part is fully corroborated, because there is independent evidence that he was seen walking about and talking with a woman who answers to Mrs Curtis's description. Afterwards, there's proof that he did, as he says he did, go straight back to his office, ring up Lord Carripore and have a talk with him – it seems he is trying to get Lord Carripore to put money into the concern. So it seems whatever happened, happened after Bryan left her at the entrance to the car park that used to be the stable yard. We know from Owen's report that both Hunter and Keene were at the Grange during the afternoon, but both say they left early. We'll have to check up on their alibis. I'm having that done, of course. But we can't at present rule out the possibility that one or the other might have been waiting for her on the road – she knew both, and would presumably have stopped for either if she had seen them.'

'But what motive could either of them have?' Ferris interrupted. 'We know they're planning – at least we suspect they're planning – arson. But up to the present they've clean records. They've only got to stop it, and they're safe as houses; why should they add murder? — It's not credible.'

'Not looking at it that way,' agreed Mitchell, 'and if they give up their arson idea, supposing they have it, and if they have nothing to do with Mrs Curtis's murder, well, then they're all right, both of them, and no concern of ours. But you can't shut your eyes to the fact that Mrs Curtis had been to Howland Yard, and what's the explanation if not that she suspected something? And if she went to Leadeane Grange, was it because she suspected something more, and knew Keene and Hunter were meeting there? And was the result some quarrel that ended – well, as quarrels sometimes do? Of course, we've got to remember Curtis himself, and his threats, as well as his pistol he says he threw away, but that may be the one that was used for the murder – a jealous-minded man on the drink is capable of anything. And then there's the unknown motor-cyclist as well.'

'Yes,' objected Ferris, 'but if it was a woman who was driving the car when we saw it pass, where does she come from? No woman in this business that I can see, except Miss Frankland.'

'How do we know it really was a woman we saw?' Mitchell asked. 'We only had a glimpse, remember, as the thing shot by. It would have been easy enough for a man to stick on that hat covering half his face – tie it on with string to make it stick perhaps – and put on the coat with the collar turned up to cover the other half, and all the rest of his body hidden. Good enough flying by at sixty m.p.h. And easy enough to stop for a second, put back the hat and coat on the body lying at the bottom of the car, and shoot the thing full speed over the edge of the cutting. The murderer slips down after it, either sets the car on fire or makes sure it's burning already, and clears away along the track.'

They both fell silent, in the imagination of both a grisly picture enough of the little Bayard Seven dashing along the road with the murdered woman's body within and the murderer disguised in her hat and coat seated at the wheel. Then Mitchell said,

'Somehow we've got to know why she went to Leadeane Grange – whether it was only to write it up or whether there was a reason. And then we've got to find out what happened there. You and I will go there to-morrow, Ferris, and see what we can find out, and meanwhile you can instruct Owen to go on working on his own.'

CHAPTER ELEVEN

Among the Sun Bathers

THE little village of Leadeane had never been able quite to make up its mind whether to be proud of its sun bathers or to regard them as a crying scandal.

At first it had come down rather heavily on the crying scandal side. There had been much indignant talk, a suggestion of a protest meeting, of an appeal to 'the authorities', though what authorities no one seemed to know. Rowdy youngsters of the type always eager to associate a righteous indignation with a display of hooliganism had begun to look forward to a little excitement. One or two windows of Leadeane Grange, the sun bathers' headquarters, had stones thrown through them; and there was one night when a gang of youths marched up and down before the house, beating tea trays, till they grew tired of that harmless and no doubt enjoyable but somewhat monotonous amusement.

Lately, however, public opinion had distinctly leaned towards taking an amused pride in the establishment. It had been written up once or twice, just lately in the *Morning Intelligence*, with a large photograph on the back page – inset Mr Esmond Bryan, the director and founder of the establishment and President of the Society of Sun Believers. Originally, by-the-way, this had been the Society of Sun Worshippers, but the last word had been altered on the representation of some of the local clergy, who feared misunderstanding.

After all, not every village in the Thames valley got 'write-ups' like that in one of the most popular of the five or six national papers that direct our destinies, instruct our tastes, and dictate to us the opinions we hold with such a depth of passionate conviction. Had not the *Morning Intelligence* called Leadeane one of the loveliest of our English villages? Had there not been a reference to its alert and intelligent inhabitants? Leadeane, gratified, but not surprised, admitted silently that it owed these not undeserved compliments to Mr Bryan, and was henceforth inclined to view his establishment with a more lenient eye.

After all, why should not a man wear sandals and long hair? Surely each of us has a right to treat his own extremities as he will?

Possibly also, for this is a materialistic age, Leadeane was not altogether uninfluenced by the fact that the sun bathers brought a certain amount of money into the village. The garage proprietor, for instance, found his turnover doubled or trebled. The Leadeane Arms did well with thirsty chauffeurs, waiting about while their employers sunbathed. Then needed supplies were as much as possible bought locally, and there were often odd jobs to be done in the way of small repairs, gardening, and so on.

Nor was there anything in an establishment so well run to which reasonable exception could be taken. Inside the old boundary wall of the extensive grounds and beyond the belt of trees that lined it, there had been erected at considerable expense a wooden fence seven feet high. The sun bathers therefore were too well hidden from passers-by for any possible offence to be given. Even the curious, who, as sometimes happened, scaled the wall and penetrated the wooded belt beyond in order to peep through any chink they could find in the fence, saw little or nothing for their pains, for beyond the fence again was another, wider belt of shrubs, and flower beds, and ornamental trees, that bounded the open, grassy expanse, sloping to the south, where the actual sun bathing took place – that is, when the sun was so kind as to permit it.

On this grassy slope then when the sun was kind the members, their friends, and visitors, disported themselves, though always very strictly obeying the careful regulations laid down by Mr Bryan, whose watchful eye was ever on the alert to see they were properly carried out. Every one on joining, every visitor as well, had to read these regulations aloud, to submit to be questioned about them so that it might be certain they were understood, and to sign a promise to obey them in the letter and the spirit. The exact number of inches below the thigh that had to be covered, the exact amount of back and chest that might be exposed, were precisely laid down, and the weight and thickness of the material of which the body clothing had to be made was specified minutely. Indeed, the regulations were more strict and detailed than probably any seaside town would have dared to enforce on its mixed bathing beach.

For those more advanced, who desired to sun bathe *in puris naturalibus*, as Mr Esmond Bryan liked to put it, the strictest separation of the sexes was enforced. For the women, the flat roof of the house was reserved. On the ground floor was the general club room and the bar, as Mr Bryan called it, where, of course, no alcoholic beverages were served – still less those sources of all ill, tea and coffee and cocoa. Than those three Mr Bryan would far sooner have served neat alcohol to his patrons, or prussic acid for that matter, holding it less deadly on the whole. But your taste for tomato juice, neat or mixed, for turnip tea, for dandelion, parsley, and nettle tea, for orange juice, for a dozen other strange and presumably innocuous beverages, could be gratified; and as you quaffed your goblet of fresh nettle brew you could satisfy your hunger with nuts, carrots, many kinds of fruits, raw chopped cabbage or lettuce, and other similar foods that must have been delicious, for they all seemed to be devoured with equal gusto. On the first floor were the executive offices, where a couple of girls tapped typewriters all day long, Mr Bryan's private quarters, the committee room where the managing committee met, and beyond this and leading out of it Mr Bryan's private office that also communicated on the other side with his sitting-room. The next floor was cut off by a green baize door beyond which none penetrated, save those ladies admitted to the privileges of the roof. The door was fastened by a spring lock, and could be opened only by a key that never left the possession of the guardian, a stout severe matron, a Mrs Barrett, widow of a police constable, who kept careful watch to see that none passed but those who had the right. On the floor above were the sun-ray lamps with which the bathers had to content themselves when the sun itself was hidden. These operated in a large apartment that had been made by knocking several rooms into one, so that they occupied almost the whole of the floor space except for a row of dressing cubicles. Finally there was the flat roof itself, fitted up with couches and screens and protected by a specially erected parapet, where in the appropriate weather one could lie and roast like any Christmas turkey. And that this sort of cooking was much superior to that to be obtained from the sun-ray lamps, Mr Bryan was never tired of proclaiming.

'As a substitute, yes,' he would say, 'but it's not violet rays themselves that count, it's the fresh air as well, the wholeness of the air vibrant with the wholeness of the light of the sun.'

It had to be admitted, though the ribald youth of the neighbourhood were fond of joking about procuring an aeroplane and flying low over the Grange some sunny day, that Mr Bryan and his colleague, Miss James, who had special charge of this department *in puris naturalibus*, took every possible care that it was all carried out with the most perfect decorum.

For those of the other sex who wished for the same treatment there had been erected an enclosure at the foot of the grounds, cut off from them by the swimming pond formed by the damming up of the Leade, the little stream from which the village took its name and that flowed through this corner of the Grange property. Originally this was meant for a fish pond, but it had been easy to transform it into a first-class swimming pool where Mr Bryan always strongly urged his sun bathers to complete their regime by a dip when season and weather permitted – and even when they didn't.

'I don't know which is the best,' he would say, 'sun bathing or open air water bathing, but when you combine the two – perfection.'

And one of his favourite plans, to be carried out when funds permitted, was to add a constant stream of salt to the water, so that the extra benefit of sea bathing might be secured.

Another favourite project of his was to erect two covered swimming baths, one for men and one for women, where sun-ray lamps could be installed, and swimmers could bask *in puris naturalibus* in an artificial sun all the year round, instead of having to wait on the fitful appearance of that luminary so fickle and doubtful in our northern land. But here again was a project that had to attend upon a doubtful future, when money might be more abundant, for the published accounts of the establishment showed that so far it had been run at an actual loss – that is, the capital employed had not only so far returned no interest but had actually shrunk considerably.

In addition to the open-air enclosure for the masculine devotees of the *in puris naturalibus* cult, a large barn standing within it had been arranged for their use with two big sun-ray lamps so that they might not be too dependent on the weather. The whole of this part was under the supervision of a Mr Zack Dodd, a huge figure of a man who once had been a heavy-weight professional boxer, who was understood to have invested a good share of his savings in the establishment, and who was notoriously on bad terms with Mr Bryan, with whom he had more than once been heard quarrelling fiercely. Indeed Mr Bryan made no secret of his desire to pay Dodd out, as Dodd made no secret of his ardent wish to get his capital back. The only difficulty in the way apparently was that the money was not available. Not that all that prevented Mr Dodd from being almost as fervent and voluble a believer in the treatment and the virtues of sunshine on the bare skin as Mr Bryan himself.

'If only I had known before about this here treatment,' he was fond of saying, 'a course of it would have made me champion of the world instead of only runner-up.'

In point of fact he had never been even runner-up, but that is a detail.

Miss James, on the other hand, was inclined to be rather cynical about the treatment, though her fine physique, for she was a tall, strong, well-made woman, though a little on the thin side, seemed to suggest that at any rate it did her no harm. She took her sun bathing treatment regularly, however, but it was understood that that was a condition of her employment. As a paid servant, not a partner like Zack Dodd, she had to obey.

Mr Esmond Bryan himself, the director, was a thin, busy little man, very quick and active in his movements, burned almost black from constant exposure to sun rays, natural and artificial, but with a mass of snow-white hair that swept down to his shoulders and of which the whiteness was the only sign that testified to the seventy odd years he admitted. Indeed, he had found people so apt to be incredulous of the age he claimed that finally, in half humorous protest, he had framed a copy of his birth certificate and hung it on the wall in his office.

'That is what sun and air have done for me,' he would say as he talked and walked with a vigour and vivacity that would not have disgraced a man who had reached but half the allotted span.

No one had ever seen him except in his present costume of wide shorts, sandals that left the top of his feet bare, a shirt cut low at the neck so as to expose throat and neck, and with sleeves that reached only half-way to the elbows. A single woollen undergarment was all else he wore; and winter and summer his costume was always the same, except that the woollen undergarment might be a little thicker in December than in June. Even when snow was on the ground he could be seen going about in the same dress, his legs bare from the middle of the thighs downwards, the snow melting on the tops of his bare feet of which the sandals protected only the soles. It was thus attired then that he went to meet Mitchell and Ferris when the next morning he was told that the police officers were waiting to interview him.

CHAPTER TWELVE

Mr Bryan Chats

IT was therefore this odd little scarecrow of a man in his sandals and his shirt open at the neck; his shorts flapping about his thin legs from which it seemed perpetual sunshine, natural or artificial, had melted all but skin and bone; his little sharp eyes alight with the fires of fanaticism; whom the two burly police officials saw come out of the house towards where they waited just outside, watching with interested eyes the beautifully kept lawn, whereon already, for though the hour was early it was an exceptionally fine day, various devotees of the sunshine cult were enjoying their little occasional, and chancy, dose of genuine sunshine.

He had already been made acquainted with their errand, and indeed the day before had been visited by another officer, Inspector Gibbons, whose report Mitchell had read over more than once. And to that report it seemed Mr Bryan had nothing fresh to add. Though he remembered Jo Frankland's visit well enough, since a journalistic visit has always its importance, he was sure no detail of the least interest concerning it had gone unrecorded.

'Not that I paid any special attention or thought much of it at the time,' he said; 'I never dreamed of course such a tragedy was going to happen, and journalists often come here now that our great movement is attracting more and more attention and getting more and more into the papers. One of my projects for the future is to establish a paper devoted solely to our great cause. There's only one thing now that hampers us in spreading our glorious gospel of sunshine.'

'The weather?' suggested Mitchell mildly.

'The uncertainty of the weather,' admitted Bryan, shaking his head with an air of gentle reproach, 'is a difficulty, a great difficulty. But what I meant was money, that's what we need to carry on the work.'

'Need money for most things,' agreed Mitchell, 'getting born's about the only thing that doesn't cost us anything. From what you told Mr Gibbons there's no chance of your being able to tell us the exact time Miss Frankland got here or exactly when she left.'

Mr Bryan shook his head.

'I made some inquiries,' he said, 'but I don't think we could get any nearer than I said before – she arrived early in the afternoon and left just before dark. Of course, if we had had any idea of what was going to happen ... but in any case we've no system of recording when our members come or go. They suit themselves, they're welcome to stay as long as they please.'

'Must have been quite a long visit she made,' Mitchell remarked.

'I left her free to go where she liked and spend her time just as she liked,' Bryan explained. 'Of course, there's the enclosure reserved for male bathers *in puris naturalibus.*'

'What's that?' asked Ferris, as Mitchell paused to make an entry in his note-book. 'Some of these new patent bath salts or what?'

'I asked Owen that,' Mitchell remarked. 'One of our young men,' he explained to Bryan, 'we got him special from Oxford to heighten the tone of the force, same being necessary now we run in as many dukes and their like for road hogging as we do burglars and their like for other offences. Owen says it means being dressed all over the way a woman's top half is dressed when she's all togged up in her very best evening frock.'

'Oh !' said Ferris, considering this. 'Oh !' he said again.

'I think, Mr Owen should be told,' said Bryan sternly, 'that this knowledge of the classics is incomplete and reflects no credit on the University. *In puris naturalibus* means without any artificial impediment to keep from the body the health-giving rays of the sun. It means that you should bathe in sun and air as you bathe in hot water in your bath at home.'

'Well, why not?' agreed Ferris, a good deal struck by the force of this argument.

'Quite so,' agreed Mitchell in his turn. 'By the way, you have two members – a Mr Hunter and a Mr Keene, haven't you? You know them?'

Mr Bryan knew them both, though only as members. He had called on Mr Keene at his place of business in Deal Street, Piccadilly, and from that call had sprung Mr Keene's membership of the society. He did not know how Mr Hunter had come to join; probably he had read of the activities of the society, or else had been recommended to join by someone. No doubt Mr Hunter could tell them which it was. Mr Bryan could not say if either Keene or Hunter or both or neither had been there to sun bathe on the day of the tragedy. They had no system at all of recording the visits of members. Members were welcome to come as often and stay as long as they wished. They could bring friends, too, though in that case they were expected to pay a small fee. There were occasionally cases of what Mr Bryan, chuckling over what he evidently considered a good joke, called 'sun crashing', but though that was frowned upon officially, no special precautions were taken against it. One trusted to the honour of the members, and besides the 'sun crasher' of to-day was generally the member of to-morrow. But it was certainly quite possible for a stranger to roam about the grounds unquestioned, or even to enter the canteen, or for that matter the offices on the first floor.

'Or my private apartments, as far as that goes; they communicate with the office through our committee room,' observed Mr Bryan, though looking rather puzzled. 'Only why should they? There's nothing to steal, and we've certainly missed nothing. Everything of any value is kept in the safe, and that can only be opened when Zack Dodd and myself are both present; we both have keys.'

'Who is Mr Dodd?' asked Mitchell.

'Zachary Dodd? oh, he's my partner,' answered Bryan

with a faint scowl that seemed to suggest he would have liked to make another answer. 'He is in charge of the gentlemen's department – *in puris naturalibus* – as Miss James is of the ladies' section.'

'Another partner?' asked Mitchell.

'No, but a most trusted helper,' answered Mr Bryan, losing his scowl at once; 'most trusted and most useful.'

He added, as Mitchell made a note of the two names, that though he knew no more of the two members mentioned, Messrs Hunter and Keene, than of any other of the numerous adherents of the cult he preached, yet he had noticed that they were friendly, and though they seldom arrived together, yet always seemed to be mutually aware of each other's presence and to prefer to lie side by side as they basked in the rays of the artificial or the natural sun.

'The fact is,' confessed Mr Bryan with a melancholy shake of the head, 'I'm afraid both smoke – I have to allow it,' he confessed deprecatingly, 'it's almost as harmful as drinking tea, I'm not sure if it isn't even worse than coffee, but people will do it, and at first one has to go slowly. But in time we'll root tobacco out.' He straightened himself up, he looked ready to rush headlong then and there into the fray. 'It will be the last evil to be overcome,' he announced.

'Well, if it's to be the last,' murmured Mitchell, somewhat comforted by the thought that this promised it a sufficiently long life, 'though I daresay my missus would rather tea got the last run.'

'Tea?' exclaimed Bryan, catching at the word, 'poison – but we make a most delicious, attractive, health-giving beverage from scraped carrot and potato peelings. Miss Frankland herself admitted when she tasted it that she thought it unparalleled – absolutely unparalleled, so much so indeed that she said she would like to try it on a literary friend of hers, a critic, I gathered. I think she said he had reviewed a volume of essays she had published recently. I asked her,' he explained, 'to have some refreshment with me after she had seen all she wished to see – one always tries to be civil to the Press; very powerful, the Press.'

'They are indeed,' admitted Mitchell, 'for what the Press says to-day, the public said the day before yesterday. Then the public knows it was right all the time. After Miss Frankland had her – er – refreshment with you, you walked with her to the car park, I think, but I gather you didn't actually see her go.'

'No,' admitted Bryan, 'our talk had been so interesting – I felt confident she would join us before long, and of course being connected with the Press I felt she might be useful to the Cause – I had quite forgotten to notice the time till I suddenly remembered I had to call up Lord Carripore, and that unless I did so at once I should probably be too late for that day.'

'Anything important?' Mitchell asked.

'Oh, just a business proposition I had to put before him,' Bryan explained. 'So I asked Miss Frankland to excuse me – we were almost at the car park – and I hurried back to the house. The car park attendant was there to help her if necessary.'

Mitchell asked a few more questions, but admitted that the report made by Inspector Gibbons seemed to have covered all essential points. Then he asked if he and Ferris, as they were there, could have a look round the place, and Mr Bryan appeared quite charmed, and seemed to think he was on the point of enrolling two new members. At great length he expatiated on the advantages, bodily and mental, to be secured by sun bathing, and Mitchell, who could usually talk as fast and long as any man, listened in silence and apparent interest. Nor did he challenge the assertion when Mr Bryan declared triumphantly that no one ever believed him at first when he gave his age as seventy.

'My hair is white,' he admitted, 'that happened before I knew how to control the bleaching effect sometimes experienced. But I'm active enough, my arteries are those of a man of thirty-five. I'm as active as any young fellow I know. Up at five every morning and never in bed much before midnight, and all through sunshine bathing – *in puris naturalibus* when possible, and natural sunshine if possible.

If not, rays from our lamp installation.'

His flow of words went on. Indeed there was no lack of vigour and animation in his talk and gestures, and his claim that he could pass for a man not more than half the seventy years he spoke of, was one certainly well founded, though whether that was due to sunshine, carrot tea, or something else might be open to investigation. He wound up by inviting the two police officials to try an hour or two's sun bathing then and there, since they could hardly hope for a better or a brighter day.

'I have two sun bathing slips I could let you have,' he offered eagerly, 'unless you would prefer – *in puris naturalibus*?'

Mitchell seemed inclined to accept for Ferris, and only his sense of discipline and his respect for his superior officer prevented Ferris from accepting on the spot for Mitchell. Bryan, evidently disappointed that neither acceptance materialized, urged that sun bathing was good not only for the body but also for the brain.

'Many business men think out their plans here,' he declared. 'I am sure you would find the experience very useful for solving this dreadful mystery.'

However Mitchell explained that he didn't think the Assistant Commissioner would approve, not while on duty anyhow, and Bryan nodded gloomily and said he was only too familiar with official obscurantism and hostility towards all the great forward movements.

CHAPTER THIRTEEN

Sybil Visits Leadeane

INDEED this thought of official obscurantism seemed to weigh upon Mr Bryan, for he grew noticeably less talkative as the tour of inspection continued with an introduction to Miss James, the supervisor of the ladies' section. She remembered Miss Jo Frankland's visit only vaguely, but thought she had spent some time in the ladies' section *in puris naturalibus*, and indeed could not remember that she had seen her go.

'Probably she just went off when she thought she had seen enough,' declared Miss James, who seemed to be feeling the heat of the day a good deal, and who replied to Bryan's remark that she looked pale and ill and ought to revive herself with a sun bath, by a snappish retort that on a day like this she was getting all the heat and sun she wanted, thank you.

A little disconcerted, Mr Bryan took an opportunity to murmur in Mitchell's ear that unfortunately owing to a temporary – a purely temporary – shortage of cash, Miss James's wages had not been paid quite up to date, and this delay seemed to have got on her nerves.

'I think she's worrying, not sleeping well,' he said, 'and she will not give the sun treatment the full trial it must have, that anything must have, to succeed.'

Mitchell was properly sympathetic; and Miss James offered to show them over her domain, if they would wait 'till the establishment closed and all the members had left.

'Though sometimes our lamps are going till near midnight,' she added. 'Business women have to come in the evenings, you understand.'

Mitchell said he didn't think it was necessary for them to examine the ladies' section. There was perfectly good evidence nothing had happened to Miss Frankland up there, and though he would have liked a list of the sun bathers present during her visit, still as no record was kept, that was evidently unobtainable. He wished Miss James had been able to say how long her visit to the upper floor and roof had lasted, but it was quite understandable that Miss James, with all her multifarious duties, had never even thought of noticing the visitor's departure. Mitchell did not consider it necessary either to visit the men's section *in puris naturalibus* – as evidently Miss Frankland had not been there, but Mr Bryan thought it was a pity, for they were going to miss meeting Mr Zachary Dodd, who was the superintendent of that department.

'You would see from his physique,' said little Mr Bryan enthusiastically, 'what sun bathing does for a man – his body, that is.'

'Body only?' asked Mitchell.

'Ah,' Bryan said quickly, 'you're thinking of what I said about sun bathing being good for mental activity as well. But Dodd – well, after all, the sun can't work miracles, can it? It must have something to go on, mustn't it?'

Mitchell agreed gravely.

'The fact is,' declared Mr Bryan, growing confidential, 'Dodd has a somewhat unfortunate temperament – overbearing, very overbearing. If we are not exactly making money as yet – I emphasize, as yet – what does that matter compared with the great missionary work we are carrying on? What is the good of being afraid of the future? But Dodd has a yellow streak in him, a yellow streak. There are times when I'm afraid his nerve will give way altogether, just with the strain of waiting.'

And as the queer little man trotted along between the two big police officers, rather like a terrier on the alert for rats between two great hounds concerned only with bigger game, Mitchell was aware of an impression that anyhow there was nothing of a yellow streak in Esmond Bryan, no chance of his nerve ever breaking under any strain, whether of shortage of cash or anything else. And that Ferris had something of the same feeling was proved by his whisper as he muttered to Mitchell,

'Bryan's the sort of little blighter who'll hang on himself till the last penny's gone. He would preach his blessed sun baths to the very bailiffs who came to sell him up.'

'So he would,' agreed Mitchell, 'you're right there – though I'm not sure about the last penny.'

They had seen enough now, however, and said so to Mr Bryan, and he regretted that he had not been able to tell them more, and Mitchell explained that often the most important thing in an inquiry of this nature was to know just that, that in such or such a quarter nothing more was to be learnt. They were close to the entrance to the car park now. Formerly it had been the stable yard, and recently one end had been roofed over with corrugated iron for a protection in bad weather. There were two openings from the yard, one the general entrance and exit at which they had now arrived, and another, a smaller one, at the further end, where a path that originally had led to the pump used for watering the horses had now been widened for the convenience of members wishing to use the west road, without having to make the turn necessary from the main road. But as this widened path was very rough, not having been properly constructed, and led through trees not yet cut down that made careful driving necessary, it was not much used.

At the entrance to the park Mr Bryan shook hands with them and departed, remarking that on almost this exact spot he had said farewell to the unfortunate Miss Frankland, whose tragic end he so greatly deplored and the mystery enveloping which he so hoped would be soon cleared up.

'The mere fact,' he added confidentially, 'that it was from here the unfortunate lady started on her tragic journey that ended so terribly has done us much harm – much harm.'

'Too bad,' Mitchell said, but he had not been listening, for all of them had just caught sight of a figure dodging away behind one of the buildings, between two waiting cars, as if unwilling to be seen. 'See that? who was that?' Mitchell asked quickly.

'Who? that man?' asked Bryan, who had seen him too and for the moment had not looked too pleased, 'oh, it's only a man I've employed sometimes to do odd jobs. Bobs-the-Boy he calls himself.'

'I thought as much,' said Mitchell, looking very grim. 'I thought I recognized him – what's he doing here?'

'I expect he's come to see if there's any work for him. I hope he's not a bad character,' twittered Bryan, looking quite upset. 'I heard him speak of this institution in a most disgraceful manner the other day, so much so indeed that I had made up my mind not to employ him any more. Monkey house was the phrase he used, most offensive and intended to be offensive, though there's no obvious connexion.'

'None, of course,' agreed Mitchell, still frowning and disturbed. 'He's not in your employ regularly?'

'Oh, no,' anwered Bryan, 'only sometimes we have difficulty with the local youths. Recently we have had to send two away in succession – staring.'

'Staring?'

'They have unfortunately,' explained Bryan, shaking his head a little sadly, 'a tendency to stare – especially when young. A decent interest in our work one does not complain of, one even welcomes, but it must be decent. I mentioned the difficulty to one of the gentlemen you spoke of – Mr Hunter. He recommended this man. Quite satisfactory and very willing at first, I thought, but after what I overheard . . . still, he seems willing to work, and one must make allowance for the dense ignorance and prejudice others with more advantages show concerning our work. I forget his real name, though Mr Hunter did tell me, but he has a trick of saying "Bob's the boy for that", when he is asked to do any little job, and so he gets called "Bobs-the-Boy". I think he hoped to get taken on as car park attendant, but of course that's quite impossible now, and besides Wilson gives every satisfaction, if only he would free himself from his degrading habits.'

'What are those?' asked Mitchell.

'He drinks beer,' answered Bryan sadly, 'several members

have complained that an odour . . . on several occasions . . . disgusting.'

'Don't know how a man can do it,' said Ferris severely, and then Bryan shook hands again and departed for the house, while Wilson himself, the car park attendant, an old soldier with only one leg, the other having been lost at Loos, came forward to show them their car where Jacks, their chauffeur, dozed comfortably in his seat at the wheel.

Mitchell produced a liberal tip, asked Wilson a few questions, found he had no more to say than he had told his previous questioner, Inspector Gibbons, and confirmed that while he remembered Miss Frankland arriving in her Bayard Seven, and remembered her parking her car under the corrugated-iron roofing as rain seemed threatening, he had not been there when she left, as he had been sent for to the house to deal with a leaking tap that was threatening to produce a flood in the basement.

'Someone had been up to something with it,' he said. 'Some of them boys from the village up to their tricks.'

It was not, he explained, that Mr Bryan and his associates were in any way unpopular in the village, but some of the youngsters there were inclined to think the sun bathing fraternity fair game for any bit of mischief, and no doubt some of them had thought it would be good fun to try to produce a flood in the Grange, with a vague idea that cold water bathing would be a pleasant substitute for sun bathing.

Mitchell seemed interested in this bit of boyish mischief. He wanted to know if there was any lad in particular whom Wilson suspected, but Wilson would give no names, apparently a little afraid that any boy he mentioned would be marched off to penal servitude then and there. In fact it soon appeared he had no reason for his suspicions of the village lads, except for the fact that the tap had certainly been tampered with, and that every one knows how intimate is the connexion between a bit of mischief and a boy.

So Mitchell thanked him and went on with Ferris to their

car, where Jacks woke up on their approach and got down to open the car door for them.

'Funny business, that,' Mitchell observed abruptly, wakening from the silence into which Wilson's tale or something else had plunged him.

'Yes, sir, very,' agreed Ferris. 'Which did you mean, sir?' he thought it prudent to add for fear of further questions.

'About that leaking tap,' Mitchell explained.

'Yes, sir, very,' agreed Ferris. 'Er – in what way, sir?'

But Mitchell had no time to answer, for as they came up to the car Jacks held out a slip of paper to him,

'Report from Detective-Constable Owen, sir,' he said, 'marked "important". Owen left it in person, sir.'

'Oh, he did, did he?' grumbled Mitchell, and took the message and read it aloud to Ferris, ' "Keeping Curtis under observation as instructed, followed him to Ealing where he visited Mrs Frankland's house. Was able to watch him with Sybil Frankland in drawing-room. Windows were closed and could hear nothing but both seemed excited. After Curtis had gone decided to wait in case of developments, and heard Sybil Frankland's voice in front bedroom saying presumably to Mrs Frankland who is in bed, suffering from shock, 'I murdered Jo, I did it'. Then heard sound of sobbing till window was closed. Waited for further developments but none occurring, left, to try to pick up Curtis again".'

Mitchell folded the report and put it away in his pocket-book.

'Did she mean it or didn't she?' he asked, though speaking more to himself than to Ferris. 'That's the worst of a woman, Ferris; what they mean and what they say are two things with a strictly limited connexion.'

'So I'm told, sir,' agreed Ferris with suitable caution, and when the car had started and they had gone a little way he leaned forward suddenly, and then turned to Mitchell, who had been too deep in thought to notice anything.

'That was her, sir, we've just passed, Sybil Frankland, I mean. It's getting dark, but I saw her plainly in that field just behind the hedge, as if she were hiding.'

CHAPTER FOURTEEN

The A.A. Scout's Evidence

MITCHELL let the car proceed another hundred yards or so and then stopped it and alighted, telling Jacks to wait there by the roadside till they returned.

'What do you think it means, sir? the other Frankland girl turning up like this,' Ferris ventured to inquire when Mitchell, after walking back to the spot where Ferris said he had seen Sybil, came to a standstill there and remained with his hands in his pockets, staring blankly over the hedge into the field beyond, rather as if he hoped to see her still there.

But at Ferris's question he roused himself and turned a gloomy eye on his companion.

'Ask me another,' he said briefly, and lapsed again into deep thought, a natural loquacity he possessed frozen by his utter incapacity to form any reasonable theory to account for these happenings.

Ferris did not venture to speak again. His own mind seemed a blank, so little did it find on which to lay reasonable hold, but he hoped the superintendent was able to see more deeply into things. Presently Mitchell roused himself and began to move slowly back towards the Grange.

'Wonder where Owen is,' he muttered. 'Never where he's wanted, of course. Dodges about and leaves silly messages and never lets you have a chance to give him fresh instructions.'

The measure of the injustice of this remark, since Detective-Constable Owen had received special orders on no account to run the least risk of rousing any suspicion of any connexion existing between himself and the officers more openly investigating the case, is the measure of the bewilderment felt by the normally fair-minded Mitchell.

Still wrapped in thought, if that can be called thought

which was but a chaos and a turmoil of conflicting bewilderments, he stopped to stare again over the hedge into the field where Sybil had been seen, as if he hoped to stare into existence some plausible explanation of her appearance.

'You know, I never thought she was mixed up in it,' he said, 'and yet she must be if she's dodging about here, or at least that's what it looks like. You are sure it was her, Ferris?'

'I don't reckon to make mistakes in identification, sir,' returned Ferris, somewhat stiffly.

'No, no,' agreed Mitchell, for indeed long practice had made Ferris's natural memory for faces as near infallible as could be. 'No, only I don't like it, I don't like it one little bit, not after what Owen reports. The whole business seems gradually concentrating on this blessed sun bathing show, and yet you don't associate cranks with crime – cranks are generally too busy with their own special fad to go in for crime as well.'

'Might make it all the better cover for crime, sir,' suggested Ferris.

'There is that,' admitted Mitchell, 'and they do seem hard pressed for money, but then again the little Bryan man was quite open about that. Still, how would murdering a working journalist like Jo Frankland help them there? A journalist wouldn't be likely to have any money, anyway.'

'No, sir,' agreed Ferris. 'It would be a big help if we could get some idea of what the motive was,' he added.

'It would,' growled Mitchell, whose temper was giving way under the strain of his perplexity, 'and if we knew how many blue beans we wanted, we wouldn't have to count 'em. Anyhow, we know Keene and Hunter both frequent this place, and we know they are up to crooked work, probably arson, or why do they want a man with a record like that of Bobs-the-Boy in their employ? But so far we've no proof, so far those two have done nothing we can hold them on, and for all we can tell they never may. It's no crime to take out big assurances on your stock, and though I daresay it's easier just at present to burn pictures and mink coats than sell them, it doesn't follow that's what they'll actually do. And if it's only that, I don't quite see what they want a man like Bobs-the-Boy to help them for. They could light a candle on top of a can of petrol all by themselves without his help.'

'Do you know how they came to get in touch with him?' Ferris asked. 'That would be a useful point to clear up.'

'Oh, that was through Mousey; Mousey sent him to Hunter,' Mitchell answered. 'Mousey says it was because he saw an advertisement for a man to do odd jobs Hunter put in the paper, and wanted to put Bobs-the-Boy in the way of earning an honest living, but of course that's just cheek and eye-wash. Unluckily Mousey knows we can only hold him another couple of months till his original sentence expires, so he doesn't care much, and very likely he's been well paid. But do Keene and Hunter come here only because it's a convenient place to meet, and they can talk without any risk of rousing suspicion, or is there someone else they want to meet as well?'

'There's another point, sir,' Ferris observed. 'Apparently Jo Frankland was trying to break off the engagement between her sister and Keene, and there is some evidence that Keene had a violent scene with her over that.'

'Doesn't seem very strong as a motive for murder,' Mitchell objected. 'Of course, in a quarrel anything might happen, only this strikes one as a deliberately planned affair. Still, we do know Keene was here that afternoon, only apparently he left before she arrived. Have to get Owen to check up Keene's movements and see if it's possible he hung about here till she left. Better have Keene's movements all day checked up as closely as possible. Gibbons might do that, so as to keep Owen out of it as much as possible. Then there's Hunter. Seems there was some sort of connexion we haven't got the hang of yet, between him and Jo Frankland, or why was she visiting Howland Yard, as there's evidence she was? Curtis evidently suspected an intrigue.

He was all eaten up with jealousy, and that day he had been drinking, but I can't see a man in a frenzy of drink and suspicion planning a murder so deliberately and carrying out so coolly so damnably clever a scheme to hide the crime. For it was clever, you know, Ferris, and if we hadn't been on the spot to put out the fire before the body was too badly burnt, the whole business might easily have passed off as an accident, and the fact that she had been shot never been noticed at all. Besides, Curtis is a big man with tremendous shoulders, and though Mrs Curtis was tall, she was thin – he could never have got inside any coat of hers without splitting it right down. I don't think it's possible it could have been Curtis we saw driving the car when it passed us, any more than it can have been the poor woman herself, since it is certain she had been shot before then. The evidence of the photograph in the *Announcer* is conclusive that whoever the driver was, it wasn't her.'

'Yes, sir,' agreed Ferris. 'Good thing you noticed that.'

'Sort of thing someone was bound to notice,' Mitchell answered, though purring a little at the compliment. 'Young Owen spotted it quick enough, without even seeing the photo, just on my describing it to him – of course, I had told him to look out for something wrong.'

'Oh, well, you know, sir,' Ferris pointed out, 'that makes all the difference – anyone ought to be able to spot the discrepancy once they were told there was something to look out for. It was spotting it the first go off without any hint was the smart work.'

'Well, perhaps,' conceded Mitchell, who secretly was of the same opinion, 'anyhow, it's good proof the murder took place some time after Bryan left her at the entrance to the car park and before we saw the Bayard Seven pelt past us the way it did. So that seems to let Bryan out, even if there were anything much to implicate him, because there's the good independent evidence Gibbons got that Bryan did actually walk across the lawn as far as the car park and that it really was Jo Frankland with him. One of the sun bathers knew her quite well, because of having worked on the same paper with her at one time, and spoke to her as she and Bryan came out of the house together. That corroborates Bryan's story, and there's further corroboration of his story that at the entrance to the car park he left her, went back to the house, and rang up Lord Carripore just as he says. He's got a cast-iron tale, and though I don't like cast iron, because the truth so seldom is, still, there you are – amply corroborated and not a weak spot anywhere. Only there's just one little point. Bryan said Wilson could have helped her to get her car out, if she needed help. Wilson himself says he wasn't there, had been called up to the house to see to a leaking tap.'

'Yes, sir,' agreed Ferris, 'and a leaking tap that Wilson told us looked as if it had been damaged on purpose. It does seem just a little as if there had been a plan to get Wilson out of the way, away from the car park, I mean, just when Miss Frankland was likely to get there. Only, was it a slip on Bryan's part when he said that, or was Wilson sent out of the way without his knowledge?'

'Beginning to look,' Mitchell mused, 'as if we had got it down to the murder having been committed in the car park directly Bryan left her. If that's so, the only question is, who was waiting in the car park when Bryan went back to the house?'

There was a touch of horror in his voice as he spoke, and in the minds of both the men was a clear picture of the assassin lurking in the car park, between two of the cars perhaps, waiting till the unsuspecting victim should return.

'A black business,' Mitchell muttered, 'but anyhow Bryan can't be the actual murderer, since the girl was alive when he left her and he went straight back to the house.'

'He might be in it all the same,' Ferris answered, 'for I'm beginning to think this business is a bit too big and complicated to have been a one-man show.'

'That's right,' agreed Mitchell, 'and it's one of the things that points away from Curtis. A crime of jealousy would be carried out single-handed.'

'Taking it as proved,' Ferris said slowly, 'that it was neither Curtis nor his wife we saw when the Bayard Seven passed us – Curtis being too big across the shoulders to wear the coat and the *Announcer* photograph proving it wasn't her herself but someone personating her – would you say that personator was a man or woman, sir?'

'It must have been a man, I think,' Mitchell answered. 'The only other woman we have any trace of in the whole business is her sister, Sybil Frankland, and it hardly seems possible to suspect her, not without a lot more evidence than we've got so far. Of course, there is the possibility, and there's the cry accusing herself Owen reports hearing, but it's odds that only means she was hysterical and excited, overwrought with the thought of what's happened, and felt she was to blame somehow. All the same, we've got to agree it does seem to require more explanation now we've seen her hanging about here, behind hedges as if she had some special reason for not wanting to be seen.'

'And dodging off just the way Bobs-the-Boy dodged off between those two cars,' observed Ferris with a grin.

'Well, we know why he didn't want to be seen,' Mitchell said impatiently, 'but it does look as if Sybil Frankland knew more or suspected more than she's told us – and if she's innocent, why's that?'

'Curtis was jealous,' Ferris remarked. 'Of Hunter apparently. But could it have been Keene Mrs Curtis was meeting at Howland Yard? If so, did Sybil Frankland suspect it, and if it's a crime of jealousy, is it her jealousy and her crime? Seems to me it would look rather like it if we could be sure it was a woman driving the Bayard Seven and not a man.'

'In my idea,' repeated Mitchell, 'it was a man, though of course no one could be sure, going at the rate it was. I take it what happened is that after he passed us, he stopped just long enough to take off her hat and coat he was wearing as a disguise, and to put them back on the body. Then he sent the car full tilt over the railway embankment, jumping out first himself, of course. He scrambled down the cutting after it to make sure it was burning all right – or perhaps to start the fire. Then he made off along the railway track. We'll go round and see the local people and ask them to try to find out if anyone saw the car starting, and, if so, what the driver looked like. It's a pity there's no way of getting in touch with Owen at the moment. I think you had better stay on and if he sees you he may guess you've something to say and show himself. If he does, tell him Sybil Frankland is here, and meanwhile I'll ring up now to have a good man put on to take care of her at her home end.'

It was evident that Sybil's unexpected appearance was troubling Mitchell a good deal, and that he did not know quite what to make of it. Perhaps it was what is called the detective's sixth sense that made him so uneasy, or, to put it in another way, just the impression that for so strange a happening there must be some cause of real significance. They had been walking on as they talked, and now had come to the local police station where by good luck the sergeant in charge had waiting for them the very piece of information they required. For it seemed that only an hour or two before an A.A. scout had been in to say that on the day of the murder a lady driving a Bayard Seven had stopped him to make some quite trivial, and not very sensible, complaint about the driving of some other car, and had given him her card. He had not paid either the card or the complaint much attention at the time, regarding the complaint as merely fussy and the card not interesting him. But that afternoon, when on the point of throwing it away with some other rubbish he was turning out from his pockets, he had noticed that the name on it was that of the victim of the sensational murder with which the papers were so occupied. He had thought it just as well to mention the fact, though he didn't know that it was of any importance, but there at any rate lay the card on the table. And if Mr Mitchell thought the matter worth following up, the spot, said the sergeant, where the A.A. scout was on duty was not far distant.

Mitchell said he thought it would be as well to hear what

he had to say, which was in fact no more than already reported except that he was quite certain, though he had not paid her any attention and could give no description of her at all, that she was most certainly a woman. On that point he was quite clear and definite.

CHAPTER FIFTEEN

'Bobs-the-Boy' Makes Suggestions

WHEN Bobs-the-Boy slipped away from the Grange car park on the approach of the two investigating police officers, he went with his swift slouching gait, so like that of some wild creature of the jungle prowling in search of its prey, to a small beerhouse that stood on the outskirts of the village, a kind of humble rival to the Leadeane Arms that since the installation of the sun bathing at the Grange had begun to take on the airs of a smart, up-to-date hostelry. Indeed the proprietor had just given a week's notice to the admirable cook he employed, since she could only serve up sound English roasts and baked, and apple pies made the way they are in heaven, so as to be able to substitute for her a chef who really understood the art of cooking – as shown by bad French on a menu, innumerable sauces differing chiefly in name and colour, and a resolute determination that nothing should appear at table resembling itself either in taste or appearance.

But from the humble beerhouse, which neither dreamed of nor aspired to anything beyond good ale and bread and cheese, a clear view of the village police station could be obtained; and of the arrival there of Mitchell and Ferris, Bobs-the-Boy was an interested spectator.

'Something on,' he decided; 'got to find out what.'

So finishing his beer he strolled down into the village, where, since naturally the one topic of conversation was the sensational murder that had brought their quiet neighbourhood such notoriety, he had no difficulty in learning, among other things, of the visit of the A.A. scout to the police just a little before.

The gossip Bobs-the-Boy had no need even to provoke, so spontaneously did it flow, varied from pointing to the A.A. man as the actual murderer to declaring that he had been an eye-witness of the deed. Having his own reasons for being interested, Bobs-the-Boy decided that as the cross roads where the A.A. man was posted were not far, it would be worth while to pay him a visit and see what could be found out from him. He slipped off quietly in that direction, therefore, though not so quietly but that his going failed to escape the watchful eye of Inspector Ferris. However, the A.A. man had been told not to talk, understood discipline, did not seem favourably impressed by his questioner's appearance, and in fact promptly extended to him a brief invitation to 'hop it'. Bobs-the-Boy countered with a truculent offer to bash in the A.A. man's face, but on that individual showing some willingness to afford him the opportunity to try, apparently thought better of it and went off with his long prowling stride that seemed so slow and unhurried and yet took him over the ground with such unexpected rapidity.

From suspicious eyes the A.A. man watched his retreat, and then going into his box rang up the police station and reported the incident.

'Up to no good if you ask me,' he said, 'sort of fellow you wouldn't like to meet on a dark night when you had had a drop too much and your week's money in your pocket. Walks like a cat, and when he grins at you, shows a black gap in his teeth, at the back, top jaw.'

'Sounds like that fellow who's been doing odd jobs at the Grange this last week or two,' observed the sergeant from the other side of the wire. 'I'll keep an eye on him.'

'I would if I were you,' said the A.A. man and went back to his job, while, unaware of the interest he had thus roused in himself, Bobs-the-Boy made his way back to the car park, where once again he met with but a cold reception, since the attendant, the one-legged Wilson, suspected him of being after the job and promptly packed him off with an assurance that no one wanted to see his ugly mug round there.

With a meekness a little surprising in a gentleman who could show such truculence on occasion, Bobs-the-Boy accepted his dismissal, merely remarking that he would go up to the house and see if there was any chance of his being wanted next day. Instead of doing so at once, however, he produced a packet of cheap cigarettes and hung about, though out of sight of the car park, till presently he saw the huge, lumbering form of Zachary Dodd, Mr Bryan's partner, coming up from the male *in puris naturalibus* section that he had specially in charge. Dodd dressed in more normal fashion than did Mr Bryan, his chief concession to progress being flannel trousers held up by a belt, and rather badly in need of a visit to the laundry, and a brilliantly striped shirt open at the neck to show a chest so hairy it certainly seemed to have need of little other covering. Increasing flesh, that did not seem as if it could possibly all be due to the kind of provender the Grange canteen offered to its clients, had deprived him of that quickness and agility whereof at one time he had possessed enough to enable him to make a very creditable figure in the ring, but he still possessed great, if clumsy, strength. To-day, however, though his grip remained formidable and his blows heavy enough, these last came so slowly, with such deliberation, they were easy to avoid, and as a fighting man his career was over. At present he did not look in the best either of tempers or condition, for his face had a pale, pasty look and his eyes were heavy and bloodshot, while he muttered to himself as he walked; and when Bobs-the-Boy moved forward so as to cross his path with the evident intention of speaking, the ex-heavyweight boxer told him with the addition of an oath or two to clear out and quick about it, unless he wanted his face pushed down his throat.

'Yes, sir, certainly, sir,' Bobs-the-Boy answered obsequiously, keeping a wary eye on the great clenched fist that might presently come travelling in his direction. 'It's about them two "busies", sir, Mr Mitchell and the other bloke what's been here to-day.'

'What about them?' growled Dodd suspiciously, 'what do you know about them anyway?'

'Only as they've been asking questions and rooting round

like as they suspicioned something,' Bobs-the-Boy answered coolly, 'and now an A.A. scout's been calling at the police station down in the village, giving them information.'

'Telling them Miss Frankland stopped and spoke to him after she left here, I suppose,' Dodd growled. 'Well, what about it? why shouldn't she?'

'I hadn't no idea,' answered Bobs-the-Boy, looking quite downcast, 'as you knew it already, that that was what he was come about. They don't know it in the village.'

'About the only thing they don't know then,' Dodd said in the same growling, almost threatening tone. 'They know it all down there and a lot more as well.'

'Well, some of them do say,' admitted Bobs-the-Boy, 'that the A.A. scout saw the actual shooting and knows just who did it,' and Dodd grunted scornfully but made no other comment. Bobs-the-Boy went on, 'It isn't only the two big bugs that have been rooting round here to-day. There's one of their lot, a bloke named Owen —'

'I've heard of him,' Dodd exclaimed with a sudden animation in his voice. 'Yes, I've heard of him.'

'So have I,' said Bobs-the-Boy slowly and darkly. He added still more slowly, his face, his half-hidden eyes, as if a veil of darkness had spread across them, 'Some day he'll hear of me.'

They were both silent for a moment or two. Dodd's manner had changed now; it was less sullen, smoother, yet doubtful, too. It appeared as if Bobs-the-Boy had acquired a new interest in his eyes and his rumbling voice had a lower note as he asked presently,

'It was Mr Bryan told me about him, he had heard something; there's not much he doesn't hear, old Bryan. One of the newspaper men was talking. . . . Well, what about it, what about this Owen?'

'Been snooping round,' Bobs-the-Boy answered, 'that's what, snooping round, trying to find out things, the swine.'

'Well, what for? why should he?' Dodd asked; and Bobs-the-Boy said nothing to that, only his half-closed eyes were intent upon the other's face. Dodd said again, 'How do you know?'

'Heard him asking questions ... talking ... he's been talking to the car park man, Wilson's his name, isn't it? Asked Wilson a whole lot of questions he did, began about the three-thirty to-morrow and what'll win, and then all kinds of things. Wilson didn't know who he was, but I did. I knew all right.'

'What sort of other things?'

'It just about came to this,' Bobs-the-Boy answered slowly, 'he wanted to know if Wilson was there when Miss Jo Frankland left in her Bayard Seven. Wilson said he wasn't, said he was up at the house, said he was sent for on some job wanted doing up there, he didn't say what it was.'

'Well, what about it?' Dodd demanded. 'Why should he be there? she could start her own car, couldn't she?'

'Seems,' said Bobs-the-Boy, 'seems there was a lady sun bathing here that day had been pals with Miss Frankland along of working somewhere together and knew her well, seems this here lady spoke to her as she was going to the car park along of Mr Bryan.'

'What about it?' Dodd repeated. 'Why shouldn't she?'

'Seems she says, this lady says, as there was someone in the car park when Miss Frankland went to get her car out after Mr Bryan left her.'

'How does she know that?' Dodd growled. 'How can she know unless she followed her? Did she?'

'No, but she heard an engine start running. And so she says if an engine started running, there must have been someone there to start it, at least, that's what she's told this snooping Owen fellow.'

Dodd said nothing. His heavy features showed little interest, only his small bloodshot eyes had grown alert and lively and one enormous hand he held out as if he wished to take hold of something in it, something that he could grip and crush. Bobs-the-Boy went on,

'Seems from what this Owen said, though that wasn't

much, but there's times when the less what's said, the more you know what's meant, and what it seems like is as they're sure her light was put out in the car park, just after Mr Bryan left her, and that there engine what was running, was running so as nothing shouldn't be heard, for their idea is she was shot just as she was getting into her car, and that there engine running – well, then the shots couldn't be heard by no one.'

'You seem to know a lot,' Dodd growled suspiciously; 'you picked up all this did you? just from hearing them talking – or was this Owen telling it all to Wilson?'

'No,' Bobs-the-Boy answered, 'not from what Owen said to Wilson, but part from what he said, and more from what he didn't say, and most from me putting it together by way of guessing like; and what if you ask me, it all boils down to is just this – the "busies" believe there was someone in the car park when Miss Frankland went to get her car, and they believe it was someone waiting for her, and they believe whoever that was is who it was who corpsed her. So what they want to know is, who was that someone?'

'Anyone in particular they think it was?' Dodd asked.

'If you ask me,' Bobs-the-Boy replied, though with some hesitation, 'I don't think they've an idea barring guesses, and what's the good of guessing, but if they got a hint ... why, then it would be bad for anyone they fixed on, and I'm glad it won't be me.'

'Maybe it will be,' Dodd retorted grimly.

'I've got an alibi,' Bobs-the-Boy retorted in his turn, with that sudden grin of his that showed so disconcertingly the black gap appearing in his upper row of teeth.

Dodd was thinking deeply.

'Going to be bad for us,' he said after a pause, 'if they really think someone was hiding in the car park and shot Miss Frankland as soon as she went to get her car after she left Bryan. It'll make a scandal, and a place like this don't want scandals, can't stand 'em. But there's one thing knocks that theory sky high – after Miss Frankland left here she stopped and spoke to an A.A. scout and gave him her card.'

'If that's so, that's that,' Bobs-the-Boy agreed. Again he showed that disconcerting grin of his; and for once his heavy-lidded eyes opened wide as they flashed a full look at the other. 'But then seems like they don't believe that was her,' he added, 'but someone else that handed out her card.'

'Oh, that's rubbish,' exclaimed Dodd hotly; 'rubbish, plain rubbish. It's this Owen fellow been rooting all this out, is it? I should like to meet him and hear what he has to say himself.'

'He keeps out of the way,' Bobs-the-Boy answered. 'Snoops around and no one knows and gets his report ready, and till it is, not even his bosses know what he's doing or what he's thinking.'

'Hasn't he reported all these cracked ideas of his yet?' Dodd asked carelessly.

'Judging from what he said to Wilson, I should say he hadn't,' answered Bobs-the-Boy. 'Fact, I'm pretty sure he hasn't. He likes to have everything complete and written out nice and tidy before he sends it in, all with lovely red ink ruling, ready to go up to the big bugs for them to see what a smart Aleck they've got working for them.'

'I see,' said Dodd; 'I know that sort. Afraid if they speak too soon, someone else will butt in and get the credit. I know 'em.'

'If you ask me,' Bobs-the-Boy said softly, 'he wants his own light putting out, wants corpsing, too, he does, snooping round . . .' his voice trailed off into muttered threats but half audible.

Dodd said,

'I'll talk to Mr Bryan. If there's a scandal about this, it'll do us a lot of harm, a lot of harm; finish us, perhaps. Anyhow, you can come out to-morrow and maybe there'll be a job for you, and if not to-morrow, then perhaps some other day, that is, if you're not particular so long as you're well paid.'

'Oh, I'm not particular,' Bobs-the-Boy answered, 'no ways

I ain't – but there's some jobs what I do with a better heart than others.'

Dodd looked at him for a moment, but made no other answer; and then lumbered heavily away towards the house. For a time Bobs-the-Boy watched him, and then himself slid away back through the car park towards the village.

CHAPTER SIXTEEN

Sybil's Promise

WHATEVER errand it was Sybil Frankland had been about so secretly in the neighbourhood of Leadeane Grange, it did not occupy her for long, since she was back again in her Ealing home early that same evening. And the next day she did not go out at all, but concerned herself with household occupations and with the care of her mother, for old Mrs Frankland was still confined to her room, still suffering from the effects of the shock of the news of her daughter's tragic fate.

But though Sybil occupied herself thus, in these calm, ordinary, everyday pursuits, signs of the sense of stress and strain under which she laboured were apparent enough. Every knock or ring at the door, though but another in that long procession of sellers of flowers, demonstrators of vacuum cleaners, collectors for charitable institutions, that every suburban household knows so well, sent her into a fresh terror, so that in either one form of panic or another she would rush to the door and tear it open as if to face the worst at once, or else seek refuge in her own room in the hope that the rather deaf daily woman who formed their sole domestic staff would neither hear nor answer the summons.

It was under the first influence, however, that early in the afternoon she ran down from her mother's room where she had been sitting, to answer a knock she thought she recognized. But it was John Curtis who was there, and when she saw him she exclaimed,

'Oh, it's you, I thought it was Maurice.'

Curtis came by her into the house. She closed the door and he said to her,

'Have you seen him?'

'Maurice?' she asked quickly, and shook her head; and Curtis went on,

'I'm looking for him, I thought he might be here. I want to find him.'

'What for?' she asked with quick apprehension, and Curtis said,

'He and that fellow, Hunter, they had a big row this morning.'

'A row? they quarrelled?' she asked, and when he nodded she said with something like fresh terror in her eyes, 'Why? what about?'

'I don't know,' Curtis said. He added with sudden violence, 'I want to know. I've got to know.'

They were still standing in the hall. Apparently it did not occur to either of them to enter one of the rooms. The hall was no more than a narrow passage leading from the front door to the little drawing-room at the back of the house, and Curtis with his heavy, massive body and broad shoulders seemed to fill it, to dominate, too, the small, shrinking figure of the girl. She said in a low voice,

'Why? why do you want to know?' and then when he did not answer but only looked at her gloomily, 'How do you know Maurice and Mr Hunter have quarrelled?'

'I heard them at it,' Curtis answered. 'I went to Deal Street this morning. I wanted to see Keene. There was no one in the shop. That girl he has wasn't there, or the shop boy or anyone. But I heard him and Hunter shouting at each other in the room behind. Hunter was carrying on like a madman, swearing and threatening. He – I think he was accusing Keene of – of something.' He paused. 'I've got to know what he meant by what he said, what Hunter said,' he finished slowly.

Sybil did not answer. Even if there had been anything she wished to say, her mounting terror would have held her silent. Curtis said,

'She was your sister ... will you ... I mean ... will you help find out who killed her?'

Still Sybil was silent, for indeed all power of speech had

left her. He stared at her intently, his gaze never wavering, and yet it was as if he saw not so much her herself, but rather some far-off vision of which she was but a part.

'I've got to know what they were quarrelling about,' he went on. 'I want to know what Hunter meant when he talked about something Keene had – done. Something ... I've got to know ... but they were shouting at each other, and both at once, and there was something, too, about that hang-dog looking fellow Keene's had working there – Bobs-the-Boy they call him. Only then they woke up to it some-one was there. Hunter opened the door and looked out, and when he saw me he gave a sort of jump. He didn't say any-thing. He just put his head down and rushed by as quick as he could. He looked half mad. In the war, years ago, I re-member seeing men look like that, under a barrage, wonder-ing where the next shell would go. Keene came out after him. He didn't know me at first, at least, he didn't seem to. He said, "Anything I can do for you?" Then he seemed to cotton to it who I was. He said, "Oh, it's you." I asked him what he and Hunter had been rowing about, and he gave just the same sort of jump Hunter did when he saw there was someone there, and then that girl who works there came in. He said to her all in a hurry, as if he were trying to say it all at once, in one word, "Oh, you attend to Mr Curtis, will you?" and then he bolted right out of the shop just as he was, without a hat or anything. I ran after him, but he was too quick, he was across the road at once and a lot of traffic came up and I lost him. I went back to the shop and waited, but he didn't come. Has he been here?'

'No,' Sybil answered.

'Do you expect him?'

'I don't think so, no. Why?'

'Jo was your sister,' Curtis said. 'You ought to help.'

'I don't know what you mean, why do you say that?' she almost whispered, and then, more loudly, 'Maurice doesn't know anything ... not about that.'

It was a long time before Curtis spoke again, and the tension in the narrow passage grew almost unbearable. Then Curtis said abruptly,

'There's something he knows or Hunter knows or both of them. I've told the police so. I went straight there and told them when I couldn't find Keene or Hunter either, though I tried his place in Howland Yard.' He added, as if in concession to her tortured, panic-stricken eyes, 'The police-inspector or superintendent or whatever he is, Mitchell his name is, he seemed to think it might be all about something else. There's one of his men he called Owen, he seemed to think he knew more about the case than anyone else, he says he's on special duty following it up – Mitchell said this Owen chap had made a report and they were trying to check up on Keene's movements the' – he hesitated – 'the afternoon when Jo ...' Again he hesitated, and then went on more quickly, 'Well, Keene was there, at that sun bathing place, I mean, that afternoon. So was Hunter. Looks as if they were meeting there, so it wouldn't be noticed. Well, where did Keene go when he left just before Jo arrived? What he says is, he meant to drive out to see a prospective client somewhere near Rugby, but half way he remembered the client was on the continent, and so he turned back and went home. He says he only drove slowly, and that accounts for the time he took; but if that's so, he drove very slowly indeed, and why should he? He didn't stop anywhere for tea or anything, he met no one likely to know him, he hasn't a scrap of evidence to confirm his story.'

Sybil interrupted sharply, throwing out a hand against him.

'Maurice didn't do it,' she said, 'if that's what you mean.'

'Well, then, who did?' Curtis retorted. 'What were they quarrelling about? We've got to know that to be sure.'

'You've no right to suspect Maurice,' she flashed at him, the kind of terrified composure she had shown before breaking out into a protesting cry. 'How dare you suspect him?'

'He's not the only one; the police suspect me,' Curtis answered with a touch of wildness in his manner. 'You know, that's tough – to have people think you murdered your own wife when – when you loved her. But they do, at least some of them do. I'm not sure about the Owen fellow whose report Mitchell showed me. He seemed to have an idea – I couldn't understand what, and Mitchell wouldn't say even if he knew himself. The other night they were just going to arrest me, only they changed their minds . . . I don't know why . . . they said it was a photograph in the *Announcer* . . . eye-wash, of course, but they must have had some reason . . . most likely they're only waiting . . . I don't care much about being hanged, but I don't want to be hanged for killing Jo, while the man who did it stops all right . . . that's all . . . well, will you find out what Hunter and Keene were quarrelling about . . . where Keene really went that afternoon after he left the sun bathing place?'

'Do you know where Mr Hunter was?' Sybil asked, though with obvious effort.

'They're trying to check his movements as well,' Curtis answered, 'at least I think so, I think this Owen man has that in hand as well. Hunter's story is that he went back to town by train, and when he got in he went to keep an appointment with a man on business, and then changed his mind, because he didn't want to seem too eager and thought instead he would wait for the other fellow to make the first move. He got some tea at a tea-shop, and then went into a news cinema for an hour, and didn't get back to Howland Yard till late, after everyone else had gone. He did some work in his own office and then went home, and all it comes to is that his story just rests on what he says himself. He can't produce any evidence to confirm it. None of us can, us three I mean. I daresay the police don't believe it's true I went straight back to the flat and stopped there till I was dead drunk. No one saw me, any more than anyone saw Keene or Hunter. And one of the three of us may be lying. But Hunter's out of it, I suppose, he hardly knew Jo, he could have no motive.'

'No,' agreed Sybil in her low, almost whispering voice, 'no, he couldn't, could he?'

'What do you mean?' Curtis asked sharply. 'Why, he

didn't know her, not to speak of.' He went on without waiting for a reply, 'She was your sister and she's been murdered . . . it's up to you . . . are you going to help to find out who did it?'

'Yes,' she said, and the soft monosyllable seemed to linger strangely in the quiet, still air of the tiny hall where they yet stood.

'Well, now then,' he muttered, staring at her afresh, as if he recognized in that little word some strange quality he did not fully understand.

Presently he went on,

'If the murderer stopped Jo's car after Mitchell says they saw it go past him, then it was probably someone she knew. She wouldn't be likely to stop for any stranger. But if she had been murdered before, and her body was hidden in the car, and the murderer was driving it, in her hat and coat he had put on as a disguise – then most likely she was shot in the Grange car park by someone waiting there to do it. Only who? and why?'

Sybil made no answer.

After a long silence he said loudly, and roughly,

'I've told you what you can do.'

After saying that, he turned and went away, banging the front door behind him. Sybil waited a little and then went upstairs.

'Mother,' she said, entering her mother's room, 'I'm phoning for a nurse to come in this evening. I think I shall have to be out late to-night.'

CHAPTER SEVENTEEN

Motor-Cyclist Found

In his room at Scotland Yard next day Superintendent Mitchell sat before his desk, regarding it with a melancholy and indeed despairing eye. It was a large desk, of the very latest pattern, provided with all those latest conveniences which make mislaying the document you specially require so fatally easy, and only recently had it been wangled, with some difficulty, from the competent authority. Now it was covered with files, files to the right, files to the left, files in front; even the wonderfully designed drawers on each side bulged with more files, reports, correspondence. Mitchell's brow perspired spontaneously just to look at them.

Yearningly he wished he were the ideal detective of popular imagination, chiefly engaged on examining the scene of the crime through a large magnifying glass, identifying invisible finger-prints, brilliantly deducing from infallible signs on a burnt match-stick the age, height, name and address, and political opinions of the user. Whereas what he had to do was to toil through all these masses of reports and try to abstract those relevant facts that might perhaps indicate in what direction the truth might best be sought.

Yet though both to himself and to the casual onlooker he presented the appearance of any ordinary business man dealing with the morning's correspondence on an extra busy day, nonetheless as he sat there with his files, his letters, his carbon copies, his card index, his desk telephone, he was just as much the grim huntsman, fierce upon the trail of the flying murderer, on the clearness of whose vision lay the issues of life and death, on whom it depended whether the spilt blood still unavenged should cry to heaven in vain or no, as the sleuth of imagination more dramatically engaged on the scene of the crime. For it was he who held the threads that ran between his desk and the score or more of busy agents, checking this fact, verifying that, putting this other to the proof, who were engaged on the case; and his was the task of weaving from the mass of disconnected, unnecessary facts presented to him the inevitable pattern that would mean life with honour for one, and for another a death of shame upon the scaffold. To the understanding eye indeed this that seemed just the everyday spectacle of a business man occupied with his letters and his files had about it something more intense and daunting and dramatic than any such scene as the fancy might conjure up of the hawk-eyed detective, strangely disguised, poring over signs indistinguishable to all others.

Not that Mitchell felt like that himself. He was wondering how any human being could bear up under this barrage of reports and documents, and thinking how jolly it would be to shove the whole lot into the waste-paper basket and get out into the open air. Enviously he thought of his juniors whose duties did not keep them tied all day to an office chair. There was that lucky young devil, Owen, for example, running round the whole time, and never any need to soil his fingers with a fountain pen except when he sat down at night to write another report to be added to the pile upon this nice new overloaded desk it had been such a triumph to get through.

Owen's last report indeed was at this moment in the hands of the only other occupant of the room, Inspector Ferris, for whom Mitchell had just sent in order that he might read it over before starting out on the day's round.

'Well, what do you make of it?' Mitchell asked when Ferris, having read it twice, put it down thoughtfully.

'Difficult to say,' answered Ferris prudently, 'but it does show I was right about seeing Sybil Frankland there, since Owen says he saw her, too, dodging round just in the same secret way.'

Mitchell glanced over his laden desk, and then, by virtue probably of a sixth sense much dealing with reports had developed, made a grab at the very one he wanted.

'From the chap we have watching the Ealing house,' he

explained; 'it says she got back last night late, arriving by the last train probably. So anyhow she didn't come to any harm there.'

'Did you think she might?' Ferris asked, a little startled.

'Her sister did,' Mitchell answered grimly. He added after a pause, 'I would give quite a lot to know what she's up to.'

Ferris, looking at the ceiling, suggested,

'Ask her.'

'Asking questions means getting lies told you. I was taught that in infant school, if you weren't,' snapped Mitchell, who this morning was both cross and worried. 'It may come to that,' he conceded, 'but it would mean letting her know she's being watched, and then probably she would stop her little game, whatever it is. Only what on earth can she be up to, prowling round the place the way it seems she is?'

Ferris, still with his eyes upon the ceiling, remarked,

'Seems it was a woman driving the Bayard Seven when it passed us; that is, if we can trust what the A.A. scout says, and I don't see why we shouldn't.'

Selecting about the one square inch of desk visible, Mitchell used it to drum upon hard with his fingers.

'It's a possibility,' he agreed. 'If Keene's guilty, she might have been willing to help him out ... even though it was her own sister ... only you won't find Treasury counsel very anxious to put that to a jury ... or a jury very anxious to accept it, either ... unluckily there's no saying where Keene was himself last night. He gave our man the slip and we've no record of his movements. You notice Owen says both Sybil Frankland and Miss James part their hair on the right?'

Ferris nodded.

'That's important,' he agreed, 'but I must say, for my part, it's Curtis himself I'm thinking most about. There's this new story that Hunter and Keene have been quarrelling. We've only his word for it. Suppose he just faked that yarn up to throw suspicion on them?'

'If it's Curtis all the time,' objected Mitchell, 'and he's the guilty man, who is the woman who seems to be in it some-

where? I'm inclined to agree with you we must accept the
A.A. man's evidence as proving there is one. All we seem to
have got so far is that the murder was committed some time
between Jo Frankland's saying good-bye to Mr Bryan just
outside the car park, and the moment when the driver of the
Bayard Seven spoke to the A.A. man – and that must have
taken some nerve when the murdered girl's dead body was
almost certainly lying in the bottom of the car at the
moment, though probably covered up in some way. Whoever it was, she evidently wanted to be taken for Miss Frankland, as she had on her coat and hat and gave the A.A. man
her card, so it's pretty certain what she was after was to
provide evidence that Jo Frankland left Leadeane Grange
safely – a little bit of extra proof, and there's nothing so suspicious as the little bit of extra proof that's faked nine times
in ten. It was faked this time all right, and I take it the
chances are the murder was committed in the car park, most
likely just as she was starting up, so the noise of the engine
would drown the pistol shot. Significant, too, that the car
park attendant was out of the way at the time; only was that
pure coincidence that gave the murderer his chance he – or
she – was quick to seize? Or was it part of a prearranged
plan? If it was the last, then it means the Leadeane Grange
lot are in it somehow. Only how? and why? Sybil Frankland's story is that the day of the murder she was at Ealing
the whole time. But her mother started out early to visit a
friend living at Purley and didn't get back till late, and the
daily woman they employ left as usual after lunch. Conse-
quently Sybil was alone in the house from lunch till nine or
thereabouts, according to her own story, and there's nothing
to show she stayed there the whole time. Nothing to show
she didn't, for that matter, but she may have been hanging
round Leadeane just like last night, for all we can tell. As
for Miss James, according to Owen there's evidence she was
busy writing letters in her own room at the Grange at the
moment when Miss Jo Frankland left there with Bryan.
Owen has a confidential report from Mrs Barrett, who seems
quite trustworthy; she's the widow of a man who served his

full time in the Force. Her statement's clear enough. There had been some sort of business meeting or committee meeting or something between Bryan, Zachary Dodd, and Miss James, at which there was a good deal of quarrelling, as apparently is generally the case. Mrs Barrett says she remembers clearly being sent down to the canteen where Mr Bryan and Miss Frankland were sampling some of the weird stuff they sell there, to tell Bryan the other two were waiting for him, and Bryan asking Miss Frankland to excuse him, and her saying that was all right and she would have another look round till he was free. After the meeting was over, Mrs Barrett, who is always on guard at the door leading to the upper part reserved for women, is quite certain she saw Miss James go back to her room. When Mrs Barrett went off duty, she reported as usual to Miss James, who was still busy with her letters in her room, and couldn't have left it without Mrs Barrett seeing her – unless she climbed out of the window or up the chimney or something like that. So far there's no trace of any other woman.'

'One may turn up,' suggested Ferris, though not very hopefully.

'May,' agreed Mitchell, 'but until she does we've got to leave her out. The man I have been hoping would turn up is that other motor-cyclist who was reported as having been seen to stop Miss Frankland when she was on her way to the Grange and to be quarrelling with her. It mayn't mean much and it may mean a lot, but we seem to have no luck trying to trace him.'

'Nothing to go on,' Ferris pointed out, 'and either he hasn't seen our appeal to him, which isn't likely seeing the way the papers have featured it, or else he has his own reasons for not wanting to.'

'It may be that,' agreed Mitchell, 'and by the way, when you meet Owen to-day, you might tell his lordship that when I gave him a free hand, I didn't mean we never wanted to see him ever again. Tell him that if it's quite convenient he had better show up here about eight this evening. I don't say his reports haven't been full and less useless than some, but there are several questions I want to put him. I haven't set eyes on him,' Mitchell complained, 'since the investigation began and I gave him his orders.'

'Very good, sir,' said Ferris, rising to go, and then Mitchell corrected himself,

'No,' he said, 'don't tell Owen to report here – tell him to come to my house at ten. But of course,' he added with deep sarcasm, 'only if it's quite convenient. Give some of these youngsters their head,' he grumbled, 'and they seem to think they can have it all their own way for ever after. But I should like to see Owen again before he's grown out of all recognition with the passing years.'

'Very good, sir,' said Ferris, and departed, thinking to himself that it really must be a difficult case when it made the old man so touchy; and a little later on a message was brought to Mitchell that a gentleman had called who said his name was Freeman, and he had come about the 'Burning Car Mystery' as the papers called it, having noticed an appeal in the Press to him to communicate with the police.

Mitchell sat up at once and told the messenger to bring in Mr Freeman without any delay. The newcomer proved to be a youngish man who described himself as a journalist on the staff of the *Daily Intelligence*. It was he, he said, who had intercepted Jo Frankland on a motor-cycle on the day of her murder; and he would have come forward before but for the fact that his paper had packed him off abroad the afternoon of the murder to interview a Russian supposed to possess certain valuable information.

'I speak Russian,' Mr Freeman explained, 'that's why they picked on me.'

'You knew Miss Frankland, I understand?' Mitchell asked.

'Just as a girl doing rather well on the *Announcer*,' Freeman explained; 'she had brought off one or two rather good exclusive stories, and I got word from a girl pal of mine that she was after another that afternoon that promised big. So I thought I would try to see if I could find out what it was. I knew the road she was taking, and I got out my motor-bike and cut her off. I put it to her that if she would let me in on the ground floor I would do as much for her some day, and she said there was nothing doing. So I said, All right, I would hang on till I saw where she went, and she said I could do that as much as I wanted, and I could go to blazes, and anyhow all she was doing was going to a sun-bathing place after the sunshine cure some people are so keen on. Well, I didn't believe her, and I said so, and afterwards I followed her just to make sure. But it was O.K., a place called Leadeane Grange where they sit and bake all day – it's been written up once or twice. I waited a little to make sure she wasn't just trying to throw me off the tracks, but she stopped there all right, and then I saw Curtis himself was there – her husband, you know; I reckoned then he had come to meet her or she to meet him, and that was all there was to it. So I went home and found the paper had been ringing me up and wanted me badly. I was on my way to Warsaw an hour later, and I heard nothing about your wanting to see me till I got back to-day and started looking through the back files to see how things had been going while I was away, and how much I owed my bookie now.'

CHAPTER EIGHTEEN

The Capital 'C'

SUPERINTENDENT MITCHELL gave no sign of how keenly this statement interested him. The thin, loquacious lips from which at times such a torrent of words could issue remained firmly pressed together, the grey eyes stayed half closed and indifferent. One or two additional questions were put and answered; it was elicited that the 'girl pal' had no idea of the nature of the 'big, exclusive story' Miss Frankland had hinted she was on the track of. To Mitchell's suggestion that perhaps Miss Frankland had not been speaking very seriously, Freeman agreed that occasionally some journalists, though not many, would 'talk big' as he put it, and hint at wonderful stories they were on the verge of obtaining that, however, never materialized into cold print. But Jo Frankland had not been like that.

'She wasn't one of the sort that's all talk and no do,' Mr Freeman insisted. 'If she said she was on a big thing, then it was a big thing she was on all right. She didn't often talk that way, but when she did, then editors sat up and took notice.'

'It would be a great help if we knew what she had in her mind,' Mitchell remarked. 'You see, it looks as if possibly it was something important enough for those implicated to think it worth while to silence her.'

'I don't see how I can help you there,' Freeman said, shaking his head. 'Whatever it was, she meant to keep it to herself. My pal, who told me about it, thought it was something that was worrying her a bit, as if she were afraid it might be too big for her to handle alone. That's why I thought there might be a chance she would be willing to take me in; that she might be glad of someone to give her a bit of backing – women have a pull in our job in some ways, but there's times when they want a man to back 'em up all the same. A woman,' said Mr Freeman, growing profound, 'has her box of tricks all right, but a man has his, too – what wheedling is to them, whisky is for us, and there's times I would sooner back whisky than wheedling. But anyway Jo Frankland wasn't having any that afternoon, told me off pretty short and said what she knew was for her and for the *Announcer* and not for anyone else. Made it quite plain that whatever she was on the track of, she meant to keep to herself.'

'Well, if you do get any hint of what it was, you'll let us know, I can depend on that?' Mitchell said, and after Freeman had promised, the superintendent went on, 'I suppose you are sure it was Mr Curtis you saw? Could you swear to his identity?'

'Well, I only had a glimpse of him,' Freeman admitted. 'He was at the entrance to a sort of yard where two or three cars were parked. He was standing in the door of some sort of shed or outbuilding of some kind he was either just going into or else just coming out of. At the time I certainly thought it was Curtis, but I didn't take much notice. I wasn't specially anxious he should see me; I didn't want him to be able to tell Jo Frankland I had actually followed her; I knew I should get my leg pulled a bit if that got known. So I cleared off again. I thought her husband being there showed she wasn't after anything big just then, or, if she were, anyhow there wouldn't be much chance for anyone else to butt in. And as soon as I got back I got the message I told you about. I saw one or two notices in the papers abroad of the murder, but they hadn't reproduced anything about your wanting to get in touch with me. I only saw that when I got back here again.'

'Well, you've removed one name from our list of suspects,' Mitchell remarked. 'There was always the chance, so long as we couldn't trace you, that the unknown motor-cyclist might turn out the man we wanted. Now we know it was you and you were on your way to Warsaw, that possibility's wiped out. And the information you've given us may prove of the greatest value.'

He thanked Freeman again, and after his visitor's withdrawal sat in silence for a long time, trying to make clear in his mind the far-reaching implications of this new intelligence.

'Doesn't look,' he mused, 'as if Curtis had been quite telling the truth when he said he went straight back home and stayed there, drinking himself stupid. Looks a little as if this proves he was on the spot when the crime was committed. That means identity established – time and motive and opportunity. Only it won't be much good relying on this new evidence unless we get something to corroborate it. If all Freeman can say is that he thought so at the time, but only had a glimpse and didn't take much notice, no jury would be much impressed. Any smart defending counsel would whittle that story away to nothing in two twos. Not water-tight,' he decided; 'we want the something more we haven't got so far before we can do anything.'

Shaking his head at the difficulty of securing water-tight evidence, Mitchell went on with his work of reading and annotating the reports received that morning. After lunch he drove out again towards Leadeane to a spot where by arrangement he was to meet Ferris who had been charged with another minor investigation. Ferris had not much of interest to report, and after listening to what he had to say Mitchell drove on with him to Leadeane Grange, where, as the day was fine and sunny, there were a good many visitors.

Discreet questioning produced no information of any value. Apparently no one had seen Curtis either on the day of the murder or any other day. There was no trace of his having ever visited the place and no one there knew him. If he had been seen, he had not been recognized. Miss James had not even known, she said, that Curtis was Miss Frankland's proper name. Zachary Dodd, driven nearly to distraction by two of his bathers *in puris naturalibus* who apparently thought their costume adequate for a walk through the grounds, expressed a fervent desire never to see a policeman again and a complete indifference about giving any help towards the discovery of the murderer.

'It's a spot of murder I wouldn't mind down here,' he grumbled; 'some of 'em don't seem able to realize all the world isn't as advanced as we are, and we just simply daren't risk a scandal.'

Of the three in charge, Dodd, Miss James, and Mr Bryan, the last-named seemed the most inclined to be helpful. He seemed indeed slightly worried at the suggestion that Mr Curtis had visited the establishment on the day of the murder and rather curious to know what made Mitchell think that was the fact. Mitchell did not explain, but though he could obtain no confirmation of Freeman's story, and though to Bryan the idea was evidently quite new, the superintendent was still inclined to accept it.

'But it won't be much good unless we can get it confirmed,' he remarked to Ferris as they were leaving. 'By the way, have you told Owen I shall be expecting him to-night, ten o'clock sharp?'

'I left a message,' Ferris answered. 'I didn't see him himself, he rang up early to say he wouldn't be able to meet me, but he would ring up again to know if there were any instructions.'

'There'll be some instructions when I see him to-night,' growled Mitchell formidably. 'The only time he's shown up since Lord knows when is last pay day. Only sign of life he ever gives now is to ring up when you're not expecting it and ask for instructions that are never ready for him at the moment. Seems he doesn't think it's any business of his superiors what he's doing so long as he turns in a report to say he's hopeful of developments.'

Ferris began to think that Constable Robert Owen was indeed in for a somewhat hectic time that night at ten o'clock sharp. But then he, too, was inclined to think the young man had been interpreting rather too freely the commission given him to undertake independent investigation. Ferris was no believer in independent investigation; he put his trust in organization, preferring team work to the most brilliant individual performance, and thoroughly distrusting

Mitchell's tendency to allow his subordinates so much liberty of action.

It would, he told himself, be altogether desirable for Master Owen's wings to be clipped; some of these young-sters were more than apt to get above themselves and to for-get their business was not to think for themselves but just to do what they were told.

They were on their way to return to their car they had left in the car parking enclosure, and Mitchell was still grumbling, half to himself and half to Ferris, at Detective Owen's continued aloofness, when he noticed that they were passing an old tumble-down shed of some sort that stood near the entrance to the parking place.

'Part of the stables at one time, I suppose,' he remarked, looking at it with more interest than seemed warranted; 'not used now, most likely. I wonder if that's the shed where Freeman says he saw Curtis hanging about as if he were waiting for his wife. I suppose Gibbons had a look inside when he was down here examining the place?'

'There was a paragraph in his report that he had exam-ined the outbuildings specified in margin and had found nothing of interest,' Ferris remarked. 'I expect this was one of them, but I couldn't say for certain.'

'Do no harm to have a look,' observed Mitchell. 'Gibbons would be searching chiefly for signs of a struggle or some-thing like that.'

There was no difficulty about entering, as the door was not fastened; could not be, in fact, since it was somewhat badly in need of repair. The interior was filled with a col-lection of rubbish, broken flower pots, empty tins, old boxes, and so on. More than one gap showed in the roof; and in one corner a broken box had been pulled forward as if to serve for a seat. Some burnt match stalks and cigarette ends were lying near.

'Someone been having a rest there,' Mitchell remarked; 'was it Curtis waiting for his wife?'

Ferris did not answer.

'If that was it,' Mitchell said again, 'if Curtis was sitting there that afternoon waiting for his wife —'

Once more he was silent, and once more Ferris made no answer, and the eyes of both men were intent upon that up-turned box someone – but who? – but when? – had been using for a seat. Then Mitchell shook himself impatiently and muttered,

'Well, that's as may be, but nothing in the way of proof. I wonder if it would be worth while testing for finger-prints?'

'Might be,' said Ferris cautiously.

'Try it,' decided Mitchell. 'See to that, will you? Not that it's likely to be much good.' He stooped and picked up one of the cigarette ends that had only been smoked half through. 'White Monkey Brand,' he muttered; 'half the people you meet smoke 'em. Nothing to be got from them.' A crumpled newspaper was lying near, half hidden in the corner where it had been thrown. He picked it up. '*Evening Announcer* for – for the day of the murder,' he observed. 'Six o'clock edition; would be on sale here pretty near as soon as in town, I suppose. Now if that paper could tell us who left it here —'

They stood looking at it as Mitchell turned it over in his hands, and Ferris said,

'Someone's been having a try at the crossword.'

The puzzle was in fact half completed, and various suggested solutions to the clues had been scribbled on the margin. One of the clues was 'Crossed the Rubicon' and the answer 'Caesar' with a flourishing capital 'C' had been duly written in. Another clue was 'Man's name', and for that 'Cyril' had been tried, discarded as not fitting in, and 'Cecil' written instead, the same flourishing capital 'C' having been used for both words.

'Seen a "C" like that not so long ago,' Mitchell remarked.

'So have I,' Ferris said; 'on Curtis's signature he put to his statement we got him to make.'

CHAPTER NINETEEN

Confidences

THE prolonged visit to this apparently uninteresting shed by the two police officials had not passed unnoticed, and almost immediately after their departure little Mr Bryan, his shorts fluttering about his bare and skinny legs, came peeping in, intent on an effort to discover what it was that had kept them there so long.

He seemed a good deal disturbed as with quick agitated movements and sharp anxious glances he looked round the shed and its contents. That overturned box which someone had apparently used as a seat soon attracted his attention, and he stood looking for some time with frowning intentness at it and at the match stalks and cigarette ends scattered near.

But these conveyed no more to him than they had done to the two detectives, and of their discovery of the newspaper with its half-completed crossword puzzle there was nothing to inform him. Shrugging his shoulders impatiently, but with no lightening of the troubled expression he wore, he left the shed. At a little distance, as he knew, Bobs-the-Boy was working, shovelling away a truck load of coal that had been delivered that afternoon. Mr Bryan went to find him. Bobs-the-Boy, seeing his employer approaching, relaxed his efforts, which had indeed never been very strenuous, and stood waiting. Mr Bryan said to him,

'Those two police officers from Scotland Yard have been here again.'

'Snooping around,' growled Bobs-the-Boy, and with a sudden energy drove his shovel into the heap of coal before him, lifted it, and banged the contents in the wheelbarrow he was filling, as if upon their heads he was emptying it. 'Snooping around,' he repeated; 'never no peace or quiet where them blokes are,' and with a blow from his shovel he

smashed a lump of coal in half, again as if it were at one of
them he was delivering the blow.

Mr Bryan gave the thin sort of facial contortion that with
him passed for a smile; for if sun bathing and diet pro-
moted health of body they certainly did not, in his case at
least, seem to induce any gaiety of spirit.

'You saw them, then?' he remarked.

Bobs-the-Boy nodded.

'But they didn't see me,' he said with a cunning grin that
disclosed the black gap where it seemed a tooth was missing
at the back of his upper jaw.

'Why not?' asked Bryan. 'They came along the path
here, didn't they?'

'I saw 'em first,' grinned Bobs-the-Boy. 'I got out ...
snooping around,' he added darkly, 'but I saw 'em first.
There's another of 'em,' he went on after a pause. 'Owen
they call him, a young 'un ... thinks he's almighty clever,
he does.' Once more Bobs-the-Boy paused, this time for the
purpose of muttering and swearing below his breath. 'Wait
till I get him alone,' he burst out suddenly, and with a
violent and abrupt swing of his shovel split another lump of
coal in two. 'Wish it was him,' he growled. 'Mr Blasted
Detective Owen.'

'I've heard his name mentioned,' Bryan observed. 'He is
one of the police engaged on the murder of that unfortunate
journalistic girl, isn't he?'

'Nothing to do with me,' grunted Bobs-the-Boy, and went
on with his work, showing in doing so an energy he did not
usually display. 'Mr Blooming Detective Owen,' he muttered, 'better look out, better take care, Mr Bleeding Detective Owen.'

Bryan stood in silence watching him for some minutes.
Then he remarked,

'You don't seem to like Mr Owen. Well, I don't myself.
I've heard of him questioning some of our members in a
most offensive manner, though it's perfectly plain the Frankland girl left here quite safe and well. Whatever happened

must have happened after she left here, and yet they keep worrying round . . . it'll ruin the establishment if it goes on.'

'Snooping around,' repeated Bobs-the-Boy, 'that's them,' and viciously he banged a final shovelful of coal into his wheelbarrow.

'Did you notice how long they were in the shed over there?' Bryan asked.

'A quarter of an hour, more rather than less,' answered Bobs-the-Boy. 'Snooping around,' he repeated, and spat with vigour to indicate his disgust at such methods.

'I can't imagine what they wanted; there's nothing there but a lot of rubbish that'll have to be broken up and burned in the furnace when it's winter again,' Mr Bryan remarked. 'Miss Frankland can't have been in there. When she was going I went with her myself as far as the car park. Luckily several of our members saw us. And if she had turned back to go to the shed afterwards for any reason, someone would have seen her. Besides, why should she? there's nothing there.'

'Snooping around,' Bobs-the-Boy repeated once again. 'Trying to find out something to make trouble with; they don't care what, so long as they can make trouble instead of letting you alone.'

'Well, it would certainly make trouble,' agreed Mr Bryan with another of his faint, wan smiles that only served to emphasize his uneasiness, 'if they did find out that the murder of the unfortunate girl actually took place in our grounds. An institution like ours must avoid scandal at all costs . . . all costs. Or else close down.'

'That's right,' agreed Bobs-the-Boy. He added meditatively, 'I expect whoever did her in is thinking much the same . . . that he's got to stop it or else close down for good.'

'I daresay,' agreed Mr Bryan, looking slightly disconcerted, and Bobs-the-Boy went on,

'I just altogether can't stand them police blokes . . . that there Owen.' He paused and once more relieved his feelings by whacking viciously at the nearest lump of coal, as if it were Owen's head. He went on in a sudden burst of confidence, 'I tell you, mister, I got all sick like thinking maybe it was me they was after, though there's nothing I ain't done, except not reporting so as to have a chance of earning an honest living, same as anyone else, so when I saw them go in there yonder I slipped round behind. There's cracks and holes in the wall at the back so as you can hear and see . . . not all, but some . . . there was something about a crossword puzzle they was doing.'

'A crossword puzzle,' interrupted Bryan sharply. 'Nonsense, why should they go into an old shed to do a crossword puzzle? That's absurd.'

'It's gospel truth all the same,' retorted Bobs-the-Boy. 'I heard part of it plain enough . . . and I heard them saying something about a bloke name of Curtis what was married to Miss Frankland, though she didn't use his name like; not respectable, to my way of thinking.'

'Do you mean they seem to think he did it?' Bryan asked eagerly.

'They was talking about him, that's all I know,' Bobs-the-Boy answered; 'only it was his name sure enough. And there's another thing I made out.'

'What was that?'

'That there intermeddling Owen don't think it was Curtis, he's got some other notion of his own he's following up.'

'Any idea what it is?'

'No-o . . . in my idea no one knows but him. But there's something seemingly he has in his mind . . . there's something or someone he's on the track of all right . . . and there's someone else as well he's on the track of; maybe he'll wish he wasn't, some day not so far off.'

'What do you mean by that?' Bryan asked, and then when the other made no answer, 'You can trust me,' he said.

'I trust them as trusts me,' retorted Bobs-the-Boy. 'My neck's my own, and if I've got to swing, then I'll swing for Owen, too, same as for that other.'

With that, as if he felt he had said too much, he fell to

shovelling coal with great vigour. Bryan watched him for a time, and then produced his pocket-book, from which he took out a one pound and a ten shilling note. After some consideration he put the former back and offered the latter to Bobs-the-Boy, who accepted it with eagerness, with suspicion, and with a good deal of surprise as well.

'If you get to know anything more, especially about any idea you think this Owen fellow you talk about may have got in his head,' Mr Bryan remarked, 'let me know. You understand my interest? A scandal might be absolutely fatal to the establishment. Fatal,' he repeated.

'Daresay it might,' agreed Bobs-the-Boy. 'Fatal,' he repeated in his turn. 'Fatal – anyway, that's what it'll be to some if Owen gets to the bottom of who it was really did in that bit of skirt.'

He chuckled as if he thought the joke a good one, an opinion Mr Bryan apparently did not share, since he did not indulge in the contortion of the muscles round the mouth that with him did duty for a smile. Instead he scowled and turned away, but had only gone a yard or two when Bobs-the-Boy called him back.

'There's something I could show you, mister,' he said, regarding thoughtfully the ten shilling note in his hand, 'something as might be interesting and then again it mightn't.'

'What is it?' Mr Bryan demanded.

Bobs-the-Boy said nothing but continued to regard with the same interest the ten shilling note in his hand.

Mr Bryan produced his pocket-book again and taking out a pound note – he had no more of the ten shilling notes left – regarded it with equal interest.

It was a silent contest of will power in which Bobs-the-Boy was the winner.

'Oh, well,' Bryan said, 'give me that ten shilling note back and you shall have this one instead.'

He held it out as he spoke and Bobs-the-Boy accepted it but omitted to hand back the other, on which indeed his grip tightened.

'Come along of this way, mister,' he said, and led Mr Bryan to a spot behind some bushes not far away where, hidden in a convenient hole, were two or three bottles.

'Whisky,' Mr Bryan exclaimed; 'they are whisky bottles.'

'They are that,' agreed Bobs-the-Boy, 'only empty now,' he added with a kind of lingering regret.

'Where did they come from?' demanded Mr Bryan sternly.

'Half a crown's what I was give to take them away,' Bobs-the-Boy explained, 'a measly half-crown, and every one of 'em drained as dry as a pub after closing hours. Half a crown, and that not give willing neither, but along of me happening along just as they was being put outside like.'

Mr Bryan was bending over the empty evidences of guilt.

'I thought yesterday I noticed something about Dodd's breath,' he said gloomily. 'Peppermint . . . I wondered why . . . I shall speak to him.'

Bobs-the-Boy grinned, looked at his two notes, and seemed suddenly to decide that the two of them deserved full candour.

'I don't know nothing about him,' he said, 'it was the lady.'

'Miss James,' cried Bryan. 'You don't mean Miss James . . .?'

Bobs-the-Boy nodded.

'Her all right,' he said, 'but don't go for to give it away as it was me put you on her. But it was down her throat that little lot went all right, and she showed it, too. Else as like as not that half-crown would have been twopence and no more,' he added, 'judging from the time it took to get that much out of her.'

'You can trust me,' Mr Bryan repeated mechanically. He looked more troubled and disturbed still. 'That's why she went to bed with a headache,' he observed, 'so early last night.'

'Got up with one more like, if you arst me,' retorted Bobs-the-Boy.

'It's all this murder,' Mr Bryan exclaimed. 'It's got on her nerves, it's got on Zachary Dodd's nerves, it's got on my nerves, too. It's the only possible explanation ... it's been working on their nerves, the thought of it.'

'I shouldn't wonder,' agreed Bobs-the-Boy.

CHAPTER TWENTY

Curtis is Afraid

WHILE this conversation had been going on between little
Mr Bryan and the man who called himself Bobs-the-Boy,
and so establishing for them a certain sense of intimacy and
co-operation, Superintendent Mitchell was back once more
busy at his desk. There, while he was occupied with fresh reports that had come in during the day, he received with
some surprise the unexpected information that Mr Curtis
had called and wished to see him.

On Mitchell's desk lay a fresh copy, just obtained from
the office of the paper, of that number of the *Evening Announcer* he and Ferris had found in the Leadeane Grange
outbuilding. The actual paper itself was now with a hand-
writing expert, together with some specimens of Curtis's
writing to compare with that in which the crossword puzzle
had been partly filled in. There was also on the desk a note
of the reply given by the publisher of the paper to Mitchell's
questions regarding the exact time at which the various edi-
tions of the *Evening Announcer*, from the noon betting
sheet of the last issue, would be on sale in Leadeane village
and in the various districts on the way there.

It was with a certain warmth of manner that Mitchell
greeted his visitor whom he had directed should be shown
in at once.

'You know, I was rather hoping for a chat with you,' he
said genially. 'Sit down and have a cigarette?'

He launched into a discourse on the pleasures and advantages to be derived from the practice of smoking, but Curtis
refused the proffered cigarette and interrupted the discourse,
for he had not come to talk of tobacco.

'What I want to ask,' he said abruptly, 'is how you are
getting on and how near you are to success.'

'By success, meaning —?' asked Mitchell.

'The arrest of the murderer,' Curtis answered, staring at him. 'Isn't that what we want?'

'It is often easy enough to arrest a murderer,' Mitchell answered quietly. 'What's more difficult is proof that that's what he is.'

'Have you got any proof at all yet?' demanded Curtis.

Mitchell, with an eye on the copy of the *Evening Announcer* lying on his desk, replied that as yet they were not sure; they had something, but whether it was proof he could not say as yet, and Curtis snorted indignantly.

'There's another thing I wanted to speak about,' he said, 'there's one of your men, Owen, I think he's called.'

'Owen? Oh yes,' said Mitchell, interested. 'Have you seen him?'

'No. I've heard about him, though.'

Mitchell shook his head.

'Owen's different from the good little girls that are seen and not heard,' he remarked, 'because he's heard of but not seen, though I've made an appointment with him for ten to-night. But what about him?'

'He's been making a fool of himself,' Curtis grumbled; 'he's been following Miss Frankland and asking a lot of fool questions.'

'But if we don't ask questions in our line,' protested Mitchell gently, 'no one would ever tell us anything, and if no one ever told us things, how should we ever find anything out? But that's what makes this case so difficult,' he added complainingly, 'no one comes forward to tell us anything.'

'Is that what you wait for?' demanded Curtis scornfully, 'for people to come and tell you things?'

'It's the only way,' Mitchell answered, 'to get those who know already to come and tell you all about it.'

Curtis fairly snorted his contempt.

'If that's the way you go to work,' he said, 'whoever murdered my wife seems fairly safe, doesn't he?'

'Oh, I don't know,' protested Mitchell as mildly as before. 'It's astonishing the things that people come and tell us, sometimes even the truth,' he added musingly. 'I've known it happen. More often lies, of course. The only people who aren't any help are those who don't tell us anything at all. I'm hoping there is something you have come to tell us, Mr Curtis.'

'Yes, there is,' Curtis answered, 'and I only hope it means something. My wife had a cigarette-case – tortoiseshell mounted in silver. It's in the possession of Mr Hunter now.'

Mitchell looked at him keenly.

'Are you sure?'

'Either it or one so exactly like it. . . .'

'Ah, yes,' said Mitchell, for the qualification seemed to him to be important. There are so many cigarette-cases in tortoiseshell mounted in silver, and he was not sure that Curtis was as yet sufficiently calm, sufficiently recovered from the shock of recent events, to be a good witness. 'You mean Mr Hunter, the wholesale fur dealer of Howland Yard?' he asked.

'I'll tell you something else,' Curtis went on. 'I'm certain in my own mind Jo was following up what she thought was going to prove a big story. It was something big she thought she had got a hint of. It was that took her out to Leadeane Grange, and I think you know already she had been to Howland Yard once or twice recently?'

'Might that not have been to get a new fur coat?' Mitchell asked. 'That's how it was put to us.'

'She had one already, she wouldn't want another.'

'Some women, even if they had two, wouldn't object to a third,' Mitchell observed.

'In any case,' Curtis said impatiently, 'she wouldn't have gone to a stranger for a new coat, when one of her oldest friends is in the fur trade. But she went to Howland Yard for some good reason, and – this is important – Hunter used to visit Leadeane Grange.'

'For the sun bathing?' suggested Mitchell.

'I don't believe that, that was only a blind; he went there to meet someone, it's up to you to find out who,' Curtis said with vehemence. 'Her sister has the same idea, she won't say so but I know she has; Sybil I mean, Sybil Frankland.

There was something Jo was following up and it was to stop her she was murdered.'

'What makes you say Sybil Frankland thinks so too?' Mitchell asked.

'Well, I know she does,' Curtis insisted. 'She won't say, but I know what she's thinking. I got her and Hunter together to see if she would recognize Jo's cigarette-case, and I saw the way she looked at him.'

'Did she identify the cigarette-case?' Mitchell asked.

'He wasn't using it,' Curtis answered. 'I asked him where it was and he said he had lost it.'

Mitchell shook his head gently.

'That's the way with you amateurs,' he said, 'probably now we've missed what might be a valuable clue. If you had come and told us first instead of letting Hunter know you were suspicious and had noticed the thing, we might have managed to get hold of it.'

'I wanted to be sure first,' Curtis said, a little disconcerted. 'I can still swear he had a cigarette-case in his possession exactly like the one belonging to Jo. And I've been through the list of things recovered from the fire. The cigarette-case wasn't mentioned.'

'I'll have another examination made,' Mitchell promised. 'It'll bear looking into, though if Hunter's guilty all that's happened is that you've warned him to destroy a piece of highly incriminating evidence. But it doesn't seem very likely, if he is guilty, he would keep a thing like a cigarette-case and use it. Of course it's possible. One can never tell. Criminals do odd things at times. Oh, Mr Curtis, there's a thing I wanted to ask, and as you're here I'll take the opportunity if I may. Do you take any interest in crossword puzzles?'

'What do you mean?'

'Just that – do you ever try to do crossword puzzles?'

'Sometimes. Why?'

'Ever try to do this one?' Mitchell asked, handing him the back number of the *Evening Announcer* that had been lying on his desk.

Curtis took it and looked at it.

'I don't think so,' he said, 'no, I'm sure ... I think I've seen it before, or something like it. Why?'

'One of the clues,' Mitchell remarked, pointing to it, 'is "Crossed the Rubicon". I suppose the answer would be "Caesar"? Do you mind writing that in?'

The eyes of the two men met, Curtis's angry and inquiring, Mitchell's merely inscrutable. It was again a conflict of rival wills, but Mitchell's was the stronger, for he knew his purpose while Curtis was merely puzzled. He began to write, using his own fountain pen, since Mitchell had offered him none and no other was in sight. When he had written the word, he said,

'What's the idea?'

'It may help me to find out the truth,' Mitchell answered gently. 'This other clue now, it says, "Man's name". "Cyril" would do, I suppose, or "Cecil", for that matter. Will you write them both in, if you don't mind?'

Curtis, frowning and puzzled, did as he was asked. In each of the three names, 'Caesar' 'Cyril' 'Cecil', he employed the same characteristic twirl to the capital 'C'.

'What next?' he demanded.

'I'll have another examination made of what was left of the Bayard Seven,' Mitchell promised, 'to see if any sign can be found of a cigarette-case. I know there's no mention of anything of the sort in the list of articles identified. Perhaps something not recognized before may be now we know we are looking for a cigarette-case. If not, we shall have to try to get hold of the one in Mr Hunter's possession. If it can be proved to be the same – that would mean a lot. But tortoise-shell cases mounted in silver are common enough, unless this one had anything special about it you could swear to.'

Curtis shook his head and Mitchell went on,

'Your statement is that on the day of the murder, after you gave up waiting for your wife outside the George and Dragon public-house on the Leadeane Road, you went straight back to your flat in Chelsea. I suggest that that is not true. Instead you went on to Leadeane Grange. You meant to wait for Mrs Curtis there. There was a slight shower of rain. It only lasted a minute or two. Partly for shelter perhaps, or because you did not wish to be seen, you went inside one of the outbuildings near the car park. While you were waiting you amused yourself doing a crossword puzzle in that night's *Evening Announcer* you must have bought in Leadeane because it was not on sale before then.'

Curtis had listened in silence. The only comment he made when Mitchell paused was,

'How did you find out?'

'You agree that is so?' Mitchell asked. 'You agree you did not tell the truth when you said you went straight back to your flat?'

'I daresay you won't believe it,' Curtis answered slowly, 'but at the time I thought it was the truth. Afterwards I began to have a vague idea – that it wasn't. I had had a good deal to drink. I couldn't remember clearly, my mind was all hazy and confused. All I knew was I had been saying things Jo wouldn't forget in a hurry. That was all I was really clear about, that and waiting for her outside that little wayside pub. It was only some time afterwards that I began to think I had been to Leadeane as well; even now I don't remember anything about a crossword puzzle. I suppose I hardly knew what I was doing, what with having been drinking and my quarrel with Jo.'

'Then you agree your first story was false and instead of returning at once to your Chelsea flat you went on to Leadeane and waited there in a kind of concealment till Mrs Curtis left?'

'So far as I know I was there only a very short time,' Curtis answered. 'I think I began to feel that Jo wouldn't even let me talk to her while I was like that. I went straight back to Chelsea and started drinking again, and I don't know much more till I heard the phone ringing and Sybil telling me what had happened. What with my head still a bit dizzy, and that coming on the top of it – you know, it is a bit of a shock to hear your wife's been murdered – well, I wasn't in any state to remember very clearly what I had actually done.'

'Is there anything else you've forgotten?' Mitchell asked dryly, and though he had not meant much when he put the question he saw Curtis shrink terribly before it, shrink in a literal way as though he grew physically smaller.

'That's not ... possible,' he croaked rather than spoke, 'not possible,' and startled at the idea, Mitchell realized that sometimes the thought came terribly to Curtis that perhaps it was in fact he who was guilty, that, distracted and half drunken as he was, he had committed the crime, in some abnormal, as it were, unconscious condition, so that all memory of it had passed from him.

'Not possible,' Mitchell decided to himself, 'couldn't be that ... yet it's what he's afraid of.'

After a long pause, while Curtis sat downcast and brooding and Mitchell in equal silence turned this new thought over and over in his mind, the superintendent said at last,

'Well, Mr Curtis, that's all I've to ask you at present. To-morrow perhaps I shall want another talk. I'm seeing Detective Owen to-night at ten to get his report, and perhaps after that we shall be able to see our way more clearly.'

CHAPTER TWENTY-ONE

Miss James's Nerves

LITTLE Mr Bryan's determination to speak very seriously to Miss James about the consumption of whisky she had been indulging in that Bobs-the-Boy had so treacherously revealed, he put into force that same evening in dramatic fashion.

While she was taking a rest, full length on the sofa in her room just by the open window after a laborious and even exciting day – a new client, enjoying a sun bath on the roof, had dropped off to sleep and wakened to find all the skin off her nose and most of it off the rest of her face as well, her reaction to these facts taking the form of violent hysterics – Mr Bryan knocked gently and, being bidden to enter, came in. Without speaking, while she watched him, he began to conduct an ostentatious search, looking behind chairs and curtains and in other obvious and unlikely places. After a time she said sourly,

'What's the game?'

'I am looking,' explained Mr Bryan, 'for bottles of whisky.'

Miss James put out her hand for her bag and produced a bunch of keys that she threw across to him with such good aim or luck that it caught him on an elbow that had but little flesh to protect it. He said something or another, and Miss James waited till he had finished. Then she said,

'There's two in the first-aid cupboard. Any one but a fool would have looked there first. One's empty,' she added, and as an afterthought, 'the other's got nothing in it.'

Mr Bryan went across to the indicated cupboard and verified these facts.

'You know what we agreed?' he asked.

'What's happened wasn't in our agreement,' she answered moodily.

'All the more reason —' he said and paused.

'There's half a dozen more coming,' she told him in the same angry, moody tones, 'marked "Malted Milk". Don't you try to stop them.'

He closed the cupboard very carefully and slowly, and came back towards her.

'I suppose you've gone quite mad,' he said.

'I can't sleep,' she answered. 'That's what's done it. I can't sleep.'

He made no comment on this, but his eyes gleamed like those of the weasel before it springs. She mumbled,

'It's all very well for you, you've no nerves. I have. I tell you I can't sleep. I just lie and I can't sleep.' Her voice rose suddenly from its mumbling to a scream. 'Not without that stuff,' she cried.

He continued to watch her in the same slow, malevolent silence. Still he did not speak, and now she struggled up to a sitting position on the sofa and sat, staring back at him.

'It's not only me,' she said presently. 'Zack's the same . . . it's all very well for you . . . you took jolly good care you weren't in it . . . nothing you saw . . . we did, Zack and me.'

'Zack's as big a fool as you, bigger,' the little man snapped out at her. 'What you want, both of you, isn't whisky, it's prussic acid.'

'Well, fetch it along, quick as you like,' she answered, staring at him still.

It was in a milder voice, as if that defiance had a little affected him in one way or another, that he answered,

'It's all right if only you and Zack don't lose your heads. We're perfectly safe.'

'Safe,' she almost screamed, her face flushing suddenly, her eyes bloodshot and wild. She was on her feet now, gesticulating with both hands, 'Safe? . . .' she repeated. 'With him . . . following . . . watching . . . waiting . . . there all the time and making sure you know it.'

'Who's that?' Bryan asked.

'You know,' she answered, 'you know all right . . . that Scotland Yard man . . . Owen they call him . . . Owen . . .

Owen ... he knows, he does ... and now he's only waiting till he's ready.'

'Nonsense,' Bryan answered, 'he doesn't know anything ... how could he? ... and it wouldn't matter if he did ... You're just panicking ... why, you've never even seen the fellow, have you?'

'No,' she admitted, 'but he's there ... all the time ... that's what gets on your nerves ... you never see him, but all the time you know he's there and all the time you keep hearing things....'

'Nonsense,' Bryan repeated. 'What's all that amount to? ... He can't know anything.'

'He suspects,' Miss James answered. 'If he doesn't, why is he always ... always just not there?'

'You're letting your nerves run away with you,' Bryan insisted. 'It's just your nerves ... that's all ... Only once you start giving way to nerves, you're no good, and you're only making it worse with whisky. All you've got to do is to keep yourself in hand.'

'Zack's just the same,' she said, sitting down again. 'He feels just the same ... He says he thinks Owen was one of the men in the private enclosure yesterday, only he's not sure which.'

'Zack's as big a fool as you,' Bryan retorted. 'You and he, you have got to stop this whisky game, both of you.'

'Can't be done,' she answered sullenly, and then, when he turned his cold patient eyes on her, she added in the same sullen way, 'Not till you've got rid of that detective fellow ... Owen ... if that's his name.'

'All in good time,' Bryan answered quietly. 'There's that new odd job man, Bobs-the-Boy he calls himself. It seems he doesn't like this Owen person any more than you do, or even less perhaps. Got you both scared seemingly, but perhaps this Bobs-the-Boy may be useful.'

Miss James began to laugh, a low cackling laugh that went on and on, breaking at times into a high note, and then resuming its low tone.

'Shut up, can't you?' he said to her fiercely.

'All right, all right,' she answered. 'But you're so funny
... You've always someone else on hand to do the dirty
work for you ... Don't forget to tell him if he can't sleep,
then whisky's the boy, whisky, not Bobs-the-Boy then.'

'Oh, shut up,' Bryan snarled at her again. 'Besides, he's
not the sort of sniveller you are, and Zack too ... he let out a
lot ... I'm not quite sure what he meant, but whatever it
was, it didn't trouble his sleep. And he thinks it's him this
Scotland Yard fellow's watching. I don't know if he's right,
but that's what he thinks, and he don't like it, either ... he
was hinting what he would do.'

'Well, then ...' Miss James said, 'well, sounds like he's
the man we want.'

'We should have to take him into our confidence,' Bryan
observed.

'If it's right what you say,' she observed, 'we can risk that
... if it's right Owen's after him, too.'

'Owen seems to have got on all your nerves pretty
thoroughly.' Bryan grumbled. 'I don't know how he's managed it ... he isn't on mine ... but then I don't cultivate
nerves ... Why do you think he's so dangerous?'

'I just feel it,' she answered. 'If he wasn't ... he suspects
... he's watching all the time, never showing himself, just
watching, asking questions, putting everything together; I
can hear him when I lie awake ... I can hear him making
notes ... only you never see him ... other people do but you
don't ... you just feel him all the time ... laying a trap
there ... noticing something here you've never thought of
yourself ... I would rather be a fox or a hare with the dogs
after me; at least they can see what's following them but you
can't.'

'He's just got on your nerves,' Bryan repeated, 'that's what
it is ... he's got on your nerves and you've made it worse
swilling whisky ... If you had kept off whisky you would
have forgotten all about him by now.'

'If it wasn't for whisky,' she retorted, 'I wouldn't ever
sleep .. If you don't sleep, then you go mad. Whisky's saved

me from that; at least, I think it has.' She stopped and gave her cackle of laughter again. 'Set on your Bobs-the-Boy to save us from Owen; if he does, then I'll stop the whisky, too.'

Mr Bryan did not answer. He was deep in thought, his sharp chin cupped in one skinny hand. There seemed something uncanny about him now; he had the air of a skeleton musing upon death.

Miss James lay back again on her sofa. The evening was warm and still and the window at her side was open. She stared out idly at the garden below where the shadows were lying thickly as the darkness increased. Presently she said, half to herself,

'I wouldn't wonder if he wasn't there now, just watching us.'

Bryan took no notice, and indeed did not seem to have heard. He was still deep in thought. After a long pause she turned her head and flung at him angrily,

'All very well for you ... you stop in the background ... you take care you don't risk your own precious skin ... It's different when you have to do things yourself.'

'I have done – things myself before to-day,' he answered calmly, 'and perhaps I shall again soon.'

'Oh, well,' she said, letting her head fall back and resuming her stare at the garden, watching it intently as if she expected to see at any moment some sign of that watcher who some secret intuition seemed to tell her was there, implacable in patience and resolve.

It was a thought that set her trembling as she lay back on her couch, and then the door opened and Zachary Dodd came in, with a kind of clumsy silence, treading on tiptoe, but making the boards creak beneath his elephantine weight, closing the door behind him with infinite caution, and as he turned from doing so knocking over a chair to fall clattering backwards. He said in a rumbling whisper as loud as most men's lifted voice,

'Has Hunter come yet?'

Neither of the others answered. Apparently they thought reply superfluous. In the same loud whisper, Dodd said,

'If he hasn't, that detective has; Owen, I mean.'

'What's that?' Bryan snapped, roused at once, and Miss James jumped to her feet.

'You saw him? you've seen him?' she almost screamed.

But Dodd shook his head.

'When I do, I'll scrag him,' he said, mingling his words with many oaths. 'I'm fed up ... You know he's always there and yet he never is.'

'If you didn't see him —' began Bryan, but Dodd interrupted impatiently.

'I tell you no one sees him,' he almost shouted. 'You only ... one way or another, you know he's been there and that's all ... when I see him, I'll do him in,' he added and confirmed it with fresh oaths.

'What's the good of talking like that,' Miss James interposed. 'You'll never see him, none of us will, not till he's ready ... then it'll be us that'll be done in, not him.'

'Well, then ...' Dodd muttered, 'well ... now then.'

'If you haven't seen him,' Bryan repeated once more, 'how do you know ...?'

'Oh, this time he left his card,' Dodd answered, laughing harshly, and while the others stared at him he produced a slip of pasteboard from his pocket and threw it on the table. 'There it is,' he said.

It bore in fact Owen's name and in addition to his address the legend : 'C.I.D. Scotland Yard'. Round it the three of them stood, grouped in a common and disturbing fear.

'Where was it?' Bryan asked.

'In my room, on the floor, down there,' Dodd answered, with a jerk of his head over his shoulder towards that portion of the grounds where was the men's private enclosure he was in charge of. 'He must have dropped it ... accident or purpose ... he must have been there half an hour ago ... Bobs-the-Boy says he saw a man walking down that way, but he thought it was one of the members and took no notice.

Half an hour or more he may have been there, looking round.'

'There wasn't anything ...' Bryan asked quickly, 'anything he could use?'

'I don't think so : how can you tell, those fellows will twist anything ... twisters ... What did he leave that card for?' Bryan said,

'Going a bit too far ... I'll have to do something.'

He said this very gently almost to himself, but the other two heard him and grew silent at once. It was as if those few muttered words had daunted them and satisfied them as well. Dodd sat down quietly on the nearest chair. Miss James went back to her couch by the open window.

'There's Bobs-the-Boy, of course,' she remarked, 'but we should have to explain a lot to make him trust us.'

'I don't want that,' said Dodd. 'Tell nothing. It's never safe.'

'We aren't safe now,' Bryan remarked in his gentle menacing voice, 'not with Owen ... Owen ... I think this Owen's getting on my nerves as well,' he said.

From the window Miss James, who had resumed her almost mechanical watching of the garden below, said softly but very intensely,

'There's a man down there ... I saw him ... behind a tree and then he slipped away.'

'A man? what's he up to?' Bryan asked sharply.

'Watching,' Miss James answered in the same low yet intent voice, 'watching ... waiting ... watching. ...' After a momentary pause, she added, 'Owen, that's who it is.'

'Owen,' repeated Dodd. 'Oh, oh,' he stammered, exactly as if he had received some sudden hurt.

Bryan was peeping over Miss James's shoulder, but now in the garden there was nothing visible, only darkness and long, growing shadows. He drew back and took from his pocket first a small pamphlet on the uses and benefits of fruit juice, and then a small cardboard carton marked, 'Raisins, shelled nuts, dried banana – one cake enough for one meal'.

This he opened and took from it neither raisins nor nuts nor dried bananas, but instead a small, deadly-looking automatic pistol.

With it in his hand, without speaking a word, he slipped from the room.

CHAPTER TWENTY-TWO

'Bobs-the-Boy' Joins

THERE was, in addition to the main stairway, a second, narrow and winding, originally intended for the use of the domestic staff of the house. It started from a passage at one end of which was the kitchen, at the other a small door leading into the garden. Down these stairs now Mr Bryan went at a light run, a small, grotesque, deadly figure, his shorts flapping about his legs like drum-sticks, his shirt open to show his narrow and sunburnt chest, the automatic pistol clasped in a hand as firm as it was bony.

A light was burning in the passage at the foot of the stairs. He switched it off before he opened the door. In a flash he was through it, running with extraordinary speed and silence across a space of open lawn till the shadows of the trees and shrubs beyond swallowed him up.

A weasel, questing to kill, could not have moved more silently or more swiftly. There was something strangely daunting between his odd appearance and attire that seemed to suggest the harmless crank concerned only with his own fads and fancies, and his purposeful and deadly movements.

He noticed that the window of Miss James's room was now closed and the curtains drawn. With a grin of contempt he thought that up there they wished to remain in ignorance of what was happening.

'Nerves,' he muttered, 'nerves. . . .' He had a silent gesture of contempt to himself there in the shadow of the trees. 'Nerves . . .' he said again.

He went on sliding from one shadow to another, from one tree to the next. His eyes, his ears, every sense was alert, tuned to an almost unnatural keenness. It was as if he heard the grass growing, the worms burrowing, the beetles and the ants scurrying to and fro on their various occasions, as if he heard and distinguished every sound that filled the night with a faint continuous murmur. Far off, and then much nearer, he heard the clocks strike ten. He circled round a bush whence no sound came, where the shadows seemed to him deeper than elsewhere. His finger twitched upon the trigger of the deadly little weapon that he held, that carried seven deaths in its metal chambers. His tongue was sticking out and a few drops of saliva dribbled from the corners of his mouth. A voice from the centre of the bush said,

'You're a bit too late, Guv'nor; Owen's done a bunk.'

Bryan swung round quickly. His finger was on the trigger of his weapon but he did not fire. Rather clumsily, the figure of a man extricated itself from the bush. Almost as much by recognition of the voice as of the figure, for the darkness here was intense, Bryan understood that this was Bobs-the-Boy. He still kept his pistol levelled as he said,

'What are you doing here? I thought it was a burglar.'

'Not you, you didn't, Guv'nor,' retorted Bobs-the-Boy. 'What you thought was that it was that Scotland Yard swine, Bobby Owen. And you was right, too, or would have been, if you had been just two minutes quicker. But now he's off and Lord knows where.'

'What's that you've got in your hand?' Bryan asked.

Bobs-the-Boy held out his arm and let fall something heavy.

'A brick,' he said simply. 'I was going to bash his nob in for him, so you couldn't have told it from a pot of paperhanger's paste . . . and so I will sometime yet,' he added with what seemed a burst of uncontrollable ferocity, 'for I'm fed up with him following me the way he is; and if I've got to swing, why, it might as well be for him, too.'

'What do you mean, "too"?' Bryan asked. He put his pistol back in his pocket and began to walk away towards the more open parts of the garden where the darkness was less intense. 'What have you done to swing for, as you call it?' he repeated as Bobs-the-Boy followed him.

'Nothing . . . that's my business, that is,' Bobs-the-Boy answered sulkily.

'You may as well tell me; perhaps I could help you,' Mr

Bryan observed, and added carelessly, 'I don't know that I like this policeman person – Owen is his name? – I don't think I like him any more than you do.'

'No reason why you should,' retorted Bobs-the-Boy, shambling along a yard behind his companion. 'I don't know if it was you and your pals did in that bit of skirt all the papers are talking about ... and I don't care ... nothing to do with me. But I do know the "busies" think you did it, and Owen thinks so, too, for I heard him talking to one of the big pots from the Yard, and that's what it came to.'

'That, of course, is quite a mistake, a regrettable, even a ridiculous mistake,' Bryan told him. They were in the middle of the lawn now, and Bryan stopped and turned to face the other. 'What were they saying – this Owen man and the person from Scotland Yard?'

Bobs-the-Boy shook his head.

'I only caught a word here and there,' he answered, 'but what it came to was plain enough, and that was that she was done in here and that you and some of your pals done it. But they couldn't think why.'

'I should suppose they couldn't,' declared Bryan with a dry little sound Bobs-the-Boy did not at first realize was a laugh. 'Of course, it's obvious there could be no reason, quite obvious, isn't it?'

'There's a many couldn't give reasons for what they done,' Bobs-the-Boy retorted with an unexpected touch of philosophy, 'but that there's what they think all right.'

'What do you think?'

'Nothing,' Bobs-the-Boy answered promptly. 'Why should I? What's it do with me?'

'What do they think about you?' Bryan asked next.

'It ain't so much what they think as what they know,' Bobs-the-Boy answered in a slow and hesitating voice; 'only I'm not sure what they do know, and it wasn't no fault of mine, for I never meant to do it. But she made me mad the way she talked and talked, and I never did a thing but what any other bloke she had aggravated so wouldn't have done just the same as me.'

'What was that?'

'It was only a sort of a clip on the ear,' Bobs-the-Boy answered sullenly. 'But down she went flop with her head against the grate and looked so queer like, I shoved off. Then afterwards I heard as how she passed out for keeps, and like as not, if them busies can, they will bring it in murder, same as it never was, nor manslaughter neither, seeing I never meant a thing except to teach her to hold her tongue. But she always was an awkward one, and after that I never reported any more according to my ticket. And if that there Owen . . . Owen —'

He repeated the name again, spitting as he did so in token of abhorrence, and Bryan continued to regard him very thoughtfully. After a moment or two Bryan asked,

'Are you sure it was Owen you saw?'

'Do you think I don't know him?' Bobs-the-Boy retorted contemptuously. 'Why, I know his mug as well as I know my own. Snooping round he was; and if he hadn't bunked off just when he did, I would have laid him out, I would, so he wouldn't ever have troubled no one any more.'

'And left us, I suppose,' remarked Bryan dryly, 'to explain what had happened?'

'We all has to look after our own troubles,' explained Bobs-the-Boy, quite calmly.

'Oh, we have, have we?' snarled Bryan. 'I suppose you thought it would be pretty smart to let the police think we were responsible when he was found in our grounds, and you knew they had these crazy suspicions of theirs already . . . I've a good mind to give you some trouble of your own to think about,' he said, and lifted his pistol threateningly.

But Bobs-the-Boy did not seem much alarmed. Perhaps he knew the threat was not one very likely to be carried out.

'Well, I didn't mean no harm,' he explained, 'but you ain't nothing to me. I don't owe you nothing. If it was pals now, that's different. I never let down a pal, never, and never will, but you and me ain't pals, so why shouldn't I look after myself first? Nothing to do with me what the "busies" thought. Your trouble ain't mine. And wasn't I doing you a good turn getting rid of a busy that's as keen on getting you as me – or keener?'

'Of course, that's all nonsense,' Bryan said.

'Oh, yes,' Bobs-the-Boy agreed, but in a tone that Bryan judged it wiser to take no notice of.

'What were you doing here yourself?' he asked instead. 'Your work was finished long ago. What were you hanging about for?'

'That was Owen, too,' Bobs-the-Boy explained, 'just as I was going I saw him there, hanging about outside, waiting for me, I reckoned. So I dodged back again and waited, and when I tried again at the back way, through the car park, there he was again, watching just the same as before, waiting, always waiting. I tell you, Guv'nor, the way them fellows wait till they get you at the end . . . so I waited, too, and I made up my mind to go on waiting till I got him alone . . . behind . . . when he wasn't looking . . . but he always was. All the time he was there, watching and waiting just the same, and so was I, till it was dark. Then he came snooping in, only I was watching still, and somehow then I fell to it, it wasn't me he was after, or else that it was you just as much as me. There was bricks lying loose I had noticed near where I was working at that coal, shifting it. So I went and got one and I made a little noise like, so as he would hear it and come along to see what it was, and then just as he got near and I was ready to lay him out, someone said something up in that room where you was all talking and leaned right out of the window and pointed. He knew then he had been spotted and off he bunked, quick as he knew how, and, if he hadn't, then he would be here still, only with his nob bashed in, same as a rotten egg.'

'Good thing, too,' Bryan commented; 'we don't want dead policemen found lying about here.'

'I would have rung you up to let you know so you would have had a chance to put him away,' Bobs-the-Boy explained amiably. 'You could easily have put him in a sack and dumped him in the pond down there . . . in the overflow channel would have been better. No fear of his being ever found there.'

It was a suggestion on which Bryan made no comment. After a time he said,

'Come into the house with me. We had better have a talk. I think this Owen is getting a nuisance, but then an establishment like this can't afford scandal.'

'No more can't I,' grinned Bobs-the-Boy. 'See here, Guv'nor, why don't you take me to work with your lot? That there Owen, he means to get us both. It wasn't murder what I did, it wasn't anything, rightly speaking, but if he can he'll bring it home to me and then I'll swing, sure as running horses. And he means to bring the other business, about that bit of skirt in the burning motor-car, home to you, for that much I did hear enough to be sure of. Not enough evidence yet, he said, and he didn't want to say what he had already, not till he was sure, but soon he thought he would be, he said, and then he would put it all before the other bloke what he was talking to and be ready to swear, he said, it would be good enough for any jury. Only till then he didn't want to say nothing, not a thing.'

'I almost think you are right,' Mr Bryan commented, 'in saying this detective must be dealt with. His idea's all nonsense, of course, but he might easily make a scandal that would ruin the establishment. One of my colleagues was complaining just now of the way he had been behaving here, actually breaking into locked premises, and so on. I really think something must be done about it; it's almost a pity you were interrupted, even though your method was rather crude. Are you sure Owen went away, or may he still be hanging about here?'

'He went all right,' Bobs-the-Boy answered. 'Faded away like the pictures off the screen when the film's run out. But he might come back, you can't tell that, though just now I'll swear there isn't no one here but only me and you. And I don't reckon he would be likely to come back, seeing he went along of having been spotted, only you can't be sure.'

'I suppose not,' agreed Bryan. 'Come upstairs with me and we'll see if we can come to any arrangement likely to suit us both.'

He led the way to the house, and close behind him followed Bobs-the-Boy, like a second, darker, more threatening shadow.

CHAPTER TWENTY-THREE

The Noise in the Inner Room

WHEN they came back to the room on the first floor where Bryan had left his two associates, Zachary Dodd and Miss James, he saw to his surprise that during his absence they had been joined by a newcomer, Horace Hunter, the wholesale fur merchant of Howland Yard.

'You,' Bryan exclaimed sharply, standing still in the doorway. 'What's brought you here?'

Hunter was at the other end of the room, standing before the fireplace. He looked flushed and excited, and had evidently been talking and gesticulating freely. Zachary Dodd was sitting at the table and Miss James was still on the couch before the now curtained window. Before Hunter could answer she called out shrilly to Bryan,

'Did you find him? But you wouldn't ... it was Owen, I know it was, and you never saw him.'

'Owen?' Hunter repeated, catching at the name. 'You mean he was here? It was Owen you saw ...? Are you sure?'

'Sure and certain, too,' Miss James answered him in the same loud, shrill tones. She added, 'He's everywhere, he's nowhere.'

'Never mind that now,' commanded Bryan from the doorway. 'You're making a bogey of the fellow; you're letting him get on your nerves. That's only silly, losing your head that way.' He flung out an accusing skinny hand at Miss James. 'You're letting yourself get hysterical,' he said, but she only muttered to herself and took no other notice.

Bryan still did not move from his position in the doorway. Bobs-the-Boy, standing a yard or two back, escaped the notice of the three in the room. Zachary Dodd grumbled in his heavy, muttering tones,

'We've got to do something about him . . . I don't know what we can do about him.'

'It was him brought Horry Hunter here,' Miss James told Bryan. 'Whenever anyone does anything, it's always because of him.'

'Is that true? What about him?' Bryan asked Hunter.

'I haven't seen him myself,' Hunter began, and Miss James interrupted him shrilly,

'Oh, you wouldn't . . . no one ever does . . . not yet.'

'Shut up, will you?' Bryan screamed at her, but her flushed face, her heaving breast, her heavy breathing all remained the same.

'I haven't seen him myself,' Hunter repeated, 'but he's been around a lot . . . I didn't know who it was at first, then I found out . . . asking questions, wanting to know . . . There's something he's got hold of.'

'That's us,' Miss James muttered, 'it's us he's got hold of.'

'Oh, shut up,' Hunter shouted at her in his turn, but he had now become very pale, and Zachary, at the table, had begun to wipe perspiration from his face.

Even Bryan was silent, and all of them had the feeling that an unknown grip, invisible, impalpable, inescapable, was closing slowly in upon them. It would not have taken much at that instant to have set them all into some such access of hysterics as that the woman amongst them was fighting against. They were like men choking in a fog from which they did not know how to seek relief, and alone, Bobs-the-Boy, looking on from behind, neither speaking nor moving, only watching, seemed immune from this miasma of panic. Bryan, glancing back and seeing him there, seemed to derive a certain courage from the other's silence and immobility.

'That won't do, no sense to it,' he repeated. 'Pull yourselves together, can't you? You're like a lot of babies frightened at a nursery tale.'

'Yes, I know,' Hunter agreed, 'but this sort of thing is a bit worrying, upsetting. If one knew what the fellow was after, I mean, what he really knew. . . .'

He took out his cigarette-case as he spoke and helped himself. Miss James pointed a trembling finger at it.

'Put it away, put that thing away,' she said, 'I don't want to see it . . . I tell you I don't want to see it.'

'Elsie,' Bryan told her, 'if you go on like this, I'll . . . I'll —'

He left the threat uncompleted, and she looked round at him with the same wild stare.

'I don't want to see that thing,' she repeated. 'Tell him to put it away.'

'Oh, all right, have your own way,' Hunter exclaimed, shrugging his shoulders, 'but it's my own, it's not that other one. This is one a girl gave me a long time ago.' He put it back in his pocket and began to laugh in a nervous jerky way. 'It reminds Elsie of another one she gave me herself just the other day. But that one's at the bottom of the river. This one's mine, and lots of people have seen me use it.'

'Why shouldn't they? What are you talking about, the two of you?' demanded Bryan.

'Elsie gave me a cigarette-case just like this one the other day,' Hunter repeated. 'She didn't tell me where she got it from, all she wanted was to get rid of it the quickest way she could. But when I looked I found inside it one of Jo Frankland's cards. I don't know what happened to Jo Frankland. How should I? I've never asked and I was miles away. But all the same when I saw that card, I went out to the Tower Bridge and flung the cigarette-case and the card with it into the river.'

Bryan turned his small, cold eyes on Miss James. He seemed quiet now and more controlled, but none the pleasanter for that.

'What fool trick. . . .?' he demanded.

'It wasn't my fault,' she answered, sulkily enough, but also a little more calmly. 'It just happened. Just as I was jumping out of the car I noticed a cigarette-case lying on the seat. I thought it was mine, it looked like it. I thought I must have taken it out of my bag without thinking and put it down there and it was mine. I knew if it was I didn't care to leave it, and I grabbed it, and then afterwards I saw it wasn't mine at all, it was – hers. She – must have left it lying there herself. I gave it to Horry to get rid of it.'

'So I did, no need to worry,' interposed Hunter.

'That thing of yours looks like it,' Miss Jones said doubtfully.

'Most tortoiseshell cigarette-cases look like each other, especially if they happen to have silver mountings,' Hunter retorted.

'It makes me remember,' Miss James said; 'brings it all back. . . . I tell you I can't stand it . . . not when I know that Owen man is prowling about without ever stopping.'

'If you don't stop it, if you can't control yourself,' Bryan snarled from his place by the doorway whence he had still not moved, 'you'll have to go the same way as Jo Frankland . . . You're getting a danger to everyone else, breaking down this way.'

'Murder me too, would you, you beast?' she asked, but without much emotion. 'That what you mean?'

He nodded quietly but rather horribly. Miss James opened her mouth wide, as if she meant to scream, but saw him looking at her, and closed it again. She seemed to collapse now; the flush on her face faded to a ghastly pallor, her heavy breathing to a kind of whimper. She did not speak at all. Zachary Dodd, equally silent, looked from her to Bryan and back again, and then wiped his face once more. His handkerchief had become a wet rag from which one could easily have wrung the moisture. The silence in the room had lasted some time when Hunter said abruptly,

'There's someone out there in the passage, listening to all this.'

'Owen,' breathed Miss James, 'that'll be Owen.'

Bryan's patience, or what was left of it, gave way, and he turned on her in a silent fury, choking and gesticulating, his angry hands hovering furiously in the air as if at any moment they might descend to fasten round her neck. But she paid him and his silent anger, though it was terrifying enough, no attention at all, only stared past him into the passage, where, from her position, nothing was visible. She said again,

'It's Owen, and he's there, all the time, listening to all we've said.'

'Of all the fools that ever lived you're the worst,' Bryan almost screamed. 'Do you think I'm as mad as you are? Do you think I've brought a Scotland Yard man up here to hear us talking? Owen, indeed! you're out of your senses if you ever had any. It's Bobs-the-Boy, the fellow who was working here. We can be useful to each other, he and us; he's tired of Owen just as much as we are, more.'

'That's right,' agreed Bobs-the-Boy from behind, 'tired of him, sick of him, never rid of him, had enough of him.'

He went on darkly muttering to himself; they could hear his voice die away in a mumbled menace. Looking at each other they listened with a kind of secret content, a threatening and evil satisfaction.

'Mr Owen seems a busy sort of man, here, there, and everywhere,' Bryan went on after a pause. 'Maybe he's a bit more busy than wise. It's not only the – accident to Jo Frankland he's bothering about. It seems there was another accident a little time ago.'

'That's right,' confirmed Bobs-the-Boy. 'Accident it was, nothing to do with me in a manner of speaking. I only caught her a clip on the ear same as you might, or anyone else without meaning nothing much, and she went and corpsed herself on it. But will them busies believe it was that way? Not them, not Owen, messing round the way he is and asking questions everywhere.'

'That's right,' agreed Bryan, 'that's the sort it seems he is.'

'Won't leave nothing alone,' Bobs-the-Boy said again. 'Don't give a bloke no chance, not while – not while Owen's still . . . alive.'

Again they were all silent, looking at each other in the same secret way as before, but not speaking. Bryan had moved now from his place in the doorway. Bobs-the-Boy was standing there instead. He did not look at any of them, but yet it seemed he watched them all from behind his half-closed eyes. All at once Miss James began to laugh, a high-pitched, hysterical laughter. Bryan came across to her side and, taking her arm, twisted it viciously. She stopped laughing and looked at him, but made no sound, though the pain must have been severe. Bryan said,

'You leave whisky alone, you hear me? or you'll get worse than that.' He gave her arm a final twist, more vicious than before, but still without eliciting from her the least sound. As if her silence exasperated him beyond control, he shouted at her, 'What's the matter with you, anyway? You've nothing to worry about. I planned it. Zack did it. You did nothing but drive the car away. And yet it's you breaks down and starts this fooling. . . . Elsie, my girl, you had best be careful.'

He dropped her arm that hung numbed and powerless by her side and moved back to the other side of the table. She said,

'You hurt me; what's the good of hurting me? It's all because I can't sleep, and if I could I daren't, because when I do I dream I am back there in the car with her all huddled up between the seats.'

'You're a nice lot to be working with,' grumbled Hunter. 'Now we all know all about it, don't we? telling the world . . . pity this Owen fellow isn't here so he could hear all the news.'

'Well, he isn't,' Bryan snapped, 'so that's all right. You mean the same fellow has been making inquiries round your way?'

Hunter nodded.

'Asking a whole lot of questions, got at some of my staff, told 'em who he was, got 'em scared. Lucky there's nothing they can tell, because there's nothing they know. But it looks to me as if he had got hold of something or knew something or suspected it . . .'

'Has Keene been saying anything, do you think?' Bryan demanded.

'He wouldn't dare,' Hunter answered, 'not him; he's too much of a skunk. He's a coward, got scared, but he would hold his tongue for his own sake. It's that other Frankland girl's got hold of him if you ask me. But I don't believe he's told even her anything.'

'Sybil Frankland you mean?'

'Yes. I think she guessed something was on, and she's made him give it up. But I don't think he's ever told her much. He wouldn't dare, he was always panicking about something, about what was going to happen, or what she would think if she knew, or some blessed thing or another. But all the same I think it's because of her, and because she let him see she had spotted something was on, that he's backed out.'

'It might be through her the other girl came fooling round here and got more than she expected,' Bryan said. He looked at Bobs-the-Boy, still silent in the doorway, and went on, 'You had better know how it all happened. We had to have some more money or else close down. I didn't mean to close down. I've spent a lot building this place up, it's a big thing, it means a lot.' He paused, and for a moment his whole expression changed; for just that moment it was as though a blaze of relief, of fanatical devotion, transfigured him entirely. For just that moment he had the look of one lifted by a passionate creed to higher levels. Then once more he was back, once more he was the hungry, questing weasel tracking down its prey. He went on, 'We made our money in the first place from one or two fires we arranged, one on a liner that brought in almost nothing because the whole thing was muddled and others we had better luck with. Only during one of them some old fool we had never heard of, knew absolutely nothing about, managed to get himself suffocated. It wasn't our fault, we couldn't help it, only you never know what an accident like that mightn't get called.'

'I know,' agreed Bobs-the-Boy gloomily, 'same here ... Something happens, you didn't never mean it ... but what do them busies up at the Yard care? ... Swing you for it all the same, so they will, if they can.'

It was a remark that did not seem to raise the spirits of

any of the others. Even Bryan looked appreciably paler as he went on,

'What made it worse was that Lord Carripore, it was his company had to pay up most, began messing about, trying to find out things, and we had to slow down operations for the time. This place costs a lot to run at present, it will till it gets fully established, and though we managed to collect a bit of coin from our operations, expenses were heavy – assessors, for instance, scandalous, what we had to pay them when they did nothing at all, nothing till it was all over and then walked off with the fat. So we had to try some more, and Mr Hunter and Mr Keene came in to help. But we wanted a good trustworthy odd job man as well.'

'Bob's the Boy for that,' grinned Bobs-the-Boy. 'It was Mousey told me you might have a job for a fellow what knew his way about. Mousey had been in it already, hadn't he?'

'Off and on,' Bryan answered with some reserve, as if he didn't care to go into details. 'Unluckily he got taken again just then, but not till he had told us where to find you. Though he seemed to have some sort of idea —'

Bryan paused and Bobs-the-Boy laughed harshly.

'I know,' he said. 'Mousey thought that Salvation Army bloke had got hold of me and I was running straight. Mind you, I ain't got nothing against running straight, only a bloke's got to live, ain't he? Well then . . .'

'That's right,' agreed Bryan. 'What we wanted was a man who would know how to break into Mr Hunter's warehouse and remove some of his more valuable stock the staff could swear was there when they closed down. After that, you were to start the fire, and no assessor afterwards could have told the difference between the cheap minks and sables we should have given you to put in the place of what you were to remove. We didn't mean to be bled by assessors any more. The same idea was to be carried out at Mr Keene's place, where there are valuable paintings, good, honest, sworn testimony would have shown were on the premises when the fire broke out but that the fire had utterly destroyed. Only your job would have been to break in and clear them out before starting the fire, so we should have had the insurance on them and the things themselves as well, to sell afterwards; and it would have been a mighty smart assessor who could have told the difference between a genuine Old Master and a copy all nicely charred up. The fires were to have happened when Mr Keene was in Paris on business and Mr Hunter somewhere else, on a week-end cruise or somewhere, so they could both have had good alibis. I suppose you knew most of that already?'

'Most of it,' agreed Bobs-the-Boy with another of his grins; 'all of it, pretty near. I told Mr Keene as much the other day. It wasn't anyway difficult to see what the game was ... smart, too, all right, smart and safe as houses.'

'Now Keene's backed out,' Hunter said gloomily. 'I told him what I thought of him. But he'll hold his tongue for his own sake.'

'They used to come here to talk it over and fix things up,' explained Bryan to Bobs-the-Boy, 'and then afterwards I would tell Zack and Elsie what had been arranged.' He paused and licked his lips that had become a little dry. 'Well, that's how the whole thing happened,' he said. 'Zack and Elsie —' He stopped again for a moment, to glare malevolently at the woman. 'I used to think Elsie had good nerves,' he went on; 'now she's gone all to pieces. Well, we were talking things over in here, in this room. I explained everything so we should all know just what was arranged and what we had to do. Then we heard a noise in the room beyond there that opens out of this one. There was a sort of scratchy sound as if a chair had rubbed against another, and then something fell on the floor and smashed, a bit of china it was, and there was a sort of cry. So that told us there was someone there listening to all we said.'

'That's right,' Dodd said, speaking for almost the first time, 'that's what we heard ... then we knew someone was there.'

In a silence filled for Bryan, for Dodd, for the woman, with a memory of that moment when they realized an unseen listener had heard their talk, they all three looked at one another, living over once again that moment of appalling knowledge. Bobs-the-Boy watched them with his everlasting grin, and then, just as he was about to break that heavy silence of dark memory in which they seemed all three so closely wrapped, all of them heard distinctly a sound from the adjoining room as if a chair had knocked against another. Almost immediately there followed a noise of china breaking, as if a flower vase or something of the sort had fallen and broken, and then a low, soft cry to tell them beyond all doubt that once again there was someone in that inner room, someone who had listened to all they said, had heard it all, and now knew all their secrets.

CHAPTER TWENTY-FOUR

'*Bobs-the-Boy*' for —

FOR a moment, a long and dreadful moment, there was a silence in that little upper room so complete and strange one might have thought the world itself had stopped.

Had the five who were present there been smitten dead upon the spot, they could not have been more still or quiet. It was as if even their hearts had ceased to beat, their breath to come or go.

Then at last there was a whisper heard. Who spoke it first none could tell; perhaps it came from them all at the same moment; a low, half uttered whisper that seemed to murmur interminably all about the room as though it would never cease, a whisper that was but one word — a name endlessly repeated.

'Owen, Owen, Owen,' it went on and on, and they all heard it, and hardly knew whether they uttered it themselves, or listened to it spoken by the others; whether they repeated it aloud again and again that it seemed to linger so in the air around, or whether they were merely conscious of it as the overwhelming knowledge of them all.

But at last Bryan spoke, very softly, his words hardly audible, yet all the same clear and distinct to the minds of them all.

'If it's Owen, if it is,' he said, staring at the door that led into this inner room, 'then he's there still, for the outer door into the passage has been locked and bolted ever since . . . ever since. . . .' He did not complete the sentence, but they all understood well enough. He added, 'There's the window, but it's barred; it was the day nursery in there once.'

'If it's Owen,' Hunter babbled, so shaken in every nerve and muscle he could hardly articulate, 'if it's Owen . . . then he's heard it all . . . he knows it all . . . what are we to do?'

'If it's Owen,' Zack Dodd mumbled in his heavy, rumbling voice that was so full of threat and menace, 'then he's got to be ... dealt with ... like her ... dealt with,' he said with a gesture of his great, clenched fist. 'It's him or us,' he said.

Miss James said,

'It's him all right ... it's him ... it's him ... he's been there all the time ... he's heard it all.'

'If it is,' Bryan said, still staring at the door, still fingering what he held still hidden in the pocket of his coat, 'he must have slipped in when you and Zack went down to let Hunter in.'

Hunter said,

'I'll go, it's nothing to do with me. I don't know anything about all this or what happened to Jo Frankland.' He said this last sentence very loudly and in the same high, almost shouted tone, he added, 'I was miles away. I can prove that. Easily. I'll be going.'

But when he made as if to rise from his chair to carry out his intention, he saw how the other three were looking at him, and he understood and sat down again very quickly.

'Oh, all right, all right, all right,' he stuttered.

'You'll see it through same as the rest of us,' Zack rumbled. 'You'd best be careful too, you sneaking cur.'

'All right, all right, all right,' Hunter stammered again, and indeed by now he was so shaken with such an extremity of terror it is doubtful if, even if they had permitted it, his legs would have carried him as far as the door.

Bryan muttered, almost whispered, his glance turned back again upon the closed door of the inner room,

'We'll all see it through together, but what a fool the fellow is to let himself be caught in there like this.'

They were silent again, silent and waiting. Hunter managed at last to gasp out,

'Perhaps he didn't hear ... most likely he couldn't.'

They took no notice, and presently Zack Dodd said, leaning across to Bryan,

'If he's got a gun, he'll shoot it out.'

'If there's firing, they'll hear it in the village,' Bryan said.

Miss James said in a kind of whispered incantation,
'Owen, Owen, Owen, Owen.'

'Oh, shut up, can't you?' Bryan snarled at her, but she took no notice and went on muttering,
'Owen, Owen, Owen, Owen.'

'We can't do anything,' Hunter clamoured in the same hoarse and strangled voice, 'even if he heard, it doesn't matter, it's only his word against ours, that's all ... I mean ... oh, my God, you don't intend ...?'

They still took no notice of him, they might not have heard him; they all continued still to watch that inner door. The expectation they all had was that it would open and that Owen, unable to escape by the locked and bolted outer door, finding the window secured by the iron bars put up when the room had been a nursery, would presently come out.

So they waited, still and watchful and intent, while Hunter crouched and trembled in his chair, and Miss James muttered still her perpetual litany, 'Owen, Owen, Owen's there ... Owen,' and Zack Dodd now and again put out his tongue to moisten his lips, intolerably dry, and Bryan moved not a muscle but sat there quite motionless, motionless now as the weasel the moment before it springs, absolutely still that is, and yet with a kind of quivering intensity of every nerve and muscle. Zack whispered across to him,

'Suppose he's got a gun ... if he has he could have us covered first.'

From his post at the door where he stood, darkly thoughtful, formidable somehow in his patient waiting, though in the shock of their realization that there was someone hidden in the inner room the others had half forgotten his presence, Bobs-the-Boy said quietly,

'That's all right, Guv'nor ... them Yard chaps never carry guns.'

'That's right,' agreed Bryan.

'I can't stand this,' Hunter cried wildly, getting this time to his feet and even making a step towards the door.

'You've got to,' Dodd growled, and beneath his baleful

glare Hunter suddenly sat down again, and from the doorway Bobs-the-Boy said,

'You're in it, aren't you? just the same as all of us.'

'I can't stand it,' Hunter repeated as wildly as before. 'What are you going to do? My God, my God, what are you going to do?'

None of them took the least notice.

Swaying softly to and fro where she sat on the sofa, Miss James was still muttering her perpetual litany,

'Owen . . . Owen . . . Owen . . . I knew all the time he was there.'

'Got to do something, ain't you?' Bobs-the-Boy demanded. 'Sooner the quicker if you ask me.'

'That's right,' agreed Bryan again.

Looking round him, Bryan seemed to be asking the opinions of his companions. No one volunteered any suggestion. Hunter noticed suddenly the time his wrist-watch showed, and understood with amazement that all this had happened in rather less than five minutes. From his place in the doorway where he still stood, Bobs-the-Boy barked out suddenly a loud and disconcerting laugh.

'Scared, aren't you?' he said. 'Well, Bob's the Boy for the job.'

Before they realized his intention he crossed the room with a light, quick step, so lightly, so swiftly indeed, that had they not seen his passage they would not have known he had moved. He swung open the door and was through it in a flash, banging it behind him, and in the room he had left the three men and the woman still there sat motionless and astonished and afraid. Even Miss James's muttering ceased at last, and like the men she sat staring at the closed door behind which might be happening – they knew not what.

Intently they listened but they heard nothing. No sound came to give them any hint of what was passing there. It might almost have been that they had dreamed that swift passage of Bobs-the-Boy across the room and his disappearance into the inner chamber, but for the fact that at any rate he was no longer visible at his post in the doorway. The mysterious quiet following his entry into the inner room increased almost unbearably the tension of their amazement, their terror, and their suspense.

'I can't stand this,' Hunter muttered, 'I can't . . . I'll go mad soon, I shall . . . mad.'

Dodd said, but not as though he much believed it,

'There's no one there after all.'

'Owen's there,' Miss James said. With the accent of a profound and unalterable conviction, she repeated, 'Owen's there . . . I know it.'

Bryan did not speak, but it was evident that even he was uneasy. Indeed the strain of waiting thus without knowing what was passing behind that closed door they watched was becoming more than any of them could bear. Hunter's features had grown contorted, convulsive, to such a degree that it was plain that, if not madness, then at least hysterics, was very near. And Bryan knew that if once one of them broke down, anything was possible. He knew he ought to take some action to check this rising tide of panic that threatened to sweep away from them all every vestige of self-control, and yet he could not. He sighed a little and saw the handle of the door turn.

Abstractedly he watched it, for long years, for something like an eternity, it seemed to him he watched that turning handle. The door swung slowly back. Bobs-the-Boy came out. He closed the door again behind him very carefully and stood looking at them. His face was quite expressionless. Not one of them dared speak at first, but their avid and dreadful eyes searched for some sign on his dress or person to tell them what had happened, and searched in vain. Bryan said at last,

'There's no one there?'

'Vases and chairs and things don't upset themselves of their own accord,' Bobs-the-Boy answered, grinning at him.

'There's someone there?' Bryan said.

'What have you done?' Dodd almost shouted. 'Who was it? what have you done?'

'Done?' repeated Bobs-the-Boy, 'why, nothing.' He let

the word drop so softly it was almost inaudible, and yet there was a thrill of something terrible in its soft sound. 'Not yet,' he added as gently, 'nothing yet.'

'It's Owen who's there,' Miss James said, 'it's him, and he's been there all the time, but now somehow he's got away.'

'Aw, cheese it,' Bobs-the-Boy retorted contemptuously, 'it ain't Owen at all. You've got that bloke on the brain all right, haven't you? Cut it out, ma'am, cut it out . . . Owen ain't there . . . it ain't no Yard man at all . . . it ain't no man either.'

'Not a man? What do you mean?' Dodd asked, and Bryan said almost simultaneously.

'Stop playing the fool . . . tell us what you mean.'

Even Hunter lifted his head that he had hidden in his hands as though he would try to conceal his own terrors from himself, and Miss James repeated the name that seemed by now the only word she had power to pronounce,

'Owen . . . Owen.'

'Lumme,' cried Bobs-the-Boy, exasperated, 'like a blooming grammyphone, ain't you? I tell you Owen ain't there, not him. There's no man there, neither, same as I told you before.'

'If it's not a man —' Bryan began.

'So it ain't,' Bobs-the-Boy interrupted, 'and for why? Because it's a girl, that's why.'

'A girl . . .?' Bryan repeated, 'a girl . . . what girl?' It was plain neither he nor the others quite understood. 'What do you mean . . . what girl?' he said again.

'That other one's sister,' explained Bobs-the-Boy. 'Her sister. Sybil Frankland, that's who it is.'

'Sybil Frankland,' Dodd repeated, 'but . . . but —'

'Her . . . her sister?' Miss James asked in a kind of bewildered whisper.

'That's right,' Bobs-the-Boy answered.

'If it's her,' Miss James said slowly, 'if it is . . . why, then I would almost rather it was Owen instead.'

'Oh, it's her all right,' Bobs-the-Boy repeated, 'fainted she has ... most likely when she knew she had given herself away knocking the chair and things over, then she was so scared she just fainted, and there she is.'

He made a slight movement aside as if inviting them to look for themselves. Bryan got up and looked past Bobs-the-Boy, standing sideways in the door. Drawing back again, Bryan said,

'It's her all right ... what was she doing there?'

'Do you think she heard what we were saying?' Dodd asked slowly; 'if she's fainted. ...'

'She heard it all first,' asserted Bobs-the-Boy, 'that's why she fainted when she knew as she had give herself away. You can bet on that, you can hear every word in there what's said in here.' He added meditatively, 'That's why the little fool fainted when she knew she had give herself away, because she had heard every word you spoke.'

'Perhaps it makes it easier, that she's fainted,' remarked Bryan, who had gone back to where he had been sitting before.

Bobs-the-Boy turned his head to look at him. For a moment, a long and dreadful moment, their eyes met ... and understood ... understood the secret message that flashed between them.

'That's right,' Bobs-the-Boy said at last, 'makes it easier in a manner of speaking, so it does.'

He made a gesture, his hand with outspread fingers circling his throat, and looked at Bryan. Almost imperceptibly Bryan nodded. More deliberately still, while the others watched him, he took a large, dirty, red silk handkerchief from his pocket and twisted it into a noose. Again he looked at Bryan and again Bryan nodded slightly, more slightly even than before. Bobs-the-Boy stepped back into the inner room once more, softly closing the door behind him.

He had not been gone more than a second or two, they were still watching the closed door behind which he was hidden, when they heard a step in the corridor without. Not only did the lips of Miss James open to give vent to a startled scream. Dodd, too, jumping to his feet, had a cry of terror

183

and alarm hovering on his lips. As for Hunter, only the choking, strangling feeling in his throat prevented him from screaming out aloud. But then the furious and frantic gesture Bryan made, one of intense command, held them silent, checked their cries still unuttered. The door opened and Maurice Keene stood there, watching them doubtfully.

'Is Sybil here?' he asked. 'Miss Frankland, I mean, Sybil Frankland?'

CHAPTER TWENTY-FIVE

Keene Suspects

WHEN he had said this he remained standing in the doorway, darkly watchful, almost in the same attitude, almost with the same expression, as Bobs-the-Boy had shown when he stood there shortly before. It might have been indeed that he had come again, though in different guise.

At first none of them made any effort to reply to Keene's question. They were too conscious of what their imaginations pictured to them as occurring on the other side of that closed door through which Bobs-the-Boy had just vanished with his knotted, noosed handkerchief in his grasp. Keene's sudden appearance at that moment of all others held them indeed appalled. Even Bryan was shaken dreadfully; the merest trifle, one way or another, would have sent them all flying in a panic-stricken madness of terror, or launched them in a wild attack on Keene himself, or indeed hurled them into other extremity of action of any sort or kind in which their overwrought and quivering nerves could have found relief. To all of them it seemed certain that the next thing that would happen would be that Keene would cross the floor of the room and tear open the closed door that alone hid what was passing in the adjoining room. This seemed to them so obvious a thing for him to do that they could not understand why he delayed, and he on his side could not understand why they all sat there, so strangely watching him, so silent and so still.

'Well, now then,' he said at last, looking from one to the other, 'now then, can't you say something?' He turned his gloomy, questioning gaze on Hunter. 'I didn't expect to find you here,' he said. 'Have you seen Sybil?'

By a great effort, Hunter succeeded in making a negative gesture with his head. He was quite incapable of speech, nor could he keep his eyes from wandering towards that closed door behind which – he jerked his thoughts away, he jerked his gaze back towards Keene, and then he shut tight his eyes for fear they should betray his awful knowledge.

Bryan spoke then in a voice that was fairly calm and well controlled.

'Miss Frankland? Miss Sybil Frankland?' he asked. 'She's not here, I don't think she's been here to-day, has she, Miss James? How did you get in, Mr Keene, if I may ask? It's long past our hours, we closed long ago.'

'I knocked, I rang, there was no answer,' Keene replied, 'so I pushed the door open and came in. I heard voices and I came up here. Are you sure Miss Frankland has not been here?'

'I think so,' Bryan answered. 'Miss James, you haven't seen Miss Frankland, have you? Her name's not in the visitors' book, is it?'

Miss James shook her head and her gaze, too, because she could not control it, went wandering in torment and in terror to the closed door of the inner room.

'What made you think the young lady was here?' Bryan asked Keene.

'I was told,' Keene answered, 'someone said —'

He hesitated and did not complete his sentence. It was fairly evident that now he was definitely suspicious, though of what he did not know. But in his heavy and gloomy gaze, a question was now apparent, and in turn he stared at each one of them, as though trying to extract an answer to what as yet he had not asked.

'Well, I'm afraid we can't help you, we know nothing of the young lady here,' Bryan went on in tones and with a manner that by now he had made nearly normal again. 'She's not one of our members, and I'm pretty sure she's not visited us to-day. If you found the door downstairs open, did you shut it again after you came in?'

'Sybil came to Leadeane by the seven-seventeen from town,' Keene said, ignoring Bryan's question, which indeed he had hardly heard or noticed, since only what affected

Sybil and his search for her had power just now to enter his mind or awaken his attention.

But Bryan turned to Dodd.

'Zack,' he said, speaking rather slowly and loudly, 'you might go and see to the door, will you? Goodness knows who else may come walking in or out.' He tossed a bunch of keys across to Dodd. 'They are labelled,' he said, 'so you can pick the right one out. It's not safe to have doors open. Sometimes it's not safe to have them locked either.'

He laid a slight emphasis on these last words as he spoke them, that his associates understood well enough. It was the key of the outer door of the adjoining room, of the door that opened on the corridor, that he was giving Dodd, so that Dodd could unlock it and allow the imprisoned Bobs-the-Boy to escape, carrying with him as he did so what there was need should not be allowed to remain there.

Dodd was not over quick of apprehension, but he understood all that well enough. He rose and lumbered heavily to the door, where Keene was still standing. Keene, though plainly more puzzled and uneasy with every passing minute, stood aside almost mechanically to let him pass on what was to all seeming so harmless and so necessary an errand. They all heard his heavy step lumbering down the passage without for a moment or two, and then pause as a fit of coughing took him. They all heard that equally plainly, and all of them, except Keene, knew that under the cover of that fit of coughing Dodd was unlocking the outer door of the adjoining room. Then they heard his heavy step go lumbering on, and they knew that now the way of escape was open to Bobs-the-Boy. Bryan began to talk in order to distract Keene's attention.

'Well, Mr Keene,' he said, 'I really don't see, even if Miss Frankland did leave by the seven-seventeen from town, why you should think she was coming here. Did she express any intention of paying us a visit? and if she did, did she say why she was coming so late? She has been here once or twice, I think, and she seemed interested, but she never became a member. Are you sure she was coming to Leadeane at all? The seven-seventeen goes to other places as well, you know. Anyhow, I don't see what we can do to help you. Of course, if we could, anything in our power, anything at all, we should be delighted. We all feel very keenly her sister's dreadful murder, and that this was the last place she visited before it happened. Indeed, I may as well tell you that affair's done us a lot of harm; illogical of course, but an establishment of this kind can't afford even the most indirect association with anything criminal, with anything not entirely and absolutely above board and respectable. You see it has meant visits from the police and questioning and what not – most upsetting. I'm not complaining, of course, very necessary no doubt and quite natural, but also very upsetting for our members, most upsetting and disturbing.'

'I believe Sybil may have thought,' began Keene slowly, 'in fact I was told —'

'Who told you?' Miss James interrupted him in a high, shrill, unnatural voice, 'who told you ... was it Owen ... Owen?'

'Owen ... who is Owen?' Bryan asked blandly, though the look he shot at Miss James was anything but bland. 'I don't know that name, do I? Not one of our members, I think?'

'Owen —' began Keene, and again Miss James interrupted him.

'If he told you, then you've seen him? Have you seen him?'

'Why, no,' Keene began once more, and yet a third time Miss James interrupted him.

'No one ever has,' she said, 'no one ... no one at all. But some day we shall all see him, all of us.'

Keene, more puzzled than ever, dimly aware of an atmosphere of suppressed terror and emotion there seemed little to account for, was again about to speak when now it was Bryan who interposed,

'But really, Mr Keene, if you have never seen this Owen person, whoever he may be and certainly not a member here, how did he manage to tell you Miss Frankland might be visiting us to-night?'

'He came to my place in Deal Street one time when I was out,' Keene answered. 'He asked a lot of questions of the girl I have there to look after things for me. She's pretty quick ... she thought he meant ... I don't know if she was right, but she's quick at spotting things.'

'What things?' Bryan asked, and the door opened and Zack came back into the room. He had regained now something of his natural, heavy swagger; the terror that had oppressed him so visibly before seemed to have passed away, and to have been replaced by a kind of ponderous insolence as of one who now felt himself secure.

'That's all right now,' he rumbled. 'All safe now,' he declared, grinning at that closed door of the adjoining room, which till now had seemed to all of them so frail a barrier between them and the discovery of the dread horror it concealed.

Even Bryan could not help drawing a long breath of relief. It was to all of them like a reprieve from a discovery that had seemed as imminent as inevitable, for what had there been to prevent Keene at any moment from walking across to that door and flinging it open and perceiving what lay behind? But now that opportunity had passed and gone for ever, passed by without his having even been aware of what to all of them had seemed so strangely obvious. Hunter lay back in his chair and shut his eyes, collapsed indeed, quite exhausted by his emotions and no longer with sufficient strength to sit upright. Zack's attitude of triumph he hardly troubled to conceal; it was as if he stood there and visibly snapped his fingers at defeated Fate. Miss James, experiencing suddenly a need for more air, flung back the curtain that had been drawn before the window, and leaned out a little that the cool air might bathe her throbbing temples and flushed, fevered face. Her action was just in time to permit her to see in the patch of light thus thrown abruptly on the lawn below, a man who ran heavily, and yet with speed, across it towards the shelter of the trees beyond, and who bore over his shoulder the body of a woman, limp and still and helpless, her head and feet dangling.

For one moment the two of them, the bearer and the borne, were plain there on that illumined patch of grass. Then they vanished into the shadows beyond. One last glimpse remained with Miss James of two feet in high-heeled shoes that hung down aimlessly, swinging a horrible tattoo against the ribs of the man, and then she sank back upon her sofa.

She had spoken no word, she had uttered no sound, and yet there was something visible about her, as it were, of the terror and the horror that she felt, a visible emanation of her dread. They were all looking at her, Keene in doubt and wonder, Bryan in cold fury, Dodd with a sort of sullen contempt. Only Hunter was unaffected, and he merely because he was insensible to all but the overpowering relief he experienced in knowing that what had before been behind that closed door was now no longer there.

Keene came forward from the doorway where till that moment he had been standing. He said, loudly and clearly,

'Something's been happening here ... you know something you are trying to hide.'

'Oh, really, Mr Keene, really,' protested Bryan with the best laugh he could summon up, but one that even to himself sounded false.

'There is,' Keene repeated with vehemence; 'there's something, and you're trying to hide it. I know there is, I can see it, the way you look. I interrupted something. What?'

'We were talking business, I think, when you came in,' Bryan replied.

'Then why did you all look the way you did? why do you all look like you do now?' Keene demanded. He flung out a challenging hand. 'I'll ask you something,' he said. 'It's been on my mind long enough and now I'll ask you. Did Jo Frankland know anything ... or suspect ...? Did she ever guess it was arson you got your money from?'

'There's no need to shout like that,' Bryan answered. 'How should I know what she knew or suspected? If she did, it could only have been if you told her things – did you?'

'She may have guessed, perhaps,' Keene admitted. 'I don't know. If she guessed Hunter and I were planning to have big fires at our places to draw the assurance money, if she managed to get to know somehow that it was you who were behind us, well, then perhaps she came here to try to find out more, and if you found her out in that —' He paused and then went on, 'I've tried to think that wasn't possible. I tried to think arson was only a bit of sharp practice with an assurance company that had lots of money already and could easily stand a loss or two. Only somehow Sybil made me see it differently. But anyhow murder's different, a long way different. If there's anything happened to Sybil, I'll go straight to Scotland Yard and tell them all I know and just what we had planned to do.'

'If you do that,' retorted Bryan, 'the only result will be, you will get a dose of penal servitude, that's all ... and I don't know that that would help you to marry the lady you're working yourself into such a state of excitement about. That is, if they believed you at the Yard, but I don't know that they would, for you've no evidence, not a scrap. I've taken care of that.'

'Bobs-the-Boy,' began Keene, and then stopped, for the unexpected mention of that name that was so heavy in all their minds so startled them that one and all they turned to look at the still closed door admitting to the adjoining room.

Again and again before then, Keene had subconsciously been aware of this trick they all seemed to have of letting their eyes turn towards this door, as though there were something behind it that held intensely their interest and their thoughts. This time his awareness of their action was more acute, made itself more felt, and he asked sharply,

'Why do you keep looking at that door, all of you? Is there something there?'

'Really, Mr Keene,' Bryan protested, 'you seem to have quite lost all common sense ... Do you think Miss Sybil Frankland's hiding there?' He crossed to the door and flung it widely open. 'Go in and look for yourself if you like,' he said. 'Perhaps you would like to search the rest of the house for her as well afterwards?'

Keene went into the room. That there was no one there was evident enough. It was a large room and held a good deal of furniture, but that was all, it seemed, till Keene, advancing across it, looking sharply around, saw lying on the floor a dirty red silk handkerchief knotted into a noose at one end, and not far away, a lady's handbag.

'That's Sybil's,' he said and picked it up. 'What is it doing here? what have you done with her? what's this for?' It was the noosed handkerchief he held up now. 'What's happened here?' he asked.

They did not answer him, but Bryan's attitude had grown suddenly rigid and in the doorway loomed the huge and threatening figure of Zack Dodd. ·

'I'll show these to Owen,' Keene said, and leapt away with all the speed he could command towards the door that opened into the corridor without, while Dodd thundered in pursuit and Bryan went sprawling on the floor from a swinging blow Keene aimed at him as he fled by.

CHAPTER TWENTY-SIX

'Bobs-the-Boy' Comes Back Again

IT was late, it was midnight past, when Bobs-the-Boy came back again across the lawn Miss James had seen him traverse earlier, carrying a woman's body slung over his shoulder.

He bore no such burden now as he came quickly and softly to the door of Leadeane Grange and knocked and rang and rang again. When he got no answer he pushed the door, as Maurice Keene had done before, and, finding it unlocked, went in quickly.

The darkness was profound, the silence unbroken, and when he called he got no answer. He had a pocket electric torch with him. He took it out and by its light made his way up the stairs. Plainly he was puzzled and a little uneasy. At the head of the stairs he waited and then called out again, and getting no answer went on to Miss James's room. The door of it hung open, and when he swung the ray from his torch about the room he saw her sitting there in a chair, quite still.

He addressed her by name, but she took no notice. He switched on the electric light and spoke to her again, but she still made no response, only looked blankly at him. He said to her,

'What's the matter? what's been happening here? where's the Guv'nor?'

She tried twice before she managed to articulate a reply, and then, instead of answering, it was other questions she put him.

'Where have you ... what ... how ...?' she muttered and again, 'Where have you ...?'

'Where have I planted her?' Bobs-the-Boy completed her question for her. 'Never you mind, don't you worry about that. What I'm asking is, where's the Guv'nor?'

She continued to stare at him, but without making any

attempt to answer. She appeared indeed quite dazed. Bobs-the-Boy seemed puzzled, and then from one of his pockets he took a small flask of brandy. Nearly half its contents he poured out and put to Miss James's lips.

'Drink it up,' he commanded briefly.

She obeyed, and the strong spirit seemed to restore to her that balance of mind which at more normal moments it might have been likely to overthrow. Her dazed look and manner gave place to one more natural. She said presently, as under the influence of the brandy her life began to flow again,

'I saw you taking – her – away. What have you done . . .?'

'You saw me when someone pulled the curtain back up here and the light showed me up, eh?' Bobs-the-Boy asked. 'Gave me a scare that did, I nearly dropped – what I was carrying, to run for it. Any one else see me?'

'No.'

'Gave me a scare,' Bobs-the-Boy said again. 'It's always the way, things happen just as they didn't ought. Just another half second and I should have been in among the trees and no one wouldn't have seen nothing. It's a wonder I didn't just drop her and run for it. Good thing I didn't though, if no one saw me but you. You're sure of that?'

'Yes. What have you . . . where have you . . . suppose they find . . .?'

'Well, they won't,' Bobs-the-Boy retorted, 'and never you mind what I done about it. What folk don't know, they can't tell. But you can take it from me – her dead corpse won't never be found by no one, not never.' He said that quite quietly, but with an accent of profound confidence and conviction it would have been difficult indeed to doubt. 'Not possible,' he repeated, 'the way I've fixed things, not possible, no more than jumping over the moon or picking winners in a string without ever going wrong.'

'Are you sure?' Miss James asked. 'You can't be sure! How can you be sure?'

'Sure and certain,' he asserted once again, 'sure and certain as me and you sitting here, her dead corpse won't never be found just simply because it never can be, not possible.'

'What do you mean? what have you done?'

'That's my affair,' he answered coolly. 'I don't tell everybody how it's done . . . no one will ever find her dead corpse; why, I couldn't even myself supposing I wanted to, which I don't. But if I did, I couldn't.' He paused to chuckle softly to himself. 'Don't you worry none about that,' he said. 'It won't be found, because – well, because it don't exist no more, it just simply isn't there to be found, that's all.'

'How can . . . you mean you've burnt it up or something? . . . you couldn't . . . not so quickly.'

'I'm not telling you no more,' he answered coolly, 'and I didn't say anything about burning anything – anyone could do that, or try rather. I'm just telling you her dead corpse can't be found because it don't exist now and that's gospel truth. Where's the Guv'nor?'

'He's gone. He thought the police would be coming. So he's gone.'

'Bunked?' cried Bobs-the-Boy, disgusted. 'Well, I did think he had more sense than that – where's he gone?'

'I don't know.'

'Abroad or somewhere?'

'I don't know,' she repeated. 'He's had his plans ready for long enough – he used to say you never know when things mightn't go wrong. Oh, he's clever, he thinks of everything. And no one will ever find him. Some snug hole he's made ready where they'll never find him.'

'And Dodd, Mr Dodd, what about him?' Bobs-the-Boy asked. 'Lost his head and bunked too, I suppose?'

'I don't know,' she answered. 'He hasn't come back; he ran after Maurice Keene, he meant to kill him if he caught him, but I don't know if he did. But he ran after him and he hasn't come back again yet.'

'Things seem to have been a bit lively after I went,' observed Bobs-the-Boy drily. 'I thought the Guv'nor had a cooler head on his shoulders, though. And that Hunter chap – what about him?'

'I suppose he went away, some time or another,' she answered. 'We didn't notice; when we remembered him he wasn't there any longer.'

'And me,' complained Bobs-the-Boy, 'fixing things up nice and quiet like, making it sure and certain no one couldn't ever be charged with putting out that girl's light, and I done it proper, too, so no one can't ever be pinched for that, and then I come back here to find everyone's done a bunk, and all the fat's in the fire all over again. Suppose the "busies" had come before, what could they have proved? but suppose they come now and find every one's run for it? Giving yourself away, I call it. What was it happened next after Zack Dodd unlocked the door into the corridor and told me to clear, same as I was only too glad to do?'

'Maurice Keene came. He was looking for her. He kept asking questions, he suspected something. Esmy Bryan wanted to know if he would like to look in the next room, as he seemed to think the girl was hiding there. Of course Bryan thought that would be all right now you had gone and taken – taken her away as well. So he told Mr Keene to go and look for himself, and he did, and he found a hand-bag lying on the floor. I suppose you hadn't noticed it. There was your handkerchief, too – the one you made into a noose. You left it lying on the floor. Keene knew the handbag belonged to – to her. You could see what he was thinking, and all at once he said he would show them both to Owen. And we knew what that would mean, and he saw us looking at him, and he understood, and he ran. He knocked Esmy over before he could do anything, and ran out of the house as hard as he could and Zack after him – we heard them run, the two of them, as fast as they could. Zack's big and heavy, but he can run fast when he has to. And that's all, for Zack's not come back as yet.'

'Well, now,' Bobs-the-Boy exclaimed, 'there's a nice mess, and just when I thought I had everything fixed right. Why haven't you bunked with the others anyhow? Bad for you as for them, isn't it?'

'I'm waiting for Zack,' she informed him. 'I thought perhaps he would come back, and if he did and I wasn't here, then he would kill me – he's my husband, you know,' she added as if to explain.

'Oh, married, are you?' Bobs-the-Boy grunted; 'married – that means you act under his influence, in law, of course. I know that much. Rummy thing, the law. But it doesn't help much. Who would have thought of Mr Bryan losing his head that way? Lay the best plans that ever were; and then they all go west, because someone acts the way no one ever could have dreamed of.'

'I would have gone, too, if I had dared,' she said moodily.

'That means you're as big a fool as he is,' Bobs-the-Boy retorted angrily. He was evidently a good deal disturbed, and for a time he was silent, deep in thought apparently.

Presently he went on. 'They had no real evidence – the police I mean. What did it matter if Miss Frankland's handbag was found here? or my handkerchief either? Couldn't I have picked it up in the grounds somewhere and brought it to you as instructed in all cases of lost property? and I might have wrapped it up in my handkerchief, mightn't I? to keep it clean. What's there in all that to make Dodd give himself away by trying to murder Keene?'

'It wasn't only that,' she answered. 'There's the other thing, too. They're suspecting us of that, too. There's one of them called Owen – he's everywhere, asking questions, questions; you can tell when you hear about them, what he's thinking.'

'What's it matter what he's thinking? what's it matter what the whole boiling of them's thinking?' scoffed Bobs-the-Boy. 'We should worry – what matters is what they've got they can put before a jury, and that's not much. Don't you realize the police haven't got to know? – they've got to make a jury know, and know on the facts put before 'em. Why, I've heard of a fellow walking straight into the Yard where they were working overtime on a job he had done, and he knew they knew he had done, and ask them cool as you like, how they thought they were getting on, and tell them just the piece of evidence they wanted to bring it home to him – only he knew they couldn't ever get it themselves, and what he said himself of course they couldn't use. You lot were as safe as he was, if only you had had the sense to sit tight instead of bolting for it – or trying to murder Keene and perhaps succeeding for all I know – and you may get away with it once easy enough, and twice with a bit of luck, but not three times, unless you've been rubbing luck off all the sweepstake winners that ever were. What evidence was there against you? Not much that I can see, unless of course you tell yourself how you did it.'

'Well, we shan't do that,' Miss James remarked, smiling a little, for under the encouragement administered by Bobs-the-Boy she had become almost normal again – quite normal, indeed, but for a certain underlying excitement of reaction that showed itself in a necessity to talk and chatter, 'not likely.'

'Was it you did in the other bit of skirt?' Bobs-the-Boy asked curiously, as if realizing that in this new garrulous mood she was likely to be willing to explain to him details he had often wondered about.

'No, it wasn't. I had nothing to do with it till it was all over,' she answered passionately. 'That's why it's so unfair I should be always dreaming of it, when I didn't even know what they meant to do until it was over. And it was all her own fault.'

'Trying to find things out that was no concern of hers?' observed Bobs-the-Boy. 'I suppose that was it?'

'Yes, somehow she guessed. I expect it was something her sister, Sybil, said or told her; most likely Maurice Keene let out something to Sybil and then she told enough to Jo for her to guess. I expect that was it, but I don't know. Then Jo came prowling about here to see what she could find out to make a big story for her paper. "The *Announcer* Unveils Sensational Plot", all that sort of stuff. And she hid in that room next to this to hear what we were saying when we were talking together. Afterwards she tried to slip out, but most likely she had got nervous and excited by then, and she managed to knock something over and we heard it. So then we knew we had to stop her. But I had nothing to do with it. What I said was we must give it up. But they said it was too late for that, she knew too much already, and Esmy kept her talking and talking, while Zack went round to the car park and waited for her there. We got the attendant out of the way up here to look after a leaking tap. I went down to hit it with a hammer and make it leak worse, but only because they told me to. I didn't know what for. Esmy left the girl outside the car park, and I came back here, and pretended to be busy with letters, and then I slipped out through the next room and the back stairs, without anyone seeing me, and across to the road, to wait there till Zack brought her car round. When he did, he told me he had shot her just as she was starting up, and I was to put on her hat and coat, and I was to speak to the A.A. scout so he would swear she had left the Grange quite safely, and then I was to run the car over the railway embankment by the bridge and set it on fire. We hoped it would pass for an accident; and that anyhow she would be too burnt for it to be noticed she had been shot first. But we had no luck, and it all came out, and even somehow they made sure it wasn't her driving the car at all, but someone else.'

'There was a little oversight there,' Bobs-the-Boy explained. 'You wore her hat tilted down on the left so that you couldn't be seen plainly by anyone you passed on the one side. But Jo Frankland's photograph showed she wore her hat tilted over on the right, and she couldn't very well have worn it the other way, unless she had changed her style of doing her hair. If it hadn't been for that, or if it hadn't been noticed, most likely Curtis himself would have been charged.'

'We couldn't understand why they seemed so certain it wasn't her in the car,' Miss James said slowly. 'I remember thinking how lucky it was the hat, low down on one side, and the coat collar coming up to meet it, nearly met, so my face was hidden.'

'It didn't turn out lucky,' observed Bobs-the-Boy, 'for it was that set them all thinking so hard. Only what's the good of their thinking, if there's no evidence to show? And the evidence they've got shows Mr Bryan leaving her outside the car park, and you back in your room when the thing happened, and nothing against Zack Dodd at all. So as long as you don't tell the "busies" yourself how it all happened, what's the panic? And there never will be any evidence about the other girl; for no one will ever find her dead corpse, and till they do, which they can't, there's nothing they can charge you with. They may know all right, but who cares about that, so long as they haven't proof? And how can they get proof? Where are their witnesses?'

Under the influence of this stream of encouragement, so well argued and presented, Miss James was quickly recovering her confidence.

'Esmy Bryan thought it was all over. He said our only chance was to go into hiding,' she remarked.

'Silly,' commented Bobs-the-Boy, 'when there's no evidence against you except anything you say yourselves.'

'You mean we're all quite safe still,' she said slowly.

'That's right,' he declared. 'You can take it from me everything's O.K., so long as you keep your mouths shut, except for Mr Bryan having bunked, and unless Zack Dodd's done anything that'll put us all in the cart again. Haven't you any idea where Bryan is? we must get in touch with him somehow.'

'I don't know at all,' she answered. 'He never told us, only that he had a safe hiding place where no one would ever find him. He seemed quite sure of that, that he would be safe there, I mean.'

Bobs-the-Boy looked rather gloomy.

'If he's got some hole all ready to crawl into,' he observed, 'some friend, a woman perhaps, ready to give him shelter, it would take the "busies" themselves all their time to find him.'

'No one ever will,' Miss James insisted, 'he's much too clever.'

'Well, that's torn it, that has,' Bobs-the-Boy muttered.

'But he told us,' Miss James went on, 'he would see anything we put in the agony column in the *Announcer* if we headed it to "Jim" and signed it "Rose Ann". He wrote out a list of a dozen places and gave each a key letter, where we could arrange to meet.' She paused and added abruptly, 'Someone's coming. It's Zack, I think. It's his step.'

CHAPTER TWENTY-SEVEN

'It's Always Owen'

THEY heard his heavy, lumbering step it was not difficult to recognize, come up the stairs and slowly down the passage. He opened the door of the room and stood there, scowling at the woman who said she was his wife, scowling still more viciously at Bobs-the-Boy. In a kind of scream his wife cried out,

'What did you do, what did you do? What's happened?'

He said, ignoring the question,

'There's Mitchell and his lot all round the house . . . waiting they are. Well, they'll never get me alive . . . nor you neither,' he added, looking sideways at his wife with a dark significance it seemed she understood well from the way in which she shrank back and trembled. 'Where's Bryan?' he demanded. 'It's all his doing, I'd like to twist his scraggy neck for him and save the police the trouble.'

But at that Bobs-the-Boy let loose a sudden torrent of invective that made even Zack blink his eyes, so violent and so fierce it was. Indeed Zack seemed even a trifle daunted by it.

'You needn't talk,' he muttered, when at last Bobs-the-Boy paused, though more apparently to take breath than from any adjectival shortage. 'You're done in same as us, you are, with all that crowd all watching outside.'

'Let 'em watch,' retorted Bobs-the-Boy. 'I'll go out presently and tell 'em trespassers will be prosecuted. It's all O.K. unless you've torn it, doing in young Keene. And I reckon most likely you haven't, or you wouldn't have come back here. That so?'

'He was too quick, he got away,' Zack answered. 'He called out back to me, "If it wasn't I've got to show these things to the police, to Owen, I'd have it out with you all right". If he had, I'd have done him in, I could do him in with one hand tied behind me. But he got away, and now he's telling that blasted Owen all about it; and that'll finish us and you, too,' he added with a vicious grin at Bobs-the-Boy, 'and I wouldn't have come back here, either, only for not having any money on me, not so much as a penny piece, and not knowing where else to go. So I thought I would risk it, and I came in the back way by the car park, but there was one of Mitchell's fellows waiting there, and then there was another close behind. So I came on here because I didn't know what else to do, but I reckon it's the end for all of us.'

'No sense in getting the wind up yet,' retorted Bobs-the-Boy. 'There's no evidence Mitchell's got yet he would dare take into court, for fear of being laughed out again. You can take that from me, that's straight goods, that is.'

He went on talking rapidly and fluently. As convincingly as before he persuaded Miss James, he now showed Zack how small was the real amount of evidence in the hands of the authorities, how little real proof in the legal sense there was against any of them.

'Not enough to charge a lost dog on,' he concluded. 'I don't say there mightn't have been if you had done in Keene, but as you haven't, that's all right. You know how this sort of thing is worked? They draw up a report at the Yard, Mitchell and the rest of them, and send it in to Treasury Counsel and Treasury Counsel read it and say it won't do, and send it back to have all the weak points tightened up, and if they can't be, well, it's all off, because Treasury Counsel aren't going to risk taking any case into court there's any chance of being turned down on. Professional reputation is what they think of more than anything else. What's Mitchell actually got – I mean in evidence he can take into court, not just mere guesses? Precious little if you ask me. Who saw anything? And where's the motive? A jury always wants to know that, and there's none the police can talk about. Even if they guess it was to keep her mouth shut, they aren't let talk about guesses. It cuts no ice what the police know, it's what they can prove – lummy, if the police could act just on what they know, a nice look out it would be for us chaps.'

'There's always Owen,' Miss James said, speaking for the first time.

'Ah, you've got Owen on the brain, you have,' Bobs-the-Boy said, looking at her benevolently. 'Bless you, scared of him, you are, and yet you've never seen him. No more have I.'

'Keene will have gone straight to him,' Zack said.

'If he has, that's all right,' Bobs-the-Boy retorted. 'Owen's one of the sort that likes to keep things all to himself till he's got everything ready. That means he doesn't speak till the last moment and no one knows what it is he's got. Very well. That's all right, gives us a chance to fix him before he ever says a word at all. See?'

They looked at him silently, a little doubtfully, and yet with a certain dreadful hope as well.

Presently Dodd dropped a single word.

'How?' he asked.

'I'll fix that, you leave that to me,' Bobs-the-Boy answered. 'All you've got to do is to hold your tongue. Most of those that hang, it's their own tongue they swing by.'

'It's easy, if there's nothing to it but saying nothing,' Zack said. 'I was never one to blab and talk,' and his wife nodded confirmation, agreeing on both points.

'Well, stick to that, saying nothing to anyone, and you'll be safe as houses, once this Owen's fixed,' Bobs-the-Boy repeated. 'Only just let me be sure I've got it right the way things happened. It won't do for me to make any bloomers.'

He asked a few questions, and Zack's replies confirmed fully the account his wife had already given.

'That's O.K. then,' Bobs-the-Boy pronounced presently. 'I've got the hang of it now, it's going to pan out just the way it ought.'

'There's always Owen,' Zack remarked, repeating unconsciously the same form of words that his wife had used earlier.

'You aren't getting him on the brain, too, are you?' asked

Bobs-the-Boy, with his familiar and always slightly disconcerting grin. 'Never seen him, have you? No more have I, but I've got my own idea about him.' He paused and his grin grew wider, displaying that black gap in his upper jaw where it seemed a tooth was missing. 'Leave Owen to me,' he repeated. 'But now our next job is getting hold of Mr Bryan again.'

The other two looked at each other blankly, and Dodd shook his head.

'I don't know how we're to do that,' he said. 'He always said he would only bolt when the game was properly up, and when he did no one would ever find him again. He said that more than once. I expect he had a bolt hole all ready; some woman most likely he knows he can trust to keep him hidden. He's got money, and he'll have it all thought out, and once he stops bleaching his hair he'll look quite different – he's nothing like as old as he pretended, you know; he put that on to make the suckers think it was all that fake stuff made him so brisk and strong; he even got his dad's birth certificate and hung it up on the wall for his own. He always said he could disappear any moment and not all the police in all the world would ever find him – I believe him, too. He had everything all thought out, and he's clever as they make 'em.'

'Sounds it would be a tough job,' agreed Bobs-the-Boy thoughtfully; 'if I were Mitchell I should be afraid of having to give him best there. If a man's got brains and money, and his plans made, and a place all ready to go to, and somebody to help him – well, then, you might as well look for the needle in the haystack. Unless he gives himself away.'

'Esmy Bryan won't do that,' declared Dodd.

'No,' agreed Bobs-the-Boy, 'not that sort – it was always supposed you and he didn't hit it together and he wanted to get you out of the show here. Was that only put on?'

Zack nodded.

'Just so as no one would think we were too thick,' he said.

'I thought as much,' Bobs-the-Boy remarked. 'I daresay

your Owen friend would tumble to that much. Only if one of us cuts and runs well, it looks bad for the rest, don't it? It's up to us to make him see everything's O.K. – always providing there's no talking.'

'There's always Owen,' Miss James put in, or Mrs Dodd, if she had real claim to that name.

'I told you I knew how to fix Owen, didn't I?' Bobs-the-Boy snapped.

'There's that girl to-night,' Zack reminded him. 'How about if they find out —'

'That's O.K., too,' Bobs-the-Boy interrupted. 'Haven't I told you I've got that fixed so no one will ever find her dead corpse? and unless they do, which now they can't, there's nothing they can bring up against you or me or anyone.'

'How can you know it won't be found?' demanded Zack. 'You're mighty clever, to hear you talk, but how can you make sure of that? It don't matter where you've hid her, any bit of luck —'

'Only,' interrupted Bobs-the-Boy once again, 'only no one can ever find what simply doesn't exist.'

'What do you mean? doesn't exist? why doesn't it exist?'

'Because it doesn't,' Bobs-the-Boy answered with the same quiet, assured confidence.

'How's that? how could you manage that?' demanded Zack. 'It's not possible, not so quick as that. How could you?'

'That's my affair and I'm not telling,' Bobs-the-Boy answered, still with the same calm and assured confidence that almost persuaded them against their will that he was speaking only the simple fact. 'Take it from me, it's all O.K. about her,' he went on. 'Only we had best get rid of Mitchell and his lot if they're still hanging about, same as I expect they are. I'll go and tell them trespassers will be prosecuted. Coming with me?'

But Dodd not only objected to accompany Bobs-the-Boy, but tried also to prevent him from going himself, arguing that it was both useless and dangerous. Bobs-the-Boy insisted, however, went off, and, a little to the surprise of the other two, presently returned, not only unarrested but smiling and triumphant.

'I cleared 'em off,' he said. 'Most likely they'll hang about in the road, but we can't help that, and maybe with luck some of the cars going home late in a hurry will run over some of 'em. I told 'em, too, I had found a girl trespassing earlier in the evening and how I told her she ought to be run in, and she was so scared she ran off and dropped her bag, so I took it up to the house. That's just in case Keene's found Owen, and Owen's reported at the Yard, but he won't, not if I know Owen. Keep it to himself, he will, till he thinks he's ready to produce his story all complete, to the last button on the last gaiter. There's always some like that, don't want to say anything till they've got their case complete. So then, when they're that way, if you can fix them first – well, there you are, you're O.K. just as if they had never found out a thing. And I've my own idea how we can fix Owen all right, good and plenty, too.'

'How?'

'If you wait, you'll see, if you've luck. First thing is to get hold of the Guv'nor again. I did think he had more sense than to go and bunk – an advert. in the *Announcer* will fetch him, won't it?'

'We can try,' Zack answered. 'He'll see it most likely and I suppose he'll answer it, unless he thinks it a trap.'

'What's to make him think that?' demanded Bobs-the-Boy. 'Only if he won't answer, and we can't find him, well, that tears it, tears it good and hard. Suppose he does see it and makes up his mind to answer, which I should think he's sure to, unless he's gone clean off his nut, what'll he do? phone you?'

'No. He said he would put a reply advert. in the *Announcer*, a lot of letters all muddled up like a cypher, only it won't mean anything except that the first letter will be the key letter according to a list he'll send us, and the middle letter will be the time, starting at one in the morning and going round the clock, and the last letter will show the minutes past, each letter covering two minutes, so that "e", for instance, will mean nine to ten minutes past and "z" from ten minutes to the next hour to the hour itself.'

'Got it all thought out,' observed Bobs-the-Boy with admiration. 'You would think anyone with his brains would have more sense than up and run at the first little thing going wrong.'

'Owen has him scared,' Mrs Dodd explained, shuddering a little as if in full sympathy, 'it's knowing he was always there, always asking questions, never showing.'

'Oh, well,' Bobs-the-Boy answered, shrugging his shoulders, 'it seems it's always Owen, just as you said yourself.'

'How's Bryan answering us, if he does, going to help you get hold of Owen?' demanded Dodd.

Bobs-the-Boy looked oddly at him.

'We'll let Owen know where we're to meet,' he said slowly, 'then he'll follow us. If I know anything about his type, he'll follow us alone. But we'll make sure of that. If he does, if he follows us alone – why, then there'll be another mysterious disappearance.' He paused and looked at them slowly, from one to the other. 'Never seen him, have you?' he asked. 'No more have I, never, no more than you. But this'll be your chance all right,' and Zack Dodd nodded in slow and ponderous agreement.

CHAPTER TWENTY-EIGHT

Mr Bryan Keeps his Appointment

IF, indeed, as is commonly reported, there are those who make it their hobby to unravel every cypher advertisement that is inserted in the agony columns of the daily Press, they must have had a bad time trying to discover the meaning of the jumble of letters addressed to 'Jim' and signed 'Rose Ann' that presently appeared in the *Announcer*. For that the first letter, a 'B', meant, in accordance with the key Zack Dodd possessed, 'Cleopatra's Needle, Thames Embankment', that the middle letter, a 'V', the thirteenth of the twenty-five composing the message, meant twenty-two o'clock or ten at night, and that the last letter, a 'C', meant half past that hour, no human ingenuity could very well have discovered, any more than it could discover in the totality of the message a meaning that was not there – did not exist, as Bobs-the-Boy so repeatedly declared did not the 'dead corpse' of Sybil Frankland.

'It's a rummy place to choose,' Bobs-the-Boy observed a little distrustfully, when Zack told him the designated spot was in front of Cleopatra's Needle. 'Do you think it's O.K., or is he just pulling our leg?'

'There may be more to it than that; this may be only the first stage,' Zack explained. 'Heard anything about Owen? Seems to be keeping quiet, don't he? He and the rest of the bobbies as well.'

But Bobs-the-Boy shook his head.

'They're busy enough,' he said, 'trust them for that, the "busies" that they are. So am I,' he added, nodding with a certain air of grim assurance. 'I've been putting out a bit of ground bait Owen's nibbling at already. It's him or us for it now, and I mean it to be him.'

He would say no more, but there was a kind of tense, grim resolution about him that impressed even Zack Dodd's dull mind, that brought, too, a certain measure of reassurance to the woman now said to be his wife.

'If it wasn't for Owen,' she remarked, 'I wouldn't be half as much afraid – but I shan't ever think we're safe till —'

She did not complete the sentence, but Zack understood and nodded an agreement.

'We can leave it to Bobs-the-Boy,' he declared; 'he means business all right – it's him or us for it, and Bobs-the-Boy intends it'll be him wins through.' He added thoughtfully, after an interval, 'I've got a hunch Bobs-the-Boy will come out on top; he's a chap who knows what he's doing, all O.K.'

This time it was Mrs Dodd's turn to nod in silent agreement, for she, too, was conscious of the same odd – presentiment, foreboding, anticipation, call it what you will – that Bobs-the-Boy would carry to a successful end the enterprise he had in hand.

Later on, when Bobs-the-Boy came to them to suggest that they should all meet on the appointed evening at the Temple station and then walk on to where the obelisk stands, watching the flow of the Thames and dreaming perhaps of the distant Nile, Zack said to him,

'Do you know they've been broadcasting for information about the Frankland girl?'

'What about it?' asked Bobs-the-Boy coolly. 'There'll be a pile of letters that high, that's all, and none of them worth the paper they're written on. Don't I keep telling you no one can find what doesn't exist?'

'I don't know what you mean, "Doesn't exist",' complained Zack irritably. 'You may be as sure —'

'Sure and certain,' interrupted Bobs-the-Boy. 'I know what I'm talking about, and you just stick to what don't exist, can't be found.'

Again he spoke with that air of complete and assured confidence that always, for the time at least, soothed away Zack's fears.

'Only I can't think what he means when he talks that way,' Zack confided to his wife when the two of them set out that evening to keep their appointment with Bobs-the-Boy at the Temple station, 'but he seems as sure and certain about it all as you are of a pint of beer after you've drunk it.'

'He makes you feel that way when he talks to you,' she admitted, 'but I wish he would tell you straight out what he means; I never heard of any way of getting rid of a dead body so that it didn't exist any longer. I shan't feel easy till I understand.'

'Most likely we shall soon,' Zack said, though the need to understand troubled him less than it did his quicker-witted partner.

They found Bobs-the-Boy waiting for them. Together they walked along the Embankment, and by Cleopatra's Needle they halted to wait. They were a little early. The hour struck, and then the half hour. A little later a taxi cab drew up. The driver got down and started whistling to himself and looking about expectantly. Bobs-the-Boy and Zack went up to him. The man said,

'I was told I was to pick up two gents here and they would know who it was I came from.'

'Mr Bryan?' asked Bobs-the-Boy.

'That's right,' said the driver, 'hop in, I'm to drive you to Oynton Square, No. 7.'

'He hasn't come himself?' Zack remarked, somewhat unnecessarily since the cab was evidently empty.

'Said he couldn't,' answered the driver, 'but he paid down, and told me I could look to you gents for something handsome.'

Bobs-the-Boy had already suggested to Zack that his wife had better be left behind in view of the nature of what in all probability lay before them. Zack agreed at once, and she herself showed no desire to accompany them.

'I don't want any more dreams,' she said. 'I'm looking to sleep better when I know Owen's fixed, but I don't want to have to dream about the way it happened.'

They left her therefore to make her own way home, while they two entered the cab. Oynton Square proved to be on the north side of Hyde Park, a vast mausoleum of Victorian respectability, enormous houses put up apparently to solve the problem of unemployment by providing endless work for innumerable servants, the vast expanse of the reception rooms on the first floors contrasting oddly with the rabbit warren of small, stuffy bedrooms above. One or two of these buildings had been expensively converted into inconvenient flats, one or two were still in occupation by inmates holding out grimly against the tide of modern improvements, and one or two more were in process of demolition. No. 7, boarded and shuttered, reared itself in uninhabited solitude, a dreary witness of the social changes a century can bring about.

But there was no sign anywhere of Mr Bryan, and when they had paid the taxi driver and told him not to wait, he remarked with some hesitation, but Bobs-the-Boy had given him a generous tip,

'It ain't no business of mine, Guv'nor, but there's been a motor-cycle following us pretty near all the way from the Embankment.'

'Oh, that's all right, we know all about that,' answered Bobs-the-Boy cheerfully, and when the taxi had departed to seek a fresh fare in that rich hour when the theatres empty, he observed to his companion, 'Take it from me, Owen's coming along all right – there's always Owen, isn't there?' he said, chuckling grimly.

But Zack did not share in this mirth. His wrath and fear rumbled heavily in his throat, and Bobs-the-Boy asked him,

'Got a gun?'

Zack nodded.

'And this,' he said, showing a brass knuckle-duster, an ugly, formidable weapon on the hand of a trained boxer.

'Let's see the gun,' Bobs-the-Boy demanded; and when Zack produced a small automatic, Bobs-the-Boy calmly opened it, slipped out the magazine, put that in his pocket, and handed back the empty weapon to the staring Zack.

'Shooting's too noisy,' he vouchsafed to explain. 'I'm taking no risks of that going off and everyone hearing it miles round. The other thing's all right. Keep it in your coat pocket, do you? good. But what we have to do to-night we'll do quick and quiet – quick and quiet,' he repeated, and though Zack muttered and grumbled to himself, he made no other protest, yielding to his companion's superior force of decision and knowledge of what he meant to do and how.

All the same he did not seem easy in his mind.

'Suppose there's other "busies" following after Owen!' he muttered.

'There won't be,' Bobs-the-Boy answered. 'I know Owen – he always likes to play a lone hand when he can, and he won't risk having others trailing along after him that we might spot and take alarm. Besides I've put down ground bait, and I know he's nibbled. If it's Owen, he's alone, and everything is going so far just as I want – only where's Bryan?'

But to this question there was no reply, for of Bryan there was still no sign. Zack began to ask for the magazine for his automatic back again, but Bobs-the-Boy flatly refused.

'I've got my plan all ready,' he said. 'I'm not going to risk having it spoiled. Guns are noisy, and noise – well, you never know who hears it. What we do to-night, we'll do quiet, and I'll promise you one thing – Detective-Constable Owen and Bobs-the-Boy will both be there, but only one will go away again.'

He spoke once again with that strange air of certainty he had, and then when there was still no sign of Bryan he commenced to fidget and move about. He was beginning in fact to feel a little uneasy, and to be afraid something had gone wrong, or that Bryan had taken alarm.

'He may have seen we were being followed, and didn't like it and cleared off,' Zack suggested.

'If it's like that, we'll have to try again,' Bobs remarked, and then, after another look round that showed no sign of anyone in sight, it struck him that possibly Bryan might have gained admittance to the house and be waiting for them inside while they waited outside. But the doors and windows all seemed securely fastened, and not until he looked more closely did he discover a bit of paper pinned to the front door. He took it down. On it, printed in block characters, was a message directing them to follow the road through Uxbridge, and then, turning from it at a described spot, to go on by a certain route till they came to a wood bordering the road. At a spot where a tall birch tree grew, half way through this wood, they were to wait by the roadside till Bryan came; and it was added that to carry out these instructions a car hired for the occasion would be waiting for them in an adjoining garage, where the staff had been instructed to hand it over to anyone claiming it in the name of – 'Owen'.

Bobs-the-Boy chuckled again when he read this name.

'Quite pretty,' he said, 'shows the Guv'nor hasn't got Mr Detective-Constable Owen on the nerves quite as much as some other people.'

'Might be better if he had,' grumbled Zack. 'And I call it a fool trick, sticking that bit of paper there. We might easily have gone away and never seen it.'

'Ought to have had sense to spot it long ago, you mean,' Bobs-the-Boy observed. 'We've wasted half an hour for want of a little gumption. Bryan's got some sense himself, and he thinks other people have brains, too, which generally they haven't.'

Zack only rumbled inarticulately in reply to this, and then they went to the indicated garage, where they found a car waiting for them. It was of a cheap and common make, but it was possessed of a good turn of speed, and as there was not much traffic about they bowled along rapidly enough. Outside the London limits, on a straight stretch of road without side turnings, Bobs-the-Boy suddenly turned the car and went tearing back at a speed even the makers would hardly have believed possible – would certainly never have dared to claim in their advertisements. Before long they tore past a solitary motor-cyclist who drew to one side to let them go by, and Bobs-the-Boy said to Zack sitting next him,

'Notice him? was it Owen? If it was, now you've seen him at last.'

Afterwards the road was quite clear, and Bobs-the-Boy presently slowed down.

'No one else,' he said, 'no one following him – Owen or not. So that's O.K., but I was always sure he would want to play a lone hand.'

He swung the car round and tore back again the way they had come. Once more they met the same solitary motor-cyclist, who evidently had turned round himself in order to follow them.

'Owen all right,' Zack muttered. 'He's trailing us for sure, that's clear enough. He's alone, too, if that's what you played for. You've brought it off sure enough.'

'I told you you could trust me to bring things off the way I wanted,' Bobs-the-Boy answered quietly, and after a long pause, Zack said,

'He's still following. You'll let him catch us up?'

'Soon,' Bobs-the-Boy answered softly, 'very soon. Don't you worry, it's all working out the way it should.'

Zack said no more, and presently, after some twists and turns, they came to what seemed the appointed spot – half way through a wood where tall trees grew on either hand. One in especial, a tall birch, shot up above all the rest. Beneath its shade, as their instructions said, they halted, and heard at once the sound of the engine of a motor-cycle that was not far away.

'Owen,' Zack said again, 'he's coming all right,' and with a low, snarling laugh let his hand touch his pocket where the brass knuckle-duster bulged.

But there was no sign of Bryan, and Bobs-the-Boy observed, when they had waited a little,

'Better see if there's some other message here, sending us off somewhere else.'

But they could find none, though they looked carefully by the light of their headlamps, and Zack cursed softly to himself.

'He's fooling us,' he said, 'and all the time Owen creeping up behind the hedge most likely or signalling for help maybe.'

'I thought I heard something,' Bobs-the-Boy agreed, listening intently. 'Sounds up above, though, in the tree somewhere,' and down the trunk of the tall birch came a small figure, dexterously sliding.

It was Bryan himself. He had waited cautiously, well hidden on one of the lower branches of the birch till he felt it would be safe to show himself. He said without other greeting,

'You've been followed. There was a fellow on a motorcycle. I heard it plainly, I could see the headlight. It stopped when you did, it was following you.'

'It's Owen, Mr Smarty Owen,' Zack explained. 'There's always Owen,' he said with a little nervous laugh. 'Bobs-the-Boy fixed it for him to follow us, so as to get him here all alone. We three can fix him all right,' he said, and laughed again.

'You mean that fellow following you on the motor-cycle?' Bryan asked, startled, and when Zack nodded, he clapped his hands together with an odd, bizarre gesture of applause. Even in the darkness one could see how his small eyes gleamed, with what a deadly purpose his small and shrunken form seemed all at once informed. 'If it's Owen . . .' he said, a gloating anticipation in his voice, '. . . why, that's fine; fine, that is.' He turned to Bobs-the-Boy. 'Smart of you,' he said, 'you're smart all right . . . you're sure it's Owen?'

'Well, as a matter of fact,' answered Bobs-the-Boy, 'it's really Maurice Keene. It couldn't very well be Owen, because,' he explained as he dexterously fitted to Bryan's skinny wrists a pair of specially small size handcuffs, 'I happen to be Owen myself.'

CHAPTER TWENTY-NINE

Conclusion

FOR a moment or two, in the shock of this announcement, of this action, both Bryan and Dodd stood perfectly still, Bryan blinking at the bright fetters on his wrists, as though he could not relate them to reality, and Dodd's mouth very slowly opening wider and wider till it gaped gigantic in the glare of the car's headlamps. Slowly, then, Dodd swayed vaguely forward, as if he meant to hurl himself on Owen, and next as slowly sideways, as if instead he meant to turn and run. Bryan screamed,

'Out him, Zack! out him, you fool! out him, why don't you?'

As he spoke he tried to wrench himself from Owen's grasp upon his arm, but that was like the grip of fate itself, and held him fast. Zack's hand dropped to his pocket, and with fresh bewilderment found nothing there – groped in emptiness. Owen said,

'Oh, that little knuckle-duster of yours; oh, I've got that. I slipped it out of your pocket while you were gaping at our friend here swarming down from his perch up in the tree. Our Super always says a good detective must be a good pickpocket as well, so I've done my best to learn.'

'Out him, out him!' Bryan screamed again, his voice more loud, more shrill, more utterly despairing even than before.

But Zack Dodd turned. His instinct now was flight. His slow mind had told him at last his only chance of safety was swift and instant flight. As he turned he began to gather up all his energies to run, to run and run and never stop. Vaguely it occurred to him that it was lucky for him that Bryan had been taken first; occupied with the safety of his prisoner Owen would be unable to pursue. A bit of luck that, he thought, and he perceived abruptly that in turning he had brought himself face to face with Maurice Keene.

who held in one hand a pistol levelled at him, in the other a pair of handcuffs.

'Put your hands out,' Keene said, 'so I can get these on, and don't try any tricks, or I'll put a bullet through you and glad of the chance, glad of the chance to give you what you gave to Jo Frankland.'

Meekly, quietly, Dodd obeyed, for there was that in the other's voice which told him there was no other safety. From behind Bryan's thin voice still screamed wild curses, strange appeals and blasphemies, filling all the silence of the night with the clamour of his rage, his terror, his despair. Owen took no notice, but urged his prisoner on towards the waiting car. Keene followed with Dodd. Dodd said to Bryan,

'Oh, shut up, what's the good of that?'

Bryan was silent instantly, exactly as if some spring had been touched that shut off the torrent of his speech. But as he stumbled into the car, he muttered, half to himself,

'Well, it was only one woman, and my work down there at Leadeane Grange was adding years to people's lives.'

After that, the only thing that either of them said was when Zack Dodd, as if the fact had just dawned upon him, said to Owen,

'You were a detective all the time then, and not Bobs-the-Boy at all. Where is Bobs-the-Boy? Isn't there any Bobs-the-Boy?'

'Oh, yes,' Owen answered, 'but some Salvation Army people got hold of him. That's what made that brute of a Mousey get after him. Mousey's so crooked himself he simply couldn't bear to think of anyone trying to go straight, so when he knew you wanted someone to send to Hunter to do some dirty work for him, he thought of Bobs-the-Boy at once and thought it was a chance to get him back into the crooked crowd again. But the Army people told Bobs to come and see us, so we got a decent sort of job for him in the north of England out of the way; and then because we thought we would like to know what an ex-crook and ex-burglar was wanted for, I was told off to take his place. And so that Mousey shouldn't get a chance to give the show away, and because he rather more than jolly well deserved it, we reported to the Prison Commissioners and got his licence revoked. But so that the real reason shouldn't be suspected we shopped him on a framed-up charge of having stolen property in his possession that we withdrew with apologies as soon as the case came on and substituted instead the real charge of "inciting to commit a felony". Nearly got us into bad trouble, though, because an M.P. got hold of the story, saw the stolen property charge looked like a frame-up, and thought there was a chance to prove we were persecuting ex-convicts – and make a name for himself into the bargain. We couldn't explain, either, because if you tell an M.P. anything, you tell his private secretary, and if you tell a private secretary you tell the typist, too, and by that time you've told the world as well.'

Neither of the prisoners made any reply, and though Owen was a firm believer in Mitchell's favourite maxim that if you only talk to people long enough they'll always finish by telling you everything you want to know and a great deal more as well, he did not attempt to continue the conversation. After all, there was little that was not already well enough known. The car stopped, and a uniformed man opened the door. They had arrived at Scotland Yard. As Dodd was alighting he said to Owen,

'What about Elsie?'

'She'll have been arrested by now,' Owen answered. 'She'll be charged with you, I expect – accessory before the fact, I suppose, or something like that. If you're really married she'll get off fairly easily, most likely – acted under the compulsion of her husband, you know.'

'We're married all right, I can prove that,' Zack answered. Then he added, 'I'm glad they won't hang her, too.'

A slow trembling shook his vast frame as he heard himself pronounce that last word. Behind him, Bryan heard it, and was shaken by the same slow trembling. Side by side they disappeared into the charge room as into the tomb.

*

An hour or two later Detective Robert Owen, restored to rank and name and place after his long masquerade as 'Bobs-the-Boy', presented himself before Superintendent Mitchell. The mere substitution of a clean collar and tie for the spotted handkerchief round his neck wrought by itself a tremendous change; a shave and a wash completed the transformation. Then, too, he had removed the daub of black stain on a perfectly sound tooth at the back of his jaw that had given the appearance of one missing there, and had contributed to his smile a sinister and menacing quality of which he had been more than a little proud when practising it before his mirror.

'Got through all right, then,' Mitchell remarked. 'I'll not deny I'm a bit relieved you've turned up all hunk-a-dory, and got your birds as well. It wasn't quite regular to allow an unauthorized civilian like Keene to chip in, and I might have got told off for it if it hadn't worked out all right. Only what can you do when a man tells you quite coolly that if he doesn't get his own way he'll give the whole show away and muzzle your chief witness as well? I really think he was quite capable of trying to get Miss Frankland to refuse to testify. And though you can get a witness into the box all right, you can't stop them messing up their story if they want to. She could easily have said she wasn't sure what she really overheard.'

'I am sure it was best to let Keene have his own way,' Owen said. 'It would have given the whole thing away, to have more than one man following, and it was just as well to let it be Keene as anyone else. They are such wary birds that if there had been any sign of more than one man trailing us they would have taken alarm at once, whereas so long as they thought it was just "Owen" being lured to his doom, they were quite happy about it. Besides, after all, I suppose Keene had some right to take a hand in the show – it was his girl they tried to murder.'

'You've seen her, haven't you?'

'Yes, sir. I called at the nursing home this afternoon. She's getting on well, they say, though it'll be a long time before she gets over it altogether. I suppose in a way she can say she's actually had the experience of being murdered. When she saw me come in that time at Leadeane Grange, it's no wonder she thought it was all over. So did I, for that matter, for though I wasn't sorry she fainted, I didn't see how I was going to get either her or myself away safely – I knew they all had guns and knew how to use them, too. And then Dodd unlocked the outer door and told me to get off quick and take her body with me and hide it somewhere.' He paused to chuckle faintly. 'They couldn't make head or tail of it when I told them her "dead corpse" would never be found because it didn't exist any longer.'

'Should have almost expected them to fall to that,' observed Mitchell. 'Anyone almost might have spotted what you meant.'

'Well, sir,' admitted Owen, 'I think I did overdo that bit – all at once I had a feeling I might be giving myself away, and so I dried up. Lucky they weren't smart enough to tumble to what I meant, though it's a wonder they didn't; most people would, I think. Of course, they had seen me carrying away what they took for her dead body on my shoulder, and I suppose they were too sure of what they had seen for it to occur to them that I meant her "dead corpse" didn't exist because her live body was in a nursing home. Then the broadcast asking for information was a good dodge; I expect that took away any doubts any of them might have developed afterwards.'

'A terrible experience for her,' Mitchell agreed. 'Did you ask her what made her go telling her mother it was she herself who had murdered her sister?'

'She mentioned that herself,' Owen answered. 'I think she had an idea I overheard her. She says she still feels it all happened through her. It was what she half told Miss Jo Frankland, and half didn't tell, that set Miss Jo trying to ferret out the truth for herself – partly, I suppose, in the hope of proving young Keene wasn't a desirable person to marry; she was quite set on breaking Sybil's engagement off if she could. I expect when Miss Sybil gets stronger she will realize she's no cause to blame herself.' Owen paused and smiled faintly, 'I don't know if you remember, sir,' he said. 'She saw me once in their garden at Ealing, just after the murder, when I was dodging round there as Bobs-the-Boy. We bluffed her by my slipping inside your car that was waiting and our people swearing, quite truly, there hadn't been anyone but police there. It seems to have worried her quite a lot, made her think perhaps she was subject to hallucinations; she was quite relieved to know the truth and that she really had seen me and not a ghost of some sort.'

'All the same,' observed Mitchell, 'I don't know so much about her not being to blame. If she had come straight to us and told us all she knew, she would have saved us a lot of work – and herself a good deal more.'

'Well, sir, I think she was too scared,' Owen remarked. 'She knew Keene was involved, she had no idea how deeply; I think she was even afraid at times he might be implicated in the murder of her sister in some way or another – and then she wasn't sure she was thinking straight, especially after we had bluffed her into believing she had an hallucination when she thought she saw "Bobs-the-Boy" in their garden. It was all that taken together drove her on to try to find out the truth by herself and in the end to do just exactly what cost her sister her life – hide in the room next to the one they were talking in to try to overhear what they said. And when she heard them telling how it was poor Jo Frankland had betrayed herself – well, I think she lost her nerve altogether. I think it was a kind of auto-suggestion made her do the same thing, just as when you're learning to cycle you're apt to run into the very obstacle you're trying to avoid. I hope I didn't go too far, when I told her I didn't think any question of any prosecution of Keene would arise?'

'No, he gets off,' answered Mitchell, 'no overt action on his part we can take notice of. Hunter, too. It ought to be a lesson to them both, though Keene, at any rate, has done his best to make good again. None of them seem to have had any suspicion of your identity?'

'I don't think so, sir, not once.'

'Not even when you sounded Keene, and Hunter as well, about making a clean breast of it? I was afraid that might set them thinking; it wasn't quite in character.'

'Miss Sybil had been saying much the same before me, and I suppose it only seemed like repetition,' Owen remarked. 'I expect they both felt they had heard it all before.'

'She was lucky to escape,' Mitchell said. 'You told her we should have to ask her to appear and give evidence?'

'Yes, sir. I explained that was necessary because a jury might hesitate to accept my story without corroboration. I told her that was why after I had got her away we didn't proceed to arrest at once, as we didn't know how much she had heard, or what she could say, and if we had enough to be sure of a conviction. So we had to wait till she was able to tell us what she knew.'

'You'll have a fairly hot time at the trial, I expect,' Mitchell remarked cheerfully. 'Police spy, agent provocateur, is the best you'll get called. Defending counsel will let himself go because he'll have nothing else to say, and you'll get a gruelling all right. We'll get our man to bring out that you had instructions to warn Hunter and Keene, and did so. Funny thing, though, I made a bloomer myself at the very beginning that would have given you away entirely to anyone smart enough to notice it. I told them Bobs-the-Boy was a burglar, and a convict on ticket-of-leave, and of course that's a thing no responsible police officer would dream of saying if it were true – cost him his position if he did, and it came out. But they let it pass all right; wonderful what people never notice. But it shows how careful one ought to be, even to keep one's thoughts right. I ought to have been thinking of you as the "Bobs-the-Boy", the released convict, it was my duty to help and protect, like any other citizen so long as he was keeping within the law. Instead I was only thinking of trying to warn Keene he was getting into bad company and had best be careful. The real "Bobs-the-Boy" seems to be doing all right. Quite a good account from where he's working up north. Good thing for him he came to us for help when that swine they call Mousey was trying to get him back into the crook world again. If he hadn't, and hadn't given me a chance to send you to take his place, we should never have known what was happening, most likely Jo Frankland's murderers would have escaped, and by this time probably we should have had two or three more big fires to investigate – and Esmy Bryan still pursuing his career among the sun bathers where, I own up, I should never have thought of looking for a super crook of his sort. I suppose you think you would like a holiday now?'

'Well, sir, of course there's the trial,' Owen said, but brightening visibly at the sound of the word 'holiday'.

'That won't take long,' declared Mitchell. 'Perfectly plain case now – Bryan and Zack Dodd will hang as they deserve, and Mrs Dodd or Miss James, it doesn't seem clear which she is, will be lucky to get off with penal servitude. After that —'

'Yes, sir,' said Owen, visibly waiting for the magic word 'leave' to be pronounced.

'After that,' said Mitchell cruelly, 'there'll be a little job waiting for you on the east coast. There's something on there apparently that's worrying the local people because they can't make out what it is. So they've asked us to send down a youngster able to show at a country house as an ordinary guest and warranted not to give himself away by eating peas with a knife or putting his feet on the dinner table or doing anything else natural and friendly and sociable. Also required to be good-looking, smart, and intelligent. Think you can fill the bill?'

'Yes, sir,' said Owen.

'Lucky,' observed Mitchell, 'that modesty isn't one of the qualities indented for. You can cut away to bed now and I'll let you know when your fresh instructions are ready.'

THE END

CPSIA information can be obtained
at www.ICGtesting.com
Printed in the USA
LVOW01s1745120916
504265LV00016B/886/P